LUXTENEBRI AND THE MOTHER MOONS

Written By: Ryan Lamar Allen

Dedication

Thank you Kasenya Nielson for all your help in preparing this novel, I could not have done it without you.

Chapter 1

ODIMUVALERE'S PATH BEGINS TO BE PAVED

I am Mezlikied, the appointed Guardian and possessor of the Heart Stone of the great moon, Erayiphim. My purpose is to guard all of the people of the tribe of the moon. Just as all the guardians appointed by their mother moons. So, we are to seek out what is known as "Potential manifestations." This is pure energy that emanates from all forms of life on Luxtenebri and the Mother Moons. It manifests itself in many forms and seems to be attracted to a wide variety of things with significant force. Here, potential pulls in energy towards it. Through these potential manifestations, people achieve countless wonders, extraordinary achievements, and remarkable discoveries. There is one with the most unparalleled potential ever seen, and this man is Odimuvalere. His narrative has been a tremendous struggle between that of light and that of shadow. If Odimuvalere were to choose the Light, he would save Luxtenebri and the Mother Moons. If he were to choose Shadow, he would bring an end to Luxtenebri and her Moons. It's been my responsibility to guide him towards the Light since he was a young man.

"Hey Odimus, take a look at this."

Young Odimus turns, and a piece of cheese strikes his cheek. It adheres and Odimus is mortified, but proceeds to tread towards the Bremium forge where his father works. As he scurries towards the forge, he peels the cheese from his face.

"What's wrong, are you just going to accept that?"

He glances at the bully. "Yes, Amulius, I suppose I just might." Subsequently, he turns and advances through the front doors of his father's forge. Amulius just snorts and carries on his way. As Odimus ambles to the back of the forge, he searches for his father and notices he is nowhere to be found. He calls for him and gets no response. "Father? Are you here?" He hears a resounding noise and realizes it is coming from the second floor towards his father's office. Ascending towards the staircase, he becomes aware of the room below and acknowledges a multitude of bricks of Bremium metal stacked on the counter. He notices a handful of relics his father had been engaged in but had not finished. Given that his father was the master of the forge and quite a successful one, it was unusual to see him not performing any labor today.

Odimus recognizes not one executive tradesperson or stagiaire tradesperson was on shift either. Now, executive and stagiaire tradespersons work for those who have attended the great University and acquired a Master Skills education which is only obtained through going to The Great Academy of Achaicus. Executive and stagiaire tradespeople can serve under the master of any profession and not have to go to the great university or any education institute, they are just never be able to receive the Master Skill position.

Odimus's unlocks his father's office door, as he starts to enter, the door is forcefully pushed back, nearly knocking him over, pinning him in between the door and frame.

His father, in an authoritative voice, questions, "Who is there? I instructed all staff members not to be present for their duties on this day. Was I not clear about my instructions?" Odimus moans in a slightly uncomfortable voice from being pinned, "Father, it is me, Odimus."

Quickly pulling the door open, "Oh, Odimuvalere, son, I'm so sorry. Come in but wait one moment". Odimus hears scurrying and rustling as if his father is hiding something. Following that, he is granted access to come in. His father is Erastus, and is now standing in the middle of the room, solely waiting for him to walk in. He looks at his father's face, it appears he is in a pleasant mood but struggling to keep a secret, he seems to be bursting at the cheeks with secrecy. "Hello, Odimuvalere, my good son. What can I do for you?"

Well, father, first, you can call me Odimus because you know I don't like Odimuvalere. It takes too much effort to say, and no one can pronounce it. It's almost sounds made-up." Erastus chuckles at his son's request.

"Okay Odimus, what can I do for you?"

"Well, Mom said she had seen three of your tradespersons heading home earlier, and she was worried since you were not home shortly as well. So, she sent me over to see if you needed anything."

Erastus smiles, "No, son, I am working on a very important relic. I sent everyone home because I had a breakthrough in the design I had been working on, and I realized I needed to focus entirely on it myself and yet not have any prying eyes. You know what I mean?" He asked, raising one eyebrow.

Odimus offers a crooked smirk, "Well, are you going to show me?

Erastus suddenly became quite serious, and a face of fear and great concern began to show in his eyes. He looks inward at his office, not directly at anything, as to attempt not to give away the relic's location. He turns his gaze back to Odimus and, with a kind, fatherly yet stern look, replies, "No Odimuvalere my son, I will not be showing you. This relic is becoming more than I anticipated. It's best you do not mention this to anyone. Now run along back home to your mother and help her with what she needs."

Odimus slowly moves toward the door and looks back, smiles at his father, and his father smiles back at him. He leaves out the back door of the forge, hoping not to run into Amulius again because Amulius is, not a very kind young man.

As Odimus is wandering down the path, he notices a flicker of light in his peripheral vision. He glances up and sees this beautiful dust-shaped feather made of pure light and energy whipping through the air down toward the old records building. He remembers once being told of something known as potential manifestation. It appeared to happen to every person a few times in their life. As he follows this feather-shaped dust, a sense of power and ability began to emerge within him. Following it farther into the woods for about fifteen minutes, he sees the feather disappear by absorbing into a tree. Curious, Odimus touches where the light had gone out into the tree and becomes very perplexed.

He looks up and realizes what kind of tree the light had led him to. It was the Tree of Erayiphim, the tree of his home moon. This tree bore Gravity Fruit. When someone eats this fruit, it gives them many abilities to control gravity. On his home moon, you were not allowed to eat this fruit until you are twelve years old because twelve years old is considered the age of responsibility. Odimus is only eleven. He knows it is forbidden, yet why would the light lead him to a Gravity Fruit Tree? "It would not lead me here to partake, for I will not partake. So why bring me to this place?" Odimus begins to look around in curiosity for he realizes he is unable to perceive anything around or behind the tree. He looks up and finds nothing to be in the branches. So Odimus climbs the tree, thinking maybe it is about gaining a different viewpoint and understanding. He scales up to the highest branch that had the capacity to support his weight and scans his surroundings as far as his vision allowed. Still, he perceives nothing.

So, he decides to climb down. As he begins his first step down, he steps upon a branch that broke right out from under his feet. He begins to fall, hurling towards the ground and hits a few branches along the way. As he's about to hit the ground, he readies himself for impact and closes his eyes. But nothing. Odimus, covering his eyes, still waiting to hit the ground, slowly realized it wasn't going to happen.

A voice speaks to him, "You may open your eyes now, young man."

As he opens his eyes, he recognizes that he is inches from the ground. He feels his whole-body lift into the air and ever so gently, he is placed down onto his feet, standing upright.

"Mezlikied is the name"

Odimus jumps back, obviously startled. Stammering to get his words together he asks, "Did you say Mezlikied? As in THE Mezlikied?"

Mezlikied, leans over gently to reach his eyes to Odimus's eye level and says, "Yes, that is my name. What of it?"

Odimus is hit with star-struck excitement. "What do you mean what of it!? You are him! You are the great Mezlikied! What are you doing here!?"

"I am present because I perceived this lovely dust resembling a feather, and upon arriving at this spot where the light merged with the tree, I became aware of a dreadful commotion, gazed upwards and witnessed your descent towards imminent danger." Odimus tells him that he, too, followed the same feather. "Is it fate, or a sign or something else?"

Mezlikied laughs "Oh no, dear boy, there is no such thing as fate. There is a great creator among our people, but this world is guided by potential manifestations. In a sense, they were designed by God, but we are left to choose whether to follow them or not. Potential manifestations are visualized by the beholder as pure energy forming together, guiding them towards a path that leads to their greatest potential. So, it seems Odimus that your greatest potential and my greatest potential paths are crossing, and if we're in agreement, it would be wise for us to seize those opportunities collectively." Odimus agrees and takes him home to mother.

Arriving, his mother opens the door and is startled by what she sees, quickly shutting the door. You can hear lively rustling and scurrying feet. There were a loud door slams and whispers behind the door to tidy the place. Odimus feels a bit embarrassed and apologizes.

Mezlikied leans in a bit and whispers to him, "A clean home is an orderly home. Your mother is doing right by herself. Nothing to be embarrassed about. No matter how much effort one puts into their home for a stranger, gratitude should always outweigh judgment towards a host. From my perspective, your mother appears to be a fine woman."

Odimus's mother bursts through the door, now exuding energy and confidence, urging them to enter. As Mezlickied enters, he quickly surveys the room and notices a few things tucked away in the corner.

"Hello Adelphia" Mezlikied shakes mother's hand and let's go. Odimus realizes this man knows his mother but opts not to inquire about it. Adelphia guides her guest to the living room and offers a seat.

"What is the reason for your presence in our home, accompanied by my young Odimus?"

Mezlikied wastes no time and confidently declares, "It appears we have shared potential manifestations, ma'am."

Adelphia's expression turns uneasy, but Odimus recognizes it's due to her impending excitement. She maintains herself, "What are you thinking, and What does that mean? The concept of individuals sharing potential manifestations is new to me. I thought they only appeared in a way that's unique to you, so how could you know you shared one?"

Odimus notices Mezlickied staring at him, clearly confused and unaware of what's happening.

"Adelphia, you are correct. I've never heard of sharing potential manifestations before either. The one I saw wasn't in my unique shape, it was the same shape as your son's. He mentioned that it led him to the tree where I stumbled upon him."

Suddenly, Odimus remembered that Mezlickied had saved him from harm and started to worry that he would tell his mother.

"I happened to catch him inches from the ground through gravity manipulation."

Adelphia jumps up toward Odimus, "Odimuvalere. What on earth happened?!" She runs over to him and immediately begins checking his body for injuries. While inspecting, she discovers a few scrapes and scratches, so she brings him to the kitchen and gives him a glowing milk-like drink. "Drink up, young man." As he consumes the drink, all wounds heal without leaving a mark. "Mezlickied, thank you for saving my son from a much worse outcome." She questions Odimus about being in the tree because of the potential manifestation. Odimus acknowledges and relays the whole story. Just like Mezlickied, his mother leans down and explains "Odimus, potential manifestations are not signs. They don't reveal anything to you. Essentially, they lead to a location, which is basically the starting line of the next path you should follow. It either connects you with someone of similar potential or marks the starting point. Do not view it as a sign."

Mezlikied acknowledges her corrections and wisdom. Countless individuals miss out on reaching their full potential because they become overly consumed with the manifestation that it is just the mark of a path to follow, which causes them to never succeed. Due to losing sight, others no longer have manifestations as their potential paths vanish. They have reached their highest potential. They stop trying or lose sight of progression.

"Returning to your question; sharing a manifestation differs from both of us being guided to the tree. It is in fact very interesting, and to say the least, I came here to Odimus's home to request you and Erastus to visit every few weeks and to train him in the ways of Erayiphim."

Odimus is surprised he knows his father's name. Now, as for the request, it's unusual for a request like this because twelve-year-old boys typically start their understanding and training with their fathers or father figures, and twelve-year-old girls with their mothers or mother figures.

"My intention is not to replace, but to visit and expand on the fathers' teachings." Adelphia briefly felt offended by the request but then grasped Mezlickied's intentions and swiftly recognized his importance as a teacher.

"Erastus should be home relatively soon. I will send for him to speed things along."

Erastus, enters the door and gracefully enters the living room, greeting his wife and two children cheerfully. "Hello, family of mine." He warmly embraces Odimus and Adoria. Adoria, who is around 3 years old, is Odimus's younger sister. Erastus gives his wife a kiss on the cheek before noticing Mezlikied sitting at the table. He comes to a halt, pauses, and becomes pale as a ghost in fear upon seeing him, thinking he has come to inquire about the relic he's crafting at the forge.

Mezlikied rises and declares, "It appears our paths are crossing again, old friend."

Odimus now knows Mezlikied, and his parents do in fact know each other.

"Erastus, I wish to take part in Odimus's age of responsibility training every few weeks. One week each month. May I respectfully request permission from you, the father and master of this home, to train the boy with you?"

Erastus is at a loss for words and stammers for a full two minutes. He is filled with pride, excitement, and astonishment that the guardian of Erayiphim is here to train his son. Nevertheless, he is still in the process of recovering from his fear of the relic. His response is not only in agreement but also recognizing verbally the great honor it would be to have Mezlickied be a part of his training. Erastus inquires if the acquisition of the heart stone for the potential successor involves taking on a stagiaire.

Mezlikied answers with a smile, "No" and then laughs politely. "Only Erayiphim can grant the heart stone. Each guardian is called by the moon upon the untimely or timely death of their predecessor." Clearing his throat, Mezlikied resumes speaking. "No one else can possess or use the heart except the guardian of the Mother Moon to which they belong. It is possible to take it. But you will not be able to hold on to it for long because it is drawn to me and me alone. I could even take it to the pit of Anglishes on Luxtenebri to the creatures of the pit, and it would still come right back to me even if I was here on the moon of Erayiphim, sitting right here in your home. I'm here because Odimus and I shared a potential manifestation."

As Erastus turns around after filling his plate, he drops it. "Shared a potential manifestation?" What do you mean shared?"

Mezlikied discerns fear and concern in Erastus's eyes. Standing up, he boldly asks. "Despite having access to centuries of knowledge, I've never encountered or heard of this happening. I have a feeling that you possess knowledge that I do not."

Erastus requests that Adelphia escort Adoria to the upper floor. "Tell Odimus to go along as well."

Mezlikied expresses his disapproval of excluding the boy from this situation to Erastus. "I work in transparency, not secrecy."

Erastus expresses to Mezlikied that secrecy is not what is happening and recommends choosing the right time and place for this issue is best. "It is for his protection."

Mezlikied looks at Odimus and says, "Do as your father instructs."
Odimus departs, retreats to his room, lying there for a while before dozing off. When he wakes the following morning, there is a note waiting for him on his desk.

> Odimus, beginning on your twelfth birthday, I will train you one week per month. It's best for me to leave and focus on my responsibilities. You are now one of them, and I will always carry out my duties. I shall see you in five moons.
> - Mezlikied

Two months have now passed, Odimus walks home one day after assisting his father at the forge. Upon turning the corner, he was met with the sight of his house being destroyed by men throwing green balls of acid. Fearing the worst for his mother and sister, he runs as fast as he can. Almost there, he can hear his mother's screams. Breaking free from the men donning Bremium armor, he rushes towards the house, only to be forcefully thrown to the ground by another man. The impact causes immediate blurred vision, ringing ears, and a pounding headache. He could sense warm blood flowing down his head and into his ear. He then feels his body being flung upwards and compelled to move forward. Making a desperate attempt to escape and return to where his mom is, he sees her, but is thrown around by an incredibly strong man, making him feel weak in comparison. Suddenly, he feels a warm, gentle touch on his back, and then the man throws him fully into that comforting embrace. There's a moment where he almost forgets this disaster is even happening. He feels his little sister in between him and the person hugging him, only to realize it's his mother.

"Protect your sister." She whispers.

As he hears those words, his mother is ripped away, and an unforgettable scream pierces his ears. He clings to little Adoria with all his strength and doesn't loosen his grip. Then, silence falls, interrupted only by the sound of his sister's sobs.

A voice starts shouting, "No, no, no, Adelphia! Please not my sweet Adelphia!"

Its father. He rushes out of the place where he was holding Adoria, carrying her toward his father. Witnessing the horror, Erastus swiftly takes hold of both Odimus and Adoria, determined to remove them from the scene where his mother lies. Erastus forced Odimus eyes closed and begs he promise not to look, before running out of their once beautiful home. Odimus and Adoria are both overcome with emotion, weeping and sobbing. Kneeling, Erastus informs them that their mother has been killed. Odimus screams and attempts to return, but Erastus stops him, "Those who follow the Acid Tree are responsible for her death. Her body is a horrifying sight that you should not witness."

"Odimus, Odimus ODIMUS!?"

"Yes, Master Mezlikied?"

Mezlikied directs his gaze at the boy, inquiring if he's reminiscing about that night.

Odimus looks at his master, "Yes, I am."

Mezlikied walks over leans in slowly, and gently puts his hand on his shoulder. "She was a fine woman and mother. It's important to think of her but avoid dwelling on the horror she endured. Keep in mind the highs and lows of our loved ones, as those were part of their journey in life. Avoid contemplating or fixating on the actions of those who caused harm or the events that led to it. It only leads to feelings of depression, anger, and hatred. No matter the cause, we must always choose love over hate."

Odimus gazes at his master, whom he has grown to greatly admire and trust in the past four years. Deep inside, he feels the truth in his words and expresses his agreement. Now that he's sixteen years old, he spends three weeks a month training with Mezlikied and one week with his father. Right after those men took his mother's life, his father fell into despair and became solely dedicated to work. In his decision, he traded the amount of training responsibilities with Odimus with Mezlikied. Erastus didn't abandon Odimus or Adoria, but he felt incomplete and tried to fill the void with his forge. Despite everything, he is still a successful man and a good father.

Mezlikied informs Odimus, "Our work is finished for today. Why don't you go ahead and run home? It's clear that you need to take some time to meditate on your thoughts and find a way to overcome them. Remember, meditation is not about forgetting sorrow but accepting and overcoming it. Those who attempt to evade, erase or stifle sorrow are led towards more challenging paths that take a significant amount of time to heal. Those who concentrate on acceptance and surpassing sorrow ultimately find themselves."

While walking home, Odimus is suddenly shoved down into the mud by Amulius. Odimus stands, "Come on Amulius, not today."

"Why, Odimus, are you thinking about your mommy?"

Odimus swiftly turns, not in anger but with a broken heart, as he questions how one could dare say something about her. "Amulius, that's a new level of disrespect." His arm is unexpectedly compelled to strike himself on the side of his face. Glaring at Amulius, he notices one of his hands is extended towards him. He shouts, "You are only sixteen! It is forbidden to use the gravity fruit other than for defense!" Then, Amulius extends his hand once more and raises Odimus off the ground, hovering approximately 5 five feet. Odimus grows concerned that Amulius might carry out his attack using gravity abilities. "But this is forbidden! a crime against our ways!" Odimus ponders on how could he cross this line to harm me and dare to mention my mother? He begins to feel a new kind of anger. Upon feeling this, he sees a dim light that starts black, almost resembling smoke. It begins dancing around his arm, moving beautifully with elegant pauses and swift spins until it reached his hand. The instant power in his hand was unlike anything he had ever felt before. Next, the faintly lit smoke rushes towards Amulius, swirls around his nose, and then vanishes. For some reason, he knew what it meant. As if he had been taught it before. He's thrown to the ground so forcefully that it takes his breath away. Slowly, he reaches for his bag, grabs a gravity fruit, and quickly takes a bite. The powers of Amulius were no longer effective against him. With all his might, he charges at Amulius and lands a powerful punch on his nose. Amulius collapses and hits the ground.

Odimus is unable to overcome the immense feeling of power and strength he possesses. He turns his attention to Amulius, preparing to continue attacking him. In an instant, he notices Amulius seizing, struggling for breath, and foaming at the mouth. Fear overwhelms him as power diminishes. Using his gravity ability, he lifts his body off the ground and makes Amulius hover behind him as he makes his way to the healing center. Amulius is quickly taken and rushed to the back by the healers at the medical center. Erastus, shortly after being contacted, shows, then Mezlickied not long after. Following their arrival, Amulius's mother and father also arrive to aid their boy. Everyone knew that Amulius mistreats Odimus. He tells them everything, excluding the shadow manifestation he witnessed. He mentions hitting him in the nose as a way to bring him down.

Erastus asks him, "Is that everything?"

Odimus is a very honest young man who has never told a lie. But today, he does. Not only did Erastus believe him, but so did almost everyone else. Mezlikied observes that Odimus has managed to keep his first secret.

The healers came out and speak with Amulius's parents. The mother's eyes fill with tears. Odimus's heart sank into his stomach in fear he had killed Amulius. The healers from Terthiath, the moon of the keepers of the Aura Tree, made bad news impossible. Therefore, Odimus seeing Amulius's mother crying brought him serious fear. No one got sick or died on any moon or the planet unless through killing serious injury, or old age.

The parents went to Odimus and conveyed, "Amulius will live. Feel free to head home, and we'll notify you of more later."

After five days, Amulius's parents visited Odimus's home and inform him that Amulius wants to meet and speak with him. Odimus then visits Amulius in his home.

Amulius turns "Odimus, I'm sorry I have bullied you. I've been teasing and tormenting you for a long time. At first, it was because you were small, then because you came from a wealthy family with a father who was a master of the forge. You always appeared to have it all and were consistently joyful and kind. Then you become a stagiaire to a Guardian. I couldn't grasp why you continually obtained everything. I thought you were happy because of all the things you had, which made me feel even more unhappy. Even after losing your mom, you still managed to be happy and kind. I felt both anger and indifference towards you. I used the fruit against you to prove my strength and superiority despite your training with a guardian. My nose bone shattered, and fragments shot into my brain. The healers successfully restored everything except for a small bump inside my skull that will cause occasional seizures. According to the healers, this mutation in the healing aura is extremely rare. Seizures are an extremely rare occurrence, with only a few individuals in history experiencing them. I'm asking for your forgiveness."

Odimus solemnly whispers, "Amulius, if you are okay with it, I would like to be friends. I will always be here for you. Will you please forgive me for allowing myself to fight back?"

Amulius hugs Odimus, starts crying, and says, "I never meant to be cruel. I don't know why I was so mean to you, I have always wanted to be your friend."

"The darkest crime against me in my life was my mother's death, and the first time I witnessed the Shadow's manifestation was when I harmed Amulius," says an older Odimus. "From that moment on, I pledged my mission to protect those who cannot protect themselves and never give in to the shadow again. Despite making that commitment that day, little did I know that my life would turn into an endless conflict between light and shadow."

Chapter 2

FUINLUNAE AND REHNBURAN

"Fuinlunae…. Fuinlunae….."
Fuin wakes.

"We need to leave immediately."

Fuin is promptly ousted from his house, encountering a scene of mayhem with people running in all directions, homes on fire, and screams echoing. Fear starts to overwhelm him. His parents quickly grab him and his two younger brothers. His father scooping up the younger ones while his mother holds his arms, and they start running. They seem to be running forever, and he ponders why teleportation isn't occurring. He yells at his father questioning this. His father stays quiet as they sprint through an alleyway. The sounds of burning homes, clashing swords, and people screaming appeared to fade. Fuin then asks his father again, "Dad, why are we not teleporting out of here?"

His father looks down at him and whispers, "Because, son, they have posted legions around about every mile marker, and if you teleport, and if they are able, then they will strike you down on site. Their goal is to capture instead of attacking, if you don't teleport. Teleporting near soldiers could lead to us being killed. Our only option is to run and not be caught."

Fuin began to be even more afraid. "Father, who is doing this?

"The Felinus tribe."

Suddenly, they hear stomping around a corner, and his father swiftly blocks their path. Flaineel, his older brother, comes bolting around it. He runs straight into his father's arms. "Father, it's true. They're announcing everywhere that teleporting will lead to being killed on sight. If not, no harm will come to you. Uncle Laric is waiting near the old bridge for us. We must hurry." They continue running across the forge courtyard, where his mother worked. Just as they were about to cross the courtyard, a soldier emerges from around a nearby building. His mother and father try to escape, another soldier emerges, revealing that are were surrounded.

"Do not teleport, and no harm will come to you," says the soldier standing closest to them." The soldier then gives the instruction to come with them slowly and peacefully, or they will be forced to.

Turning to their father, his brother assures him that there are no soldiers near the bridge, proposing that they teleport and guarantee their safety with Uncle Laric. His father looks at him and says, "No, Flaineel, we must not risk the lives of your younger brothers."

"Father, trust me." before stepping back and attempting to teleport. The closest soldier lifts his bow, shooting an arrow as Flaineel calls out to come with him and vanishes, arm outstretched towards his family. His younger brother's shoulder is pierced by the arrow. In agony, he cries out, causing his father to place him on the ground to tend to him. He looks at his wife and orders her to teleport to the bridge with the boys. Without any hesitation, she snatches her wounded son, grabs hold of the youngest, and reaches for Fuinlunae. He rejects her hand and holds onto his father and in an instant, they vanish. He and his father are now being thrown to the ground, and they are forced to wear Anti-Void clasps. They are swept away and confined within cages.

"Fuin, son, it's time to wake up." This time, he is gently awakened and finds himself at the entrance of a cave.

"Where are we father?"

"We are somewhere on Luxtenerbi near the shadowlands."

Fuin is now very scared since he had never been off his Mother Moon, Rehnburan. The soldier yells at the other people of Rehnburan to keep moving as he witnesses their struggle to reach the cave's opening. His father lifts him up on his feet. He hears his mother yell his father's name and sees his mother and two younger brothers running towards them. His father rushes over and embraces his wife.

"What happened? I thought you got away?"

"When we arrived, your brother Laric and his family were already being captured" his mother tells his father. "A soldier noticed us and forcefully pushed us down, whispering that I was fortunate to be a woman with children, or else he would have killed us instantly. Then proceeded to tell me to stay quiet and compliant and that I will survive the day. 'Don't attempt teleportation again, as you may not be as fortunate with your next landing.' So I did as he said. After that, they loaded us into a carriage and brought us here." His mother then looks around and asks, "Flaineel isn't here?" his father shakes his head no. "Where is he then?"

His father looks puzzled and asks, "Was he not with Laric?"

She shakes her head no. As soon as they finish speaking, Fuinlunae hears men shouting, "They are here!" He then begins to see soldiers thrown through the air. People started to panic, unsure of what was going on. Next, Fuinlunae witnesses numerous men teleporting, engaging in combat, and attempting to initiate resistance. Amidst the chaos and fighting, he spots his brother, Flaineel, in the middle of the battle.

As soon as that happens, he sees his father stand up and join the fight alongside Flaineel. It looks as though they were fighting like dragons against lions. Their fight was to defend their home and their people. Then, all the men start to stand up and fight, and it seems like victory was nearly achieved. Without warning, a figure of shadow consumes the surroundings, and the men fall one by one, as if powerless. With eyes glowing bright orange, the shadowy figure moves with great force and power, defeating man after man.

Fuinlunae witnesses the figure approaching his father and brother, prompting him to rush towards them in an attempt to save their lives. At that moment, he experiences the Void Fruit's power surging from within, pulling him into the void. In an instant, he had his brother in his grasp and forcefully brings him down to the ground. He feels being unable to move when they hit the ground. When Flaineel sits up, he grabs Fuinlunae to lift him, and he notices the blood. Flaineel proceeds to inspect Fuinlunae and discovers the injury inflicted by the shadow figure.

"Fuinlunae, no.. no."

Fuinlunae gazes into his brother's eyes and proclaims that he had experienced the incredible power of the fruit for the first time, and that he used it to save his life and how grateful he was to use the power to save a life. He then slumps over and dies.

Flaineel looks up to see his father has been killed as well. He gazes around and witnesses the sight of his fallen people. One man after another. He shouts at the men, ordering them to stop fighting, and then proceeds to physically intervene, forcing them to cease. Upon seeing the men stop, he yells, "Look at all our men. We need to cease fighting." The shadow figure then also stops and transforms into a man. A powerful man, wearing a Bremium helmet crafted with exquisite skill and adorned with black power stones. It was the King from the Shadowlands. All of the people willingly surrender and are taken to the mines.

Over time, Flaineel rises to become the leader of the entire Rehnburan tribe. He educates his people about his brother's actions and words before his passing. The tribe of Rehnburan must embrace using the Void fruit solely for defense and protection as their sacred way of life. For when his brother Fuinlunae died, his eyes were so full of joy that he had harnessed the power of the void fruit to save Flaineel's life. He saw in his brother's eyes as he looked down at his wound knowing he was going to die. His words were not of fear or anger, but instead, his last words were an expression of gratitude for the chance to save a life. This teaching belongs to the Rehnburan tribe and has been so since their capture.

"Thank you, Fuinlunae. Would you prefer Fuin?"

"You can call me Fuin."

Mezlikied acknowledges Fuin and expresses appreciation for the records from his great-grandfather. "I see that you are named after your great-grandfather's brother."

"Yes, I am. It's an honor to bear his name."

"We have many records here at Ministad Reisling. The records are so numerous that even immortals would spend countless lifetimes reading them all. We never accept records without conducting thorough checks to confirm their authenticity and truth. We at Ministad Reisling have thoroughly examined your great-grandfather's journal entries about young Fuin. We unanimously confirm their authenticity, not just in terms of historical facts, but also your great-grandfather's accurate perception of those events. Thus, the Kaleidoscope Council of the Ministad Reisling graciously and respectfully welcomes these journal entries into the esteemed library archives."

For a moment, Fuin mourns the loss of his great grandfather's journal but then realizes he knew every word. His feelings of mourning transform into pride when he hears that his grandfather's journal would be located in the Ministad Reisling.

"So, you and Odimus have become pretty close friends over the past few months while you both study here at the Ministad Reisling?"

Fuin responds with, "Not only has he been a good friend, but also a wise one. Despite the significant age difference, myself being seventy-five years older, his commitment to his studies at the Great Library is commendable."

Mezlikied seemed to stand straighter, feeling a sense of pride for his stagiaire. Then proceeds, "He has grown immensely over the course of his five years here at the Library. Have you considered the offer he made you the other day? Have you made a decision?"

"Mezlikied, I've made a decision - I'll be his dedicated guard on this journey he plans to embark on."

Mezlikied tells Fuin, "It's good to know that you've made a decision. Having a Master of the Void will be beneficial for him on this journey. I need to emphasize one more time how serious the risks we could face on this journey are."

"All variables have been considered, and I firmly believe that pursuing the artifacts that King Kyron has asked us to recover, is a noble pursuit."

Mezlikied stops him during their walk to the library's front doors. "You must not speak to any one of the things the *Tree of Light* has shown Odimus. The road will be treacherous if the Shadow King finds out about these things before we begin our journey. I fear that if the Shadow King was made aware of our plans before their initiation, it could impede our progress permanently. We must tread carefully and skillfully in order to get ahead of him."

"Rest assured, Mezlikied, I haven't spoken to anyone about these matters."

"Good, it is crucial to keep our plans exclusive to the loyal followers of the *Tree of Light.*"

Chapter 3

ITHILWEN

"Father, can you tell me about the Relic and Rune wars?"

King Kyros begins, "A little over five thousand years ago, there was a great kingdom, one that had never been known nor has been since. The King of the land, both powerful and ambitious, was driven by his thirst for power. The kingdom was built on such a grand scale that it could provide comfortable and lavish living for two billion people. In the kingdom of Anglishes, there existed a remarkable forge where relics of all types were crafted, including runes. All individuals in the entire kingdom possessed Bremium jewelry, armor, and relics.

Their power and influence extended so far that they became the ruling kingdom of all Luxtenebri and the thirteen Mother Moons. For at this time, Terthiath had not yet been destroyed. The kingdom's grandeur led to the daily creation of relics and runes on the king's orders. The number grew so much that they had to store them in vaults all over the city. Below the city, a tremendous earthquake occurred, or so they believed. The creatures of the pit emerged from the ground, earning the name we use for them today. In those days, no one had known they even existed. The ground surrounding the city was torn apart, and homes and buildings were easily destroyed. They began to destroy everything in sight. The pit's creatures were so mighty that even runes and relics barely scratched them, leaving the people of Anglishes outnumbered. Some escaped, while the rest were fatally attacked. The creature's destruction resulted in the entire city sinking into the ground, now known as the Pit of Anglishes.

The loss of the ruling kingdom and the abundance of relics and runes sparked a power struggle among the people in Luxtenebri and the Mother Moons. This war was so immense that it resulted in the downfall of all kingdoms and governments in Luxtenebri and the Mother Moons, plunging all the people into conflict. In a valley near the **Tree of Light**, The Valley of Yurthalla, an extraordinary battle never before had, occurred. A massive gathering involving billions of men and women engaged in mortal combat.

All individuals with the ability to fight were aligned with one army or the other. Only a few injured men, elderly, non-warrior women, and children were scattered across Luxtenebri and the Mother Moons. Our ancestor, the great king of Zequiberus, desired an end to this great war. An ignorant yet just man, he poured his life into a legendary rune to awaken its full power. The great king believed it would incapacitate the opposing army and make them easy to capture. He advised his son to remain in the kingdom and take charge instead of going to battle. When he sacrificed himself, the rune exploded and released an energy blast that struck all living beings on Luxtenebri and the Mother Moons. The energy blast's collision with Bremium resulted in the death of anyone it reached who had Bremium on their body. There were only a handful of survivors that day. At the moment of his father's sacrifice, the great king's son took off his crown, the only piece of Bremium he had on him. As one of the few remaining royals, he enacted laws to prohibit the creation of runes and aided in the reconstruction of kingdoms across all of Luxtenebri and the Mother Moons. Not many years later, The Kingdom of Light and the Kingdom of Energy were built by your Uncle and myself. Which is why today they are the sister governing kingdoms. That is the story of the relic and rune wars. Now it's time for you to lay down and go to sleep, my little princess."

"Father!" Ithilwen shouts as she runs into his arms.

King Kyros delicately pulls back and fixes his gaze on her. "It's amazing to see how much you've grown, my dear. Has it really been 3 years at The Great Academy of Achaicus?"

"Yes, Father, three years have passed."

"How's my brother? It has been the same amount of time since I last saw him."

Ithilwen explains how Uncle Kyron appears to be doing exceptionally well.

"Good to hear." Once again, King Kyros glances at her and remarks, "Wow, it's hard to believe that only yesterday you were ten years old and still asking for bedtime stories. Now, you stand before me, a 35-year-old woman. I'm amazed at how quickly time has passed. Share with me the knowledge you have gained about Klibous, our esteemed sun."

"I understand that our sun is pure energy instead of gas, unlike most others in the known universe. A black hole devoured a tremendous quantity of Bremium. Which is an incredibly powerful element, defied the gravitational pull of the black hole and became its core, causing the black hole's gravitational power to make Bremium spin rapidly and generate energy. The energy was produced by it, which the black hole attempted to reclaim. Bremium, as the dominant power, pushed the energy away from the black hole, resulting in an eternal tug of war and the creation of a pure energy sun outside the black hole."

"That is correct, my dear. Now, what about relics? How are they made?"

"The creation of relics is made possible through Bremium tools."

"Can't it be melted?"

"No, Father, it cannot be melted. Relics can only be made from Bremium, and its characteristics can only be altered using other Bremium. No other material has the capability to change it. Bremium tools, like utensils, are required to shape relics by influencing it by an individual's will. The power of the relic increases with its intricacy and beauty."

"Can you tell me where the Bremium tools were discovered?"

"The tribe of Ichassarae from the Ice moon of Ichassarae is responsible for the discovery and creation of Bremium tools."

"Now, Ithilwen, enlighten me on where one can find all the knowledge and learning we know today."

"The place where I have dedicated three years of my life to studying, which is the Great Academy of Achaicus."

"Where can one find a comprehensive collection of records, history, and wisdom?"

Ithilwen tells Kyros, "We go to The Ministad Riesling, which is also called the Library of Great Understanding."

Kyros questions further, "Tell me about the trees that correspond to each of the thirteen moons."

Ludaea, the Fire Moon, is the first thing to mention, along with the great governing kingdom that falls under our kingdom. Glodatri is the moon of the Earth Tree, Erayiphim, housing the Gravity fruit and a republic government loyal to the Kingdom of Light. The twin moons are mutually attracted, causing them to orbit each other. The twin moons, Napthlaphane and Dalanias, are home to the Flight Tree and Wind Tree, respectively. On Luxtenebri, they have a United Kingdom with their capital city located on the floating island of Naphdali. The Water Moon is called Manekaizah, the ice moon is called Ichassarae, the electricity moon is called Levkaetus, and the Elastic Tree moon is called Alnisher. Sohmencharis is the name of the moon of the duplication tree. Rehnburan, the powerful Void Tree Moon, is where the Void Monks live. Zequiberus, our Mother Moon, is home to the Plant and Animal Tree. Luxtenerbi is now home to the Kingdom and Trees of the Aura Tree, which used to be on the destroyed and now barren moon Terthiath."

"Good Ithilwen, you paid attention to your studies, tell me about your life the past three years."

"I met a man named Othare, the crowned Prince of Ludaea, The Fire Moon."

"My dear, that would be a clever match."

"Well, that's the thing, father, we are engaged. We connected because of my friend Adoria. Her brother Odimus and Othare were friends, and from there, our story was born."

"Congratulations! We should host him for dinner, and I'll make an effort to embarrass him and remind him that he has to impress me."

"Father, you will abstain from doing that."

As they walk, her father gently nudges her, hoping she'll accidentally collide with a pillar in the hall. She returns and bumps into him, Shoulder to shoulder Kyros asks, "I'd like to know more about Adoria. Can you elaborate?"

"She's a friend I made at the Academy, starting with Calligraphy studies, then discovering we were also in chemistry and philosophy, our friendship developed rapidly."

"And what do you think of this, Odimus?"

"Adoria and I spent nights studying at their home near campus, so I got to know him a little. He is a Stagiaire of the great Mezlikied…."

"Wait, Mezlikied now has a stagiaire working for him? Mezlikied and I have been friends for a long time, it's amazing to hear this news. It seems that Odimus is a remarkable boy. Is Odimus also attending the Academy?"

"No sir, he is currently studying at The Ministad Riesling under Mezlikied."

"Odimus is also a study of the great library. Even more remarkable than attending the academy. The study program has strict approval criteria, and it is very impressive that he was accepted there."

"Yes, him and Fuin, another person I've become acquainted with."

"Fuin, huh? How many additional friends do you have?"

"There's one more, his name is Orthalla. His story is actually quite tragic, despite him being a good man."

"What do you think of Fuin? Give me some information about him."

"He hails from Rehnburan."

He quickly interjects, "Ah, a monk who follows the Void, very respectable people. How about Orthalla?"

"Out of respect for him, father, I believe his story is one that only he should share."

"Come, daughter, let's go to the courtyard and train. It's been three years, and I think it's time for you to learn not just the skill of a weapon but also the skill of wisdom in battle. Retrieve your training relic."

Ithilwen takes hold of the staff of Saita, the staff used by all warriors for training. This relic possesses the power to transform into any relic and replicate the sensations, weight, and even motion of any weapon you can think of.

"Okay, have your staff become a battle axe, and I will train with a long sword."

Ithilwen swings towards her father with impressive skill, but Kyros remains stationary, adjusting only his knee, hip, and shoulder. Each swing and hit fails to have any impact on him. With each passing moment, her frustration intensifies. Once she mentions the word "sword," the staff enables her to move swiftly and gracefully, as if wielding a one-handed sword. Kyros commands the staff to shrink to a Bowie knife, and it obeys. He demonstrated even greater resistance and skill than she remembers. Ithilwen's anger causes her to lose control, and she starts to attack as if to harm her father. Kyros strikes Ithilwen's sternum, barely taking a step forward but sending her flying through the air, landing on her back.

He goes to her, "True strength in a warrior lies in their will, not their physical power. Bremium is more malleable to one's will than it is to being hammered or beaten with force. I chose was to use smaller weapons every time you changed yours." Despite her appearance, Ithilwen proves her toughness by laughing and offering her hand to be lifted by Kyros.

"Have you been training in the ways of Zequiberus, our Mother Moon?"

"Yes, Father, I have remained committed to our customs."

"Show me!" With no hesitation, Kyros creates vines from the ground to ensnare Ithilwen, who resists by summoning a tree branch at her feet. Then Kyros undergoes a transformation, becoming a humanoid Manticore, while Ithilwen takes on the form of a humanoid Cipactli.

"Ah, I see you've developed a preference."

"Yes, father, I think it's a good choice for me, although the Manticore is also appealing."

"It's not about the form you choose, but how you use it." Using a powerful flap of his wings, he propels himself toward her at an unprecedented speed. She quickly dodges his attack by rolling and then surprises him with a swift strike from her tail.

"I'm amazed! Where did my daughter acquire such wisdom??"

While mentioning Fuin's name, she swings the Staff of Saita, calls out the battle hammer, and swings the newly transformed weapon at him, but he swiftly intercepts it and counters with a knee to her abdomen. Recovering, she proceeds to swing her weapon. They find themselves entangled in an epic training battle. Changing forms between Manticore and Cipactli. The staff's weapon influence is frequently changed, and they train with great vigor. Many soldiers, politicians, and tradespeople gather in the training courtyard to witness this battle between father and daughter. Finally, Kyros stands firm and demonstrates his impressive skills by delivering a powerful punch to Ithilwen's jaw. She is hit with such force that she changes back into a human. Blood spills from her mouth. Kyros advises her to train with Kyaphus at home to address her weakness on the left side. Ithilwen proudly stands up, showcasing her strength as a noble princess, and gives a slight bow to her father, who returns the gesture with a smirk.

"My darling, I love you, and your time at the Academy has brought about significant improvement in your fighting strategies. To whom do I owe gratitude for teaching my daughter such skill and power?"

"My friend Odimus," she says.

"I really must meet this Odimus. Where does he come from?"

Ithilwen informs her father, "Odimus comes from Erayiphim."

Kyros says respectfully, "It makes sense he would come from Erayiphim, seeing that Mezlikied is the Guardian of the great moon, but I mean, where on Erayiphim?"

"I'm not sure, but his father is Erastus."

Then, showing less poise than she had ever seen, he whips around to face her, "He is Erastus's boy?"

"Yes, Father, he is. Why?"

"Erastus was my master of the forge, teaching me everything I know. He helped me become a master and assisted in creating my Relic, the Shield of Light. He is also the master that made the Sword of Light, which your uncle Kyron possesses. Recently, he made a new one that is said to be equal to both the Shield and Sword of Light."

"Yes, that relic is now in the possession of Odimus. His mother lost her life because of it."

"I'm familiar with that unfortunate tragedy. It seems like my cousin is becoming more and more merciless. Have you told him?"

"No, I have not told him of your cousin."

"Why not?"

"Because he is not the one who killed her."

Kyros goes to tell her, "He is the one responsible for ordering the search for the relic."

"Yes, Father, but I saw it unwise to mention my Father's cousin is the King of Shadow."

"Ah, so you did not tell him out of fear of the truth. Daughter, never be ashamed of the truth and don't be a fool of secrets. Secrets cause more damage when revealed later than when initially challenged to be disclosed, regardless of the cost."

"Father, it was not my fear of how it would reflect on me, but rather my struggle to find the right words to share with a friend who is a victim of such a tragedy."

"So, you didn't tell him from the fear of hurting him by bringing up the experience again?"

"Exactly."

"Well, that one is difficult. The truth remains that secrets hurt more in the long run, especially when there's a friendship involved."

"Next time I see him, father, I will figure out how to tell him."

"Who has taught you such wisdom?"

"You have Father." She says with a sigh of love and humor.

"Let us head upstairs, Ithilwen, for I perceive you have something you wish to ask me before you retire."

Ithilwen and Kyros step into her chambers. He looks around and smiles, "You have grown, and I am proud of you. Tell me what's on your mind."

Ithilwen doesn't takes the opportunity immediately, "Father I don't just want to read and study. I have extensive knowledge in science, crafting, forging, calligraphy, history, art, and wisdom. I'm tired of always having my nose buried in a book. I long to go out and have an adventure, seeing the world. Since I was little, you have taught me to use weapons."

"It was just to ensure your safety. You're a princess in the Kingdom of Energy sworn to serve the Energy Tree. Moreover, it is the sister kingdom to the Kingdom of Light. All of Luxtenebri and the Mother Moons are ruled by your uncle, King Kyron. You're expected to possess superior knowledge, wisdom, and understanding than all others. Not gallivanting around trying to act like a soldier or adventurer. First, you need to finish your responsibilities and duties at the Academy, and then prepare to run a kingdom."

"Father, I'm not the one who is the crowned princess. It's Mivanya. Both you and your mother, along with Mivanya, are not only chosen but also immortal. As for me, I am not. Governing this kingdom like you is something I could never do. My lifespan will last between four to and five hundred years."

"Darling, four hundred plus years is an incredibly long duration."

"Yes, it is, but eventually, it will come to an end, and I will age, but you will not. Going on an adventure before taking the right-hand seat next to Mivanya and her King is my ultimate desire. Father, my fiancé is a skilled soldier from the Fire Tree Moon Tribe in the Kingdom of Ludaea and will stand by me. Then there is Odimus, who has in his possession the relic made by his father. He himself is mentored by the great Mezlikied. Then Mezlikied, Adoria, Orthalla, and finally, Fuin will all be part of this adventure. This is a strong party, do you not trust me with any of them?"

"Ithilwen, I cannot entrust my daughter to any man or warrior. Even the great Mezlikied is not deserving of my trust with you. Your kingdom needs your gifts, Ithilwen, you are one of the greatest minds of our age."

"Father, once again, it is not my kingdom but Mivanya's rightful claim. What must I accomplish to earn your blessing?"

Kyros scoffs, then turns at Ithilwen, grabs one of her hands and says, "My love, you have had it since the moment you asked. I will never control you or tell you how to live your life. It is my duty as both the king and your father to ensure that the princess, my daughter, considers the consequences before leaving the kingdom. It's crucial for me to confirm that what you're asking for is truly what you want and not influenced by others. Despite my respect and care for Mezlikied, he has a tendency to meddle. I will always be there for you, but I needed to look into your eyes to see if there was even a hint of doubt. It's clear to me now that there is none. Othare and the others must promise two moons to stay here so that all can train with our elite soldiers. I will observe their training before you go. Because I trust you and not them. Deal?"

Ithilwen is speechless with surprise and stands tall with pride. She graciously thanks her father, kneeling before him in gratitude. Following proper customs, he raises her and assures her of his love and support in helping her to become an asset to this party. He then turns and leaves her room. Upon his departure, she notices her mother and her sister, Mivanya, waiting outside the door, both giving her a slight bow. They exchange smiles and then proceed to follow the king. Ithilwen, realizes her mother and sister were right outside the door, eavesdropping. She closes her room door slowly and sits on the edge of her bed, abandoning her previous demeanor with a joyful yip. She leaps back onto her bed, laughing. Her mother and sister linger outside the door listening in further for a moment. She can hear them giggling while they walk down the hall.

Overwhelmed with excitement with her father's approval, fear suddenly creeps in. However, thoughts of Odimus make her feel safe, and her fear dissipates. Othare comes to her mind, causing butterflies in the stomach and reigniting her excitement.

Chapter 4

ORTHALLA OF TERTHIATH AND THE SHADOW LANDS

Terthiath was once a beautiful moon, for the moon was the home of the Aura Tree. This tree possesses remarkable healing abilities. Terthiath's people serve as healers throughout all of Luxtenebri and the Mother Moons. Long ago, a benevolent king on Terthiath died, and his son inherited the kingdom. He had great potential, but his thirst for power led him down a dark path to the Shadow Tree. He sought the King of Shadow in order to get a fruit from the tree. No one was ever granted permission by the King to eat the fruit. Since he was the King of Terthiath, he allowed him to have a fruit. However, the king had deceived him. He had a different purpose in mind as to why he permitted him the fruit.

The king of Terthiath, being a brilliant scientist, returned to his home on Terthiath and headed to his laboratory. However, curiosity can be dangerous for individuals like him. Using a large Bremium bowl, and the King planted an Aura Tree in a special garden to protect other plants from its roots. Then, he proceeded to crush the shadow fruit and blend it with a mixture of soil and plant-assisted nutrients. Pouring this mixture all over the roots of the Aura tree. The tree quickly started to change and mutate, causing a violent reaction. It even emitted a sound resembling a voice, unlike any known human or animal. Every bone and nerve in the King's body trembled with fear at the sound. However, the King was not only brave, but some might even consider him mad.

Witnessing the mutation caused by the shadow fruit and the transformation of the aura tree, he felt a surge of excitement. People who have experienced the cry of a tree while observing the mutation of any tree from the Mother Moons from the Shadow Tree's roots will confirm that this sound does not bring excitement or joy. The sound of each tree that is planted from the stolen moon is dreaded even by those who serve the tree of shadow. It was the king of Terthiath who first mutated a tree from Luxtenebri's Mother Moons.

Once the tree had fully undergone its mutation, the Aura fruit lost its glimmer and had grown to be about five times larger than a regular aura fruit. This caused the King to exclaim, "What a behemoth!" This is why the fruit is now called the behemoth fruit. The King started experimenting extensively with the fruit, observing its impact on other creatures. As expected, the creatures he tested on grew into behemoth-like mutated beings filled with rage. Initially, the King conducted experiments solely on tiny bugs and creatures but eventually shifted his curiosity towards the mighty Taviathon.

There is one dominant majestic creature that inhabits each moon. The Taviathon was this great creature of Terthiath. He presents the behemoth fruit to a Taviathon, which grows to over twenty feet tall and transformed into a humanoid figure while retaining some of its original features. The Taviathon developed a thick skin resembling scutum instead of fur. It grew incredibly powerful, capable of demolishing a building in a single strike. This change and mutation filled the King with pride for his creation. He referred to his creation as the Terelaviathon. It started raging and causing destruction, but he had anticipated that and secured it with Bremium chains, rendering it unable to break free. After destroying everything it could, it raged for what seemed like an hour. When the creature grew tired, it settled down and started breathing with a growl. With tears in his eyes from overwhelming emotions, he approached the beast. He managed to touch it, causing it to flinch and him to do the same, yet it still permitted contact.

He spent two months training the beast to be calm and obedient. It was only in its initial consciousness that it displayed such anger and rage. None of his previous experiments ever demonstrated peace. However, the Terelaviathon transformed into a peaceful creature. This mighty beast, ridden by the King, possessed exponential power that made armies flee. The King of Shadow arrived to find out what the King of Terthiath had done, and initially, he was angry. However, the King of Shadow was known for his self-control, grace, and occasional charm. Slowly, he placed his arms behind his back and discovered that the King of Terthiath had achieved a feat no one else had, sparking his own desire. He paid a visit to the King's home, and was graciously welcomed inside.

He is informed by the King of Shadow, "I want you to create more Terelaviathons for me. Since you approached me and I unquestioningly accepted your request for a fruit from the Shadow Tree, you must now do the same."

The King was filled with terror as he saw him walk towards his majestic creature and start to pet its snout. The beast naturally exhibited submission. The King was filled with fear at the sight. He acknowledged his command, "Yes, your majesty." The King of Shadow leaned forward and placed his forehead on the beast's snout. Taking a deep breath, the beast exhaled with a sense of relief or contentment upon being touched by its master. Feeling the beast's response to him in this manner, he stood up straight and turned ever so slightly to the fellow King, saying, "You must make me fifty."

The King of Terthiath immediately understood that this was a plan to establish a powerful force for unlimited conquest. "I will Follow your command," he responded once again. "I request that you refrain from touching anyone from Terthiath and make us your sister kingdom."

The king of Shadow, walking towards the front doorstops, doesn't turn nor move and says, "You do this for me. I will make Terthiath a sister kingdom, and you, its King."

The King of Terthiath decided to prevent the replicated reaction of his first mutated beast by placing fifty Taviathon fetuses in pods to grow slowly, nourished by the fruit as it matured into full-grown calves. This way, they would not be mutated in an instant and rage uncontrollably. They grew close to maturity, and one day, one of the King's sons was playing nearby, the boy ventured into the lab. While playing with a ball, he accidentally pressed the activation button, releasing the beasts. Startled, he fell to the floor and then ran to his mother. A few hours later, an unprecedented commotion erupted in the kingdom. The King, having knowledge of the situation, immediately called for an evacuation. Nearly everyone escaped to Luxtenebri, and the calves quickly reached full size within days, which they became unstoppable. Everything in their way was completely destroyed. They devoured and annihilated every living being, contaminating the entire moon's water. With his great beast and armies under his control, the King stayed back, fighting for weeks. Nothing could prevent, or stop the unity of forty-nine Terelaviathons.

The King of Shadow heard of this, smiled and said to his first general, "Lust for power is quite difficult to resist don't you think?"

"Indeed, it is your Majesty."

The king then states, "The king of Terthiath proved to be less resistant to my trap than I had anticipated. Seems I gave him too much credit. As I predicted, the Moon and its kingdom have been destroyed."

The first general compliments the King in saying, "Your cunning, your majesty, is unparalleled."

Many thousands of years later, Orthalla, who is eight years old, is summoned by his parents to come outside and get ready for the ritual, as the Behemoth Fruit will now have an effect on him. Despite having Behemoth parents, Orthalla isn't one until he eats the fruit. His parents tell him to go outside with the rest of the children. His mother interrupts the father and says she wants to talk to him and explain what is about to happen. The father complies and departs from their residence.

She leans down to her son, "I'm to tell you a story, my little joy. Following the destruction of our home, Terthiath, the King of Shadow, brought the Behemoth Tree to the shadowlands and planted it here. He successfully apprehended fifty individuals from our Mother Moon, both male and female. The consumption of the behemoth fruit led to our transformation. We are a small but powerful group, and have undergone mutations. Today, you are eight years old, and the fruit of the Behemoth Tree will affect you, and you will become like your father and I. But I will not allow this to happen. Quickly, we must go out the back door, and I will get you to safety." Grabbing Orthalla, she hurries out the back door and continues running with haste. Orthalla's mother successfully reaches the new homeland of the Aura Tree for the people of Terthiath on Luxtenebri.

Upon reaching the gate, she is suddenly confronted by a swarm of soldiers who quickly stop them. She begins pleading, desperately affirming that she means no harm. Nevertheless, the soldiers start their efforts to bind her. Rather than engaging in a fight, she simply begs for them to cease. But the soldiers show fear in their eyes, and she knows they are not going to listen. She begins to lose faith and begins the process of giving up.

At this very moment, there is a great old man in the city of Terthiath, which is named after the Mother Moon. Outside the gates, he witnesses many people starting to watch this unfold. The man possesses the highest level of wisdom in the entire kingdom. Rushing out the gate, he commands them to cease their actions. The soldiers acknowledge the identity of this man, and despite lacking authority, no man is more respected than him, except for the royal family. His name is Anniphus. The soldiers halt when Anniphus commands.

Orthalla's mother notices him, and tears well up in her eyes as she pleads, "Please, sir, please."

She repeats this plea numerous times until Anniphus interrupts, "It's okay, Madame." He gently places his hands on her back, and she starts to calm down. Anniphus insists on unchaining her, emphasizing that she is not an animal but a human being, and even claims she is a descendant of our ancestors. The soldiers, along with everyone watching, display pure disgust. Not for Anniphus, but for Orthalla's Mother, whose name is Hayleta. Anniphus ignores and inquires, "Madam, please tell me, what do you require?"

She then reveals a large young boy from behind her grasp. In her embrace, he takes on the appearance of a tiny baby, yet when faced with Anniphus, he appears as a young boy standing four feet tall. Anniphus perceives that he has not undergone any mutations.

Hayleta informs him, "He is eight years old and needs to be freed and returned to the people of Terthiath to serve our Mother Tree. Will you please look after him?"

Without hesitation, Anniphus agrees to care of the boy. "Years ago, I lost a son. We will care for him as our own."

Orthalla gazes into his mother's eyes and expresses his appreciation with a heartfelt gratitude. She was aware that he had no desire for the Behemoth Fruit, and all the while, she, too, was drawn to the Aura Tree deep in her heart. Standing there, they knew the other's deepest desire to be liberated from the Shadowlands. Hayleta stands and abruptly turns back to return to her husband. Her feet pound the ground like thunder while sounding the most terrible wails of agony. The sound of her wails fill the city, carrying with it a deep sense of mourning. With a single tear streaming down his face, Orthalla looks at Anniphus. It was clear to Anniphus right away that this boy possessed great strength and would grow to be a formidable man.

Twenty years have passed, and Orthalla is lying in bed. He notices a subtle thumping sensation in the ground. He experiences a sinking feeling in his heart and rushes to the front door. As he opens the door, his mother is standing there. Quickly going to her, they embrace. Orthalla is now towering at 7 feet tall, weighing in at 300 pounds of pure muscle, and her chin still rests on his head while her arms engulf him entirely. The embrace lasts longer than they realize. They release each other, and he steps back, his gaze fixated on her face, where he sees a blend of joy and despair in her eyes. He understands and warmly welcomes her into the house.

Although his home was built to accommodate his size, his mother still finds it slightly difficult. They sit and talk all night. On Luxtenebri, the night is unlike any other as darkness never blankets the entire horizon, except for the shadowlands that perpetually dwell in the absence of sunlight. The people are not affected by this. As most moons do not have a sunset at night due to the planet and moons' orbital rotation around the sun, only one side remains sunless.

They are both fatigued after staying awake throughout their scheduled sleeping period. However, Hayleta insists on continuing this reunions conversation. Orthalla obliges and goes to the cabinet, selects a small slice of the energy fruit, and kindly offers it to his mother.

"Is this fruit of the Energy Tree?"

He nods.

"I've only ever eaten the Behemoth Fruit. Never before have I eaten a fruit of any other Tree of Power." Her excitement soars as she contemplates giving it a try. In an instant, she becomes awake and alert, feeling a surge like a powerful energy source had been attached to her back. Her power, strength, and stamina also appeared to increase. Hayleta was in awe of the effects and conveyed her gratitude to her son. "You said earlier you were admitted into the great academy?"

"Yes, I was admitted a couple of years ago. Anniphus submitted a referral for me, and the Academy quickly sent an acceptance letter."

Hayleta's pride for her son was so great that she starts crying.

"My return home led to my imprisonment by the King of Shadow. Being here and seeing you only brings me great joy. I escaped only recently."

Orthalla promptly gets up and rushes into his room, emerging with a complete Aura Fruit. "Mother, the Aura Trees have the capacity to heal anyone, regardless of their ailment. I want you to take this one. I've dedicated years to studying the Aura Tree, believing it can cure you of the Behemoth Tree. You noticed that the energy fruit had regular effects when you consumed it. I think consuming the Aura Fruit will help you recover from the mutation."

"Do you really believe that son?"

"Yes, I do."

With tears in her eyes, she takes the fruit from his hands and admires it. The skin emitted a beautiful aura, resembling a small rainbow fire. She was just about to eat the fruit, lifting it towards her mouth when of a sudden, the fruit begins to wiggle violently and underwent a mutation into a Behemoth Fruit. She was startled by the reaction, causing her to drop the fruit, jump up from her chair and hits her head on the ceiling, causing some damage. Embarrassed, she tells him, "I'm so sorry son."

"No, no, mom, don't be. It's ok."

"I made a decision about where I wanted to go before coming here, son."

"Where is that?

"Since the Rehnburan people have vowed never to fight but to defend, and considering their limited presence on the moon, I've chosen to support them in their oath and live among them as their defender. During my journey, I crossed paths with a few of their tribal leaders, who assured me that I was accepted among them. So, I have decided to live there."

"Mom, I think that is an excellent idea. I made a friend named Odimus myself at the academy. Yesterday, they invited me to go on an adventure with them, which they've decided to embark on. That's why I returned home, to see Anniphus and talk with him and Mom. I mean...forgive me"

"No, son, she raised you."

"Well, I arrived home to meet with them and discuss Odimus and the team's objectives."

She perks up remembering, "I have something special for you."

"What is it?"

From her backpack, Hayleta reveals a battle axe like no relic he has ever seen before. "Son, this is the battle Axe of Quyta. This relic is ancient and predates the kingdom of Anglishes. There are very few Axes equal to it. It even has a rune already imbued into it. But I have never known what it does. I just know the Axe is very powerful. It has been locked away on Terthiath since its destruction. Prior to arriving here, I visited our Mother Moon and discovered the home of my great, great, great grandmother so that I could find this for you."

Orthalla lifts the relic from her hands, and it starts vibrating, then levitates for a few seconds before returning to his hands.

Hayleta informs him that it has acknowledged him as its owner. "I must make my leave, son. Make sure to look after yourself, and if you happen to pass by Rehnburan, drop in and see me."

They embrace, and his mother says goodbye. Once she departs, he shuts the door and, yearning to witness its power, gives it a gentle swing, a surge of energy emanates from the axe, slicing his kitchen table in half and shattering the window behind it. Baffled, he gazes at the table and window considering he was several feet away and had not even touched the table with the axe.

Laughing, his mother peers at him through the broken glass, "Well, you know what its original design is, now just need to figure out what that rune does. I love you, my little joy." she then pats the window seal and departs for good.

Chapter 5

ODIMUS AND ADORIA ARE ACCEPTED

"Odimus, it's finally arrived. Hurry up man."

As he walks into the room with Adoria, Odimus proposes, "we should go get father first, don't you agree?"

Then she turns to Odimus and inquires about his whereabouts. They both walk up the stairs and knock on their father's chamber door. He grants them permission to enter.

"Go ahead, what is it?"

In his hand, they observe a rod with intriguing markings. He places it down without attempting to conceal it.

"Yes?"

Adoria quickly goes to him and announces that a letter has arrived. Erastus expresses excitement and instructs her to open it. She tears open the letter and starts reading. The Great Academy of Achaicus has accepted the applicant, Adoria, as stated in the letter. Both Erastus and Odimus congratulate her with exceptionally aggressive pats on the back. After a moment of hesitation, Erastus flinches and turns but then follows through and grabs the rod he had previously been holding.

Looking at Adoria and saying in a stammering voice, "This is for you, a gift for getting accepted. I was holding onto it till your letter came in."

Adoria takes it from her father and inquires its abilities since it's clearly a relic. Erastus then proceeds to explain its numerous functions and demonstrates a few of its abilities.

"It is the sole whip-type relic that summons a chain of Bremium, acting as a grappling hook, and allowing you to control your ascent and descent. It has the ability to function as a zip line, carrying you over long distances, and can also be used as a staff weapon for you to beat on Odimus with." They laugh at this playful additional function. "It's a blank slate because there are no runes fused into it.

Adoria gazes at the relic her father crafted and embraces him. Adoria brings the relic close to her heart and utters words of gratitude.

"Now, how are things going between you and Mezlikied, Odimus?"

"I believe this is the right moment to let you know, Father, that I have been accepted to study at the Ministad Resiling."

Erastus and Adoria are completely astonished and fix their gaze on him, fully alert. "Son, why didn't you tell me about your application?"

"Mezlikied requested me to be his stagiaire at the library and in the ways of Erayiphim. During our visit, the Kaleidoscope Council interviewed me and unanimously extended an offer of attendance. So, therefore, it wasn't me. It was Mezlikied."

Adoria hits his arm and asks, "When did you find out, and why are you just now telling us?"

"I don't know, and I thought you would like to hear I was going with you to the Kingdom of Light, just at the other great institute of study."

Erastus fixes his gaze and continues to stare at him for a moment and then proceeds to say "You never cease to amaze me, son but just so you know, just because Mezlikied requests you to study at the great Library doesn't mean you get accepted. Guardians and even Kings have tried to use their influence to get their stagiaires into the great library for thousands of years. The Kaleidoscope Council must recognize something in you as well. It appears that your studies with Mezlikied have made an impact."

With a smirk, Odimus casually shrugs.

"I am a proud father to say that my son is studying at The Ministad Reisling, and my daughter is studying at The Great Academy Achaicus. What a proud day it is. Your mother would be crying right now, making us all happily uncomfortable, wouldn't she?"

They all three chuckle lightly, then share a moment of sincerity for their mother with their father.

A sudden knock downstairs, interrupts the silence, prompting Odimus to investigate. Upon opening the door, he is greeted by Mezlikied, "Ah, come in, master." Mezlikied enters and inquires the whereabouts of his father. Odimus is somewhat taken back by this request, as it is highly unusual for him to ask for his father. "He is on the upper floor." and without delay, Mezlikied walks up the stairs.

"We require privacy momentarily. Please remain out here."

Adoria exits the room and turns to Odimus, "What is that all about?"

Odimus wide eyed responds "Beats me!"

Speaking in a raised voice, "Erastus, you were right. I finally found the record of what you spoke about sharing potential manifestations fifteen years ago when Odimus was a young boy!"

"Mezlikied, please lower your voice. What was said? and who said it?"

"The legendary warrior of ancient times! The one who possessed the Axe and Shield was discovered in the City of Light. He was the owner of the relics that no one can activate and now sits upon the throne."

"Truly?"

"Yes!"

"What was the information provided about him?"

"The records of that time are very scarce. However, the ones I found mention he was the salvation of every tribe from a formidable enemy that nearly wiped out the entire population. According to the story, he and another person experienced sharing a potential manifestation, which started a great journey for him to save everyone from complete destruction. There is even less information about the other individual who shared the potential manifestation with the Legendary warrior of ancient times. However, it does say this individual was his guide and teacher."

"Is that the only information provided?"

"Yes, it appears so. Odimus and I sharing a potential manifestation implies that he is starting a journey that could potentially lead to the protection of us all, and I am supposed to be his guide and teacher, just like the previous one."

"Mezlikied, I believe these records to be true because many years ago, I stumbled upon a somewhat similar story, albeit less detailed."

"Erastus, pardon if I'm a bit forward, but if information is found there in the great library of Ministad Reisling to show that sharing a potential manifestation is potential that Odimus is going to be needed. Then we can assume he is going to one day save Luxtenebri and the Mother Moons from destruction."

"Yes, of course, Mezlikied, but this is still all speculation."

Mezlikied declares further, "No false or slightly altered records of the Ministad Reisling have ever been accepted into the library. All claims are verified as true before admission."

"You need to see Mezlikied, that it is speculated that the shared manifestations serve as evidence of a hero's journey beginning, after recognizing it is not speculative, the only recorded occurrence of this was the story of the Legendary hero of ancient times. You must not assume these things correlate; instead, stay vigilante and by his side while away at the institute."

"Of course, Erastus, I will take care of the boy."

Several days later Mezlikied instructs Odimus. "It is time for us to leave for the great library. Adoria, you're coming with us since the library and academy are close by.

Erastus enters the conversation, "I have bought both of you a house a little off campus for the two of you to share. That way, you don't have to share rooms with strangers or stay on campus. It's no secret that neither of you appreciate people invading your personal space."

"Thank you, Father," says Adoria.

"Now, Odimus, step over here a moment," Erastus then brings out a sword and hands it to Odimus. "This, my son, is yours,"

Mezlikied gently pushes Adoria to the side and, almost correcting Erastus, asks, "Are you sure this is wise to give to him now?"

"If the records are true, then yes, as much as you mean to this family and as much as I respect your council, I remind you that I am the boy's father."

Bowing respectfully, Mezlikied motions for Adoria to accompany him outside. With a hint of worry on her face, she departs.

"Odimus, this is what those men sought the night they took your mother's life." Odimus forcefully returns the relic to his father, refusing to accept it. "Listen to me." Erastus, notices his son's quick reaction to obey him, "I'm amazed by your obedience with exactness, son. You are an exceptional man, unlike my younger self, who was quite defiant, causing your grandfather much trouble." He pauses momentarily, "This relic has been proven to be the third greatest ever made. Only the Shield of Light and Sword of Light are equal to it. This, my son, is the powerful sword of Valiance. Its abilities surpass my knowledge, as its abilities grow, so I cannot provide a detailed explanation of all that this relic is capable of. However, I know from what I have learned, it is equal to the two legendary relics of Light. It's every ability will become known to you through proper training with Mezlikied. That, is why those men came. They didn't come for your mother, nor did they come for me. They came for the sword. Those men, upon capture, all admitted the man that took your mother's life was out of line, and even the King of Shadow counseled against their actions."

"Father, what does he have to do with this?"

"Son, the King of Shadow is the one who sent those men. He wants this relic. It was one of my stagiaires that leaked its existence to him. He sent those men to buy it from me. When I refused, they went rogue, fearing they would be punished if they did not return with the sword. Even the King of Shadow had those men brought to the courts of justice in the city of light. In all governments and kingdoms, murder is an extremely rare occurrence and a prohibited act, except in times of war. You must comprehend that there is no blood on that sword. Justice has been served for your mother, even though it has left a void in my heart. I know that Justice has been found. All this time, I have been making this sword specifically for you. It wasn't intended to be this powerful, but as it was predicted years ago, it exceeded my expectations, leading me to send all my worker's home. The leak to the King of Shadow happened on the same night. Odimus, this sword is rightfully yours. Only two relics were ever made equal to it, and this one is meant for you. Also, very few know of this relic. Due to the court cases involving your mother, only a handful of kings and royal families are aware of it. King Kyros, an old friend of mine, sat on the justice seat that condemned those who had done wrong. He advised me to keep the sword after I attempted to give it to him. He refused, considering what you've been through. He suggested I give it to my son and tell him to use it in honor of his mother."

Taking a moment to observe, Odimus swings the sword and is struck by a remarkable feeling of unparalleled strength, and he knows it is coming from the sword. Suddenly, the sword radiates a light that appears to dance around his hand and arm before eventually sinking into his flesh. The power of the light was so immense that it made his muscles weak.

His father chuckles, "Well, it appears that it belongs to you whether you like it or not."

Odimus glances at his father, filled with wonder, " I feel that it belongs to me, and I am willing to accept this sword as mine." He then holds the sword in both hands stretched out to his father, bows to him and says, "Father, I will use this sword to honor Mother. Thank you." As he looks up, he sees his father struggling to hold back tears. Odimus embraces his father before leaving through the front door.

Odimus walks out the door, he calls for Drilgom, his creature companion from the Moon Erayiphim. Drilgom is a Ngawboves, the great creature of Erayiphim, with the ability to harness gravity. Mezlikied stops and questions the wisdom of bringing Drilgom. "I never go anywhere without her, so the answer is yes."
Mezlikied responds with a smile, "Only if you're sure."

Adoria turns to Drilgom, "Come here, girl!" Drilgom quickly moves towards Adoria and stands next to her.

Odimus murmurs "traitor" under his breath. Laughing, they make their way to the ship that will transport them to Luxtenebri.

Odimus and Adoria have been studying at their respective institutions for several months now. While sitting at his table, Odimus heard the door slowly open and two girls laughing. He turns to his study partner Othare and says, "Sounds like Adoria has a guest." Both of them sit upright, pretending not to have noticed their arrival. Adoria walks through the door with a woman that Odimus can't help but stare at because as she walks in, immediately a leaf of shadow and a leaf of light appear on the floor at her feet, opposite sides of each other, and begin to spin around her. The leaves leave a trail of shadow and light behind them. They are swirling around her, leaving her standing in a spiral cylinder. Both leaves get to the top of her head and disappear.

At that moment, he realizes Adoria is telling him to chill out his eyes. The woman standing there is blushing and giving him an odd expression as well. He quickly realizes that he has been staring at her, observing the potential manifestation around her. He tries stammering his words to explain he wasn't looking at her but the potential manifestation around her. However, he is unable. His study companion nudges him to halt his embarrassing attempts to explain himself, and then Othare stands up to introduce himself. Odimus feels so embarrassed that he resumes his reading.

Despite the awkward introduction, Othare begins flirting with the attractive new woman. Adoria then introduces her friend to the group, identifying her as Ithilwen. Without delay, Othare moves back and proceeds to bow. As per custom, he starts to bow at the hip with seriousness, showing proper respect to a princess. Odimus notices jumps up, and bumps the table, causing it to shift and make a loud noise. He starts to bow, and Ithilwen gives the appropriate dismissal sign, encouraging them to relax.

Adoria reminds everyone "We're not in a formal setting, so there is no need for customs."

Ithilwen, feeling a bit embarrassed, asks Othare how he recognized her. She took great care to ensure that nobody found out at the Academy. It's easy to go unnoticed with a population exceeding three hundred billion people. Family crests are frequently displayed on clothing in society. She chose not to wear her crest for a typical Academy experience.

"As the crowned prince of Ludaea, it's my duty to know you, Ithilwen."

"I've made great efforts to hide my royal status while studying here."

Odimus expresses his apology in admitting to not knowing Ithilwen, inquiring about her reign.

For the first time since they met, Othare shows his friend a sense of disrespect, "Forgive his ignorance, my lady. He is a very wise study companion but seems to be foolish in his knowledge of his ruling government's family line."

Ithilwen respectfully raises her hand to Othare, signaling him to stop speaking. Turning to Odimus, "I am a princess from The City of Energy. My father is King Kyros."

Embarrassment overwhelms Odimus as Kyros is one of his heroes. "I apologize, milady, for not knowing you, your father is a matchless hero in today's world, and I am very familiar with him."

"No, it's not a big deal, truly. There are two kingdoms on Luxtenebri and thirteen Mother Moon kingdoms, or governments, it is quite exhausting to keep up with."

Adoria, who has been casually sitting on the countertop, finally speaks up, "Well, this itself is exhausting, so Ithilwen, I suggest we study in the living room." Many months ago, Ithilwen shared her true identity with Adoria and asked for her help in ending the uncomfortable royal formalities as they occurred. Adoria's behavior was not one of disrespect; instead, it was her way of helping her friend. Othare sits beside Odimus and gives a gentle slap to the back of his head. Odimus and Othare then start laughing uncontrollably.

Ithilwen, Othare, Adoria, and Odimus have been spending a lot of time together since this evening. Almost two years have passed. The four of them, including Mezlikied, are sitting in a café for lunch, with Odimus being the only one who doesn't go to the Academy. They gather every day for lunch at a café conveniently located near both the academy and the library. As they are sitting there, Ithilwen looks up and becomes entranced by a potential manifestation. However, the most alluring part of this manifestation is that she notices it is in the shape of a leaf. Othare, who is now Ithilwen's boyfriend, sees her turning a bit pale. He leans in and gently asks her if she is ok.

She stammers to look into his eyes and whispers, "Do you see this too?" Over the past couple of years, Ithilwen has grown very close to Odimus and Mezlikied, and along the way, they have told her how their shared potential manifestation brought them together.

Witnessing Ithilwen's uneasy demeanor, he scans the room in confusion and is taken by surprise by the sight of a leaf gracefully dancing on the table. At this point, the entire table falls silent, and Odimus, who is facing the other way to order a refreshment, turns and also notices the leaf. Everyone in the group appears to see the potential manifestation and is now fixated on it. Odimus feels his heart sink as he notices everyone sharing this manifestation. The waitress, unable to see what they're looking at, grows concerned and inquires about their well-being, Mezlikied, whose eyes stay fixated on the leaf, hushes her and bids her to leave. The group is unable to speak, but then the leaf unexpectedly jumps into Odimus's chest like a gentle hop. At that precise moment, a man reaches out to touch Odimus's shoulder and requests his name. Mezlikied leans over and dismisses him.

The man refuses, "Excuse me, may I ask your name?"

Odimus turns to him and gives the large man his name looking at him with astoundment at his size. The man pulls up a chair and introduces himself as Orthalla. He promptly and forcefully states, "I pursued a peculiar potential manifestation in the form of a leaf, which, as I came into this Cafe, it rested upon you. Leaves are not my potential manifestation symbol. Can you explain this?"

The whole group is astounded someone else saw this, then, to their uttermost surprise, another gentleman standing behind them says, "I too followed a leaf of potential manifestation here that rested upon you, sir."

Mezlikied immediately and, with an intense manner, demanded, "We must change the location of this conversation."

The group was frozen and confused by the event. Mezlikied barks, "Now!"

They all quickly stand and leave, with Ithilwen leaving payment in the form of a Bremium coin before exiting the Café. Mezlikied proposes that it is very important to find a secure location for their discussion. Obvious concern starts to grow among the group.

Orthalla, being a man not easily troubled states, "My father's home of study is here near the library. He is one of the servants of the Ministad Reisling."

Mezlikied steps through the group towards him and asks, "Who is your father?"

"Anniphus the Wise."

Mezlikied puts his closed hand over his heart and slightly bows with his head, looking toward the ground, and says, "The son of Anniphus the Wise is a friend of mine. I am Mezlikied, Guardian of Erayiphim and a servant of The Ministad Reisling."

Orthalla, having had heard of him, says, "Follow me."

Everyone except Odimus is now very confused by these things, but they follow Mezlickied's instruction.

They approach the home, Anniphus opens the door and as they all stand for him, he laughs and asks them not to do that in his home. Everyone, except for Ithilwen, ceases their respectful bows. He approaches her and whispers, "Acknowledging your identity, I observe that propriety is highly valued in these circumstances for you princess. You are dismissed from your bow." In turn, he presents the designated bow to royalty, and she raises him according to customs. Shifting attention away from everyone else and directing it towards Mezlikied. Without hesitation, Mezlikied announced that a potential manifestation was shared with the whole group.

Anniphus sits upright and almost shocked, "Shared?"

"Yes Anniphus, shared." Says Mezlikied

"This event is only known to have occurred once in recorded history. The knowledge was only shared by the legendary warrior of ancient times and one other individual."

Mezlikied agrees by saying, "Both Odimus and his father Erastus are aware of this."

"Erastus, you say? The great master of the forge? I am amazed at the lineage you come from, my boy. It appears that their potential is guiding you and others towards you. We either need to fear greatly, have great assurance and feel peace, or both." Anniphus rises and recounts the tale of the legendary warrior before removing a book from a stand holding it and it alone. This book is anything but ordinary. The book has a ring binding and is made of Bremium metal plates instead of paper. The man standing behind the group, Fuin, also observed the potential manifestation. He was standing with his arms folded, dropped them and verbally, almost uncontrollably expressed his bewilderment "It can't be!"

Anniphus, surprised the man knew of the Bremium plates, looks up. "So, you are familiar with this book?"

"Only those with the greatest desire for wisdom's paths know this book," Fuin says.

Everyone, except for Orthalla, had no knowledge of this book, including Mezlikied. Anniphus informs them this is more than just a book; it is a precious relic called the Book of Ministad. Everyone knows of this book, they were just unaware of what it looked like. Anniphus sets it down before the group.

Mezlikied looks up to Anniphus and asks, so you are the holder of the book?"

"Yes, I am."

"Did you obtain this from the library?"

"Yes, Mezlikied, I did."

Mezlikied readjusts himself in his seat, unconsciously showing envy. Odimus elbows him and snickers seeing him react in this manner. A few others also chuckled. It was obvious. Anniphus even has a smirk on his face at his reaction.

"Can anyone here tell us what this relic is capable of?"

Two others attempt to answer, but Fuin does not allow anyone else to speak. "It is connected to both the Great Library and the Great Academy. Any and all information known to all of Luxtenebri and the Mother Moons is found in both institutions, and this book can access everything they both have to offer. Additionally, if any records are discovered in an unfamiliar language, simply placing the parchment on the cover briefly and removing it will result in an instant translation of the parchment's contents, thanks to its access to boundless knowledge that surpasses the two great Institutions. Many great mysteries have been solved and uncovered for the Institutions through this book. The foundations of both Institutions are built upon it. If it were not for this book, we would not understand what we know today. Many mysteries would have never been solved, and many things would have been undiscovered. Luxtenebri and the Mother Moons, through this book, have amassed immense knowledge, even providing answers to unasked questions. Despite its limitations, it is believed to possess knowledge thousands of years ahead of our current state. The unknown mysteries have only not been revealed because the right questions have not yet been asked of the book. The book's mysteries can only be revealed by those with the greatest concentration and purest heart."

"Yes, Fuln, that Is correct. So far, I've only discovered a handful of new pages and knowledge within the book. Yet, I have acquired the skill to make the book provide me with answers based on the existing knowledge we have already obtained. It is how to obtain the unknown knowledge that I have struggle to understand."

Fuin leans in closer and asks if he can try. The moment he touches the book, it breaks its bindings, and all of the individual Bremium plates begin to float around him in all sorts of directions; the three rings float before Anniphus and line up perfectly in line before his right eye as if to show Anniphus to look down the rings. He looks down the rings he sees they are focused on Fuin's heart. As he gazes down the ring bindings, he can see that Fuin's heart is full of light, almost equal to that of the *Tree of Light's* fruit. Then, it quickly returns to the table and rebuilds itself. The entire group, in awe of this moment, directs their gaze at Fuin and then simultaneously shifts their attention back to Anniphus.

Anniphus looks at Mezlikied, "Never seen that before." With a slight laugh, he chokes on his words for a moment and says, "Well, if you'll excuse me, I must consult the Kaleidoscope Council on this matter. Since you are on the council, would you consider coming with me, Mezlikied?" The remaining members of the group dedicate time to introductions and becoming acquainted.

Chapter 6

THE TREE OF LIGHT.

In his bed, Odimus begins to dream of a beautiful and radiant light beyond description. The beautiful light disappears from his sight as he leaves from within the glorious sun Klibous and quickly turns his gaze towards the *Tree of Light*. Although he had never seen the *Tree of Light* in person, the description he received was not anything close to what he was witnessing before his eyes. It was incredibly beautiful, towering over one hundred stories tall, which reached a height of about fifteen hundred feet, surpassing any tree he had ever seen. He was aware of this because he had a moment to perform the rule of thumb while standing in front of the tree. As soon as he determined the tree's height, he found himself transported to the base of its roots, where he witnessed, within the trunk of the tree, something even brighter and whiter than the tree itself. Slowly, it left the tree trunk and found a place in his hands. It was immediately clear to Odimus that it was the Heart Stone of Luxtenebri. He came to the realization that the *Tree of Light* was the guardian of Luxtenebri, just as Mezlikied was the guardian of Erayiphim. Throughout his time at the great library, he had never learned of this information. After leaving his hand, the heart stone went back into the tree trunk.

He was forcefully expelled from the presence of the *Tree of Light*, causing his stomach to churn with fear and anticipation, which caused him to become nauseous until the expulsion abruptly ceased. After feeling the motion stop, he swiftly opened his eyes and beheld the entirety of the planet from Luxtenebri's orbit. His consciousness entered the soil as if stepping into a fourth dimension and followed the roots of the *Tree of Light* until it reached the end. Then, looking closely, he perceived another set of roots that were dark and with barb-like roots. They were very tiny, nearly impossible to see with the human eye. If the 4th dimension view hadn't been magnified, he wouldn't have observed the roots. The dark roots began to intertwine with a single one, linking it to the *Tree of Light*.

He was hurried away once more, and that familiar feeling in his stomach resurfaced, yet Odimus chose to keep his eyes open this time. He departed from the land, then rushed down to the opposing side of the ***Tree of Light*** and arrived in front of a different tree, yet he sensed the ominous presence of this other majestic tree. It was immediately clear to him that this was the Tree of Shadow. He began to feel a sensation like it was trying to devour him. He grew terrified, believing the tree would end his life.

For the final time, he was rushed back to the orbit of Luxtenebri. He felt information fill his mind, telling him the Shadow Tree lacked sentience and functioned solely as an instinctive weed, devouring everything in its path. He then shifted his focus to the ***Tree of Light*** and perceived it as having a certain level of sentience or self-awareness. Sentience was never attributed to any tree before. Sentience was known to be within the moons, which is how they determined their selection of guardians with Heart Stones. He quickly realized that the ***Tree of Light*** was sentient because it was the chosen guardian of the heart stone of Luxtenebri. Immediately upon realizing this, his gaze was forced to stay looking upon the ***Tree of Light,*** and an image of the roots flashed in his mind, giving him a piercing headache. For a brief moment, he observes the light emanating from the ***Tree of Light*** flicker and fade. Then, his gaze is forced to look upon the Tree of Shadow following yet another flashing image of its roots in his mind, giving him an even greater headache. The planet is overrun by the roots of the Shadow Tree, causing the ***Tree of Light*** to die and wither away. The subsequent consumption of Luxtenebri caused an overshadowing of the mother moons as well; they all commence to whither and conclude in the same way. Odimus sensed the ***Tree of Light*** mourning the loss of the Mother Moons and heard its plea for him to save them all. Next, a glimpse of the King of Shadows appeared as he stands before his armies, pointing towards the ***Tree of Light*** and ordering its destruction. He sees the shape of the Shadow Tree behind him and feels connected to its narrative as if the tree of shadow and the shadow king have become one, and now, through a sentient being, the purpose of the tree flows through the shadow king. Suddenly, an unbearable pain engulfs his head, unlike anything he's ever experienced, and all he sees is a Leaf of Light and a Leaf of Shadow in front of him right before he awoke.

As he awakens, a cry of agony escapes Odimus. He is extremely weak and can hardly move. Adoria hurriedly comes to his aid but soon realizes her efforts are futile after getting him into bed. He is running a fever and sweating excessively. At the Academy, she learned that Luxtenebri and the mother moons had been free from illnesses for thousands of years due to the use of the Aura Tree, so she has never encountered a real fever. Rushing downstairs, she quickly grabbed a slice of Aura Fruit and mashed it into a drink. She raises it to Odimus, and the cup seemed to possess a comparable essence to the fruit. Thus, Odimus recognized its nature and consumes it. They were surprised to find that the drink proven to be useless. Adoria, in a state of panic, unsure of what to do as the Aura Fruit has never failed to heal anyone. She informs Odimus that she will summon Mezlikied.

Mezlikied walks into his chambers a little over five minutes later. He places his hand on his head and exclaims, "You are right. Are you sure you gave him the proper amount of Aura?"

Adoria panicking, responds affirmatively to her master.

In a state of great fear, Mezlikied declares, "We must transport him to Terthiath, the Aura city. Request the presence of Orthalla to aid us, as he belongs to this tribe and kingdom."

Adoria quickly goes to fetch Orthalla. Odimus, weak and barely able to move, senses them soaring in the wind, mistaking them to be on a ship. However, he feels his hand on something as soft as feathers and beholds the majestic Volantuiva, the magnificent creature of Nathlaphane. Being on the mighty Volantuiva fills his heart with excitement, as he has always wanted to see one. Quickly, his excitement returns to agony. He hears Adoria's voice telling him they're almost there and to hang on. Leaning slightly to see what she is speaking of, he witnesses a fire resembling a rainbow engulfing the entire city, confirming it as Terthiath, the Kingdom of the Aura Fruit. He loses consciousness.

Odimus wakes up slowly and is surprised to find Ithilwen sleeping in the chair beside the bed. As he surveys his surroundings, he notices only her.
"What is going on?" he lets out verbally.

Suddenly, from the floor at her feet, shoots up Othare, "Odimus!" He leaps onto the bed to embrace him. He reciprocates the hug feeling extremely weak.

Orthalla leans up from the other side of the bed and stands upright, then sits on the bed's edge. Adoria stands up from the same side as Orthalla, following Fuin from the foot, then sits on the bed's edge. A faint creak escapes the bed before it collapses, its four legs giving in. "Orthalla!" they all say in unison, and burst into laughter. At that moment, the door swings open. Mezlikied arrives, instantly inquiring about the welfare of his beloved Odimus.

"I'm fine. How long was I unconscious?"

Ithilwen leans near him and says gently, "Five days, we have been stricken with confusion… and fear"

Another confirms by saying, "Ithilwen has been present in the room the past four days, assisting the Aura tribe medical team in their efforts to combat the fever. They were clueless about your illness, and then last night the fever suddenly disappeared."

In a sudden moment of clarity, Odimus remembers what he saw. "Mezlikied, I witnessed a vision from The ***Tree of Light***."

"You what?"

"A vision, by the **Tree of Light**. It revealed to me that it was in the possession of the Heart Stone of Luxtenebri, making it the Guardian of the moon. Just as you hold the Heart Stone of Erayiphim, making you the Guardian of Erayiphim." All went silent. "From deep within the planet's soil, the roots of the Tree of Shadow are attacking and seeking to destroy the **Tree of Light**. The King of Shadow is responsible for the Tree of Shadows' strong and extensive root growth. The King is planning to destroy the **Tree of Light** and conquer all of Luxtenebri and the Mother Moons. The fall would result in the extinction of all life on the planet and the Mother Moons. I was weakened and feverish from the vision, sharing the fear of the **Tree of Light** and the desperate pleas of the Mother Moons for me to save them." Odimus starts to make an effort to get out of bed. "We need to inform King Kyron in the City of Light right away." Despite everyone's attempts, he cannot be convinced to stay. He assures them that he is okay, stressing its utmost importance to inform the King. Luxtenebri having a Heart Stone was unheard of in all the library's records, including those known by Mezlikied. Despite skepticism, he entertains the idea that Luxtenebri could, in fact, have a Heart Stone since it is a part of the Mother Moons each with their own stone. He looks at Odimus with more fear than concern now because of what Odimus has been shown. Recognizing Odimus as an honest individual, he bends down slightly, reminiscing the times when he and Odimus were younger. He quickly comes to realize he was no longer a boy, and was not able to bend down very far. With a gentle voice, he says to Odimus, "We will figure this out as we always do together." He places a hand on one of his shoulders and looks to Ithilwen. "Can you arrange a meeting with your uncle?"

She responded with, "I can, of course."

The group are to go home and retrieve their ceremonial robes to interact with the royal family. They are to meet him at the gates of the *Castle of Light* in one week.

Exactly one week later, they all gather at the castle gates. Standing in awe, they behold the magnificent gates of the castle walls swing open. Odimus looks to Mezlikied, curious about the large Bremium gates and how it was possible to have constructed them.

Mezlikied informs him, "Your grandmother, with your father as her stagiaire, led a team of one thousand masters of the forge in constructing the gate doors of Bremium over a span of ten years. If anyone tries to attack this city, the gates can generate a shield to cover the entire area since the castle is at the center of the city. This city has remained unchallenged since it was built. Many have tried to conquer the **Tree of Energy**, where Ithilwen's father is King, but none have been able to defeat him."

As the gate doors swung open, Odimus marvels at their artistry. Ithilwen emerges from the gate doors with the grandest white light shining behind her, casting her as a dark, shadowy figure. Ithilwen can be revealed to him as his eyes adjust to the magnificent light. Once more, he catches sight of the dancing feather of light and feather of shadow around her, just as he did when they first met. His heart sinks into his stomach, but he regains his composure, remembering she is engaged to Othare. At this moment, he notices Othare approaching her from behind the gates. He walks up to Odimus and urges him to witness the magnificence of the Castle behind the gates. Using a headlock, he maneuvers Odimus towards the gate's doors. When he sees Ithilwen's eyes, he notices a blend of happiness and sadness. Othare pulls him into the city, she waves at Odimus gently, and he waves back. While they approach the Castle doors, he notices smaller versions of the same doors at the gate and is once again amazed by their craftsmanship. He runs his hands along the doors, exploring every nook and cranny of their magnificence. His father's abilities continue to astonish him.

"This is our family legacy in the greatest kingdom ever known." Adoria proudly proclaims.

Odimus encourages her to follow in their father's footsteps and believes she will excel, as her forging abilities have impressed the entire academy and even rival their father's skills. With a humble tone, Adoria looks towards the door and confesses her aspiration to acquire the same level of craftsmanship as her grandmother and Father. Odimus takes hold of her hand and declares that she will. At that moment, they realize the doors have no handles.

Looking back at Ithilwen, they see her chuckling. "I'm guessing you all aren't accustomed to Bremium crafted doors?"

From others in the group, a few chuckles were heard because of the two.

"How are you not familiar with Bremium doors being the children of the greatest master of the forge!?" Othare playfully asks.

Adoria sassily responds, "I'm not done with my studies, so excuse me if I don't know much about Bremium doors, and it so happens they are exclusive to royals and vaults."

Othare walks over and tells Odimus to open it for them through his will. He, knowing his skill in willing Bremium was unmatched, was eager to observe the doors' reaction. Following Odimus' orders, the doors begin to open. Ithilwen and Othare exchange looks of surprise and confusion. Othare seeks Mezlikied out for understanding. He ignores them, walking forward. Standing in the doorway curiously observing their opening for Odimus. His expression indicates more bewilderment than confusion.

Another confidently and playfully walks through, saying, "I guess he is born a noble of will, not noble of blood."

Odimus, baffled in confusion "...What?"

Ithilwen responds, "Only those with noble bloodlines can open Bremium doors made for castles. Opening a door through sheer will has never been accomplished by anyone not born of noble blood. It appears that Othare has assumptions about you, which is why he instructed you to open them."

Others declare, "The growth of my experiment and observations is ongoing."

"But what is it that you're talking about?" Questions Odimus. As he stands in the doorway, everyone else enters the Castle. Ithilwen and Othare pay no mind to him as they hold hands. Odimus, now more demanding, says, "Come on, tell me about the experiment!" Everyone is now inside the Castle, and therefore, Odimus gives up asking and hurries to catch up.

The King and Queen are standing on the stairs. A proper homage is paid to the King of all Luxtenebri and the Mother Moons. This bow is not situated at the hip. The men placed their right knee on the ground, left hand flat on the floor, and bowed their heads to the floor. The women rest on their heels with their backs straight upwards, eyes up to show equality with men who kneel on one knee before the King and Queen. All of them are raised by the King in accordance with proper customs. Without hesitation, he instructs Odimus to stand and join him and the rest to accompany the Queen. "Odimus, I've heard that you had a vision from the *Tree of Light*."

"Yes, Your Majesty."

"Formalities aren't necessary here, Odimus, although appreciated. Generations of your family have been friends to me here in my kingdom. I knew your grandmother's parents when they were young."

Hearing this surprises Odimus. Kyron looks at him, "I have had my records concealed of my lineage to protect my family from enemies. But I will tell you that the Mother Moon of my ancestry was Ichassarae, and your great great great grandmother and I went to school together. We'll keep this our little secret, okay?"

"Yes, King Kyron, I will keep this a secret, wow!"

"Now, I've heard a great deal about you. I have heard about the Sword of Valiance and the tragedy behind it. My condolences. I heard you are the youngest person in centuries to be accepted to the Ministad Reisling for study." The king's slight smirk gives away his knowledge of the hidden feelings for Ithilwen, "I see you are leaving a lasting impression on my niece." Despite that, Odimus maintains a composed demeanor, controlling all of his thoughts and emotions. The king stares momentarily, chuckles, and then shifts his gaze away. Continuing, the King inquires more about the vision, and they proceed from the outside hallways into a large courtyard, where Odimus witnesses the **Tree of Light** in all its glory, exactly as he had seen in his vision. Thousands of potential manifestations burst forth and danced around the tree, creating a beautiful and magnificent display. All the manifestations went exactly into the trunk of the tree, where the Heart Stone was located. The King observes Odimus as he approaches the tree and realizes he was witnessing something extraordinary. Kyron steps beside him, "Share with me all of what you saw in your vision." Odimus composes himself and recounts to the King exactly what he witnessed the potential manifestations displayed.

The king's expression shows growing concern. As Odimus closes his statements, Kyron responds, "So my cousin is plotting to destroy the **Tree of Light**? Despite centuries of peace and collaboration, he now plans to attack us, even though we allowed him to create his own Kingdom. The tree seems to have knowledge of this and is frightened."

The *Tree of Light* suddenly emitted an intense glow, causing Odimus and the King to shield their eyes. As the light dimmed, The Heart appears before them both. The courtyard guards are so astonished that they drop to their knees in reverence. Everyone understands what is being shown to them. All who witness this event feel as though they are being enlightened and privileged to know that the *Tree of Light* was the guardian and protecter Luxtenebri. The *Tree of Light* reveals the Heart Stone to confirm Odimus's vision to the King, and then slowly returns to the tree trunk, leaving Kyron and Odimus speechless. It takes nearly half an hour for them to come to speak. King Kyron finally breaks the silence. "I am committed to protecting the *Tree of Light* and will take all necessary actions within the confines of this city to ensure its safety. Odimus, it would be very foolish of you to reveal what I'm about to ask of you." Odimus turned to the King, eagerly seeking answers or guidance. The King seats himself on a bench close by and instructs the guards to depart. They take their leave.

"Odimus, you hold one of the most remarkable relics ever known. I am in possession of the Sword of Light, and my brother has the Shield of Light. Both were made by your father. It is believed that only the Book of Knowledge and your sword can compare. Additionally, there are mythical objects like the ancient warrior's axe and shield that reside on my throne. Despite their inactivity, it was claimed that they rescued our ancestors many millennia ago. Through careful examination of the axe and shield, we learned how to construct relics similar to them by using Ichassarae's tools. Relics provide different benefits compared to the fruit born of the Trees of Power. The creation of runes is forbidden due to the relic and rune wars, but obtaining them is not. You just have to register them upon finding. Only occasionally are they taken due to the runes being too powerful. However, very seldom are runes found. They can bestow even greater abilities to relics and Bremium armor. In the Ministry Resiling, there is a record of every rune ever made. There are known among those records, many runes with untold abilities. I am asking you to go on a journey to collect these runes and use them to save the *Tree of Light,* which will save Luxtenebri and the Mother Moons.

I have lived for thousands of years, and the *Tree of Light* called me to be the King of the city that protects her. We were among the first immortals, my brother, cousin, and I, after the Relic and Rune Wars where so many perished; we were just little children then. When my cousin went exploring, they stumbled upon the *Tree of Shadow*. He started serving after eating the fruit. The *Tree of Light* inspired me to build a city and appoint my brother as the King of the *Tree of Energy*, establishing sister kingdoms to protect the land. It seems the vision I was given, was to protect it from my cousin. Until today, I had not understood the purpose of the vision I received, and only my brother knew about it. I didn't know that the Heart Stone was hidden in the tree, either."

"Odimus, you have been chosen for the mission. I request that you gather the runes with a trustworthy party. During the wars that aimed to conquer the *Tree of Energy*, I did the same thing with my brother and your father. Our team consisted of elite soldiers who also collected ancient runes." The *Sword of Light* is lifted by Kyron, unveiling a rune embedded in the hilt. "When you obtain a rune, it can be fused into a relic. A relic can only admit one rune, but when fused with one, it can gain an ability or an additional ability." Kyron releases the sword, it obeying his commands, floats in the air. "This is the sword's original abilities, crafted by your father, as you see before you,"

Suddenly it caught fire with a blue-like flame so intense that even five feet away, Odimus had to lean back. The fire ability is due to the rune. Kyron informs that "The fire is ideal for the sword, allowing me to ignite it from afar to combat enemies with a blazing force." Rapidly spinning, the sword generates a vortex of fire before suddenly stopping. "There are very few that hold such power, Odimus. The sword of yours possesses great potential as well."

"The body is unable to cope with more than one relic weapon due to the draining effect. The body is not drained by armor as it lacks abilities. But when you combine a rune with armor…." Kyron activates his Bremium armor, transforming from regular clothes to instantly being covered in it. Odimus receives instructions from Kyron to strike him with his sword. Despite his hesitation, Odimus follows the instructions. With a powerful swing, he is halted just before striking the armor as if unable to touch it. "There is a forcefield enveloping my armor, extending seven inches in every direction. It possesses void-like capabilities." Odimus was amazed. The King's will powers down the armor, and he moves closer to Odimus. "Once abundant, runes are now scarce and can still be discovered in ancient ruins. It is known that there are many across Luxtenebri and the Mother Moons. Many years ago, I went on a search for them with my brother, your father, and our team. We found many, but it proved to be a very treacherous and dangerous journey. The man you refer to as master was also part of that team."

Mezlikied and his father had never mentioned this before, leaving Odimus stunned. "Don't worry if they never told you; they were sworn to secrecy. Odimus, your task is to form a team and collect one rune for each relic weapon and Bremium armor, just like mine did years ago to defeat an army that tried to seize the *Kingdom of Energy* and *Kingdom of Light* from us. Thankfully, they were unsuccessful at the entrance gate to the *Kingdom of Energy*. Without our runes and relics, we would have failed. I am confident that this is the right course of action for what is coming." Odimus comprehends King Kyron's instructions and proceeds to perform a proper bow on one knee, but the King refuses. In the traditional way that a King bows, he kneels before Odimus. Few have seen this ever happen. Odimus, taken back, looks at King Kyron confused and shows ignorance of what to do. Kyron softly requests to be raised in the appropriate manner. Odimus obliges and does as he saw the King do earlier. Upon rising, he shares, "The revelation from the **Tree of Light** being sentient, and the role of being the guardian of *Luxtenebri* is all thanks to you. Today, I owe you a gesture of honor fit for a king." Odimus thanks him, very uncomfortable yet with composure.

While returning to the group, King Kyron inquires Odimus if he had been tested at the age of eight with a leaf from the *Tree of Light*. Odimus confirms, stating that it withered in his hand, but before that, it had retained its light for so long that they believed he was chosen until it eventually withered away.

King Kyron ponders, "I wonder if the tree's intention was for you to reside outside the kingdom rather than within its walls. So that you may discover your path back. Come with me." He then takes a leaf and sets it in Odimus's hands. Unlike when he was a child, the leaf didn't wither. "Odimus, it appears you are destined to serve in the City of Light."

Shocked and perplexed as to why the tree didn't choose him as a child, perhaps if it did, his mother would still be alive. Without delay, he pushes these thoughts aside and directs his gaze towards the King.

"It appears that you are meant to be here in the City of Light. However, it is customary for every boy and girl at the age of eight to undergo this test, and if chosen, they live here with their family. Considering your advanced age and the departure from tradition, I'll give you the freedom to decide if this is where you want to be after your journey. For now, I'll keep this our secret."

Odimus shows appreciation to the king, and they return to the group. King Kyron observes the interaction between Odimus and his friends, which reminds him of moments from many years ago when he was with his brother Kyros, Erastus, and their friends. He notices numerous similarities between Odimus and his friend Erastus. He proceeds to call Odimus over one more time and quietly suggests, "It seems you already have a team in place. I heard you all shared potential manifestations; looks like your team was assembled for you."

Odimus steps back, takes a breath, turns to look at his friends and back at the King and whispers with a smile, "Ya know your Majesty, I think you are correct."

Before their departure, the question befalls King Kyron, "How was it possible for Odimus to will the castle doors open?"

King Kyron looks to Odimus and back to Othare. "Usually only noble blood can will a castle's Bremium door open, but so can a chosen one of the *Tree of Light*." Odimus is neither, so one must wonder if he IS one or the other after all." The king performs the formal dismissal signal by raising his hand, prompting everyone to bow and exit. King Kyron summons Ithilwen and, after sending the others away. Othare and Odimus glance back as the King shares a secret with her. She seems shocked but regains composure quickly, bows, and catches up.

Questions are asked but she dismisses them, "That is a matter between the King and I."

The party is now back at the Café, sitting around the table a few days later, Odimus decides to speak up. "Mezlikied and King Kyron have advised me, and now I will disclose what the King has requested." He proceeds to recount the things King told him and everything they witnessed at the *Tree of Light*. These things leave them all so amazed they're at a loss for words. Odimus invites them to join him on his journey. They, once again, sit in silence, stunned.

Orthalla speaks up first, "I have decided to seek my father's counsel before giving my answer."

Ithilwen and Othare also choose to consult their fathers before responding. Odimus approves of this idea and encourages Adoria to do the same.

As he looks towards Fuin, who quietly mutters, "I will contemplate on these things through meditation and then proceed to give my answer."

Both Odimus and Mezlikied agree that making well-considered choices is better than hasty decisions. Each of them depart in their own direction, agreeing to reunite here in one moons time.

Chapter 7

KING KYROS AND THE GUARD OF LIGHT

"Welcome to my home," declares King Kyros. "I've been informed about each and every one of you by my daughter. I am thankful for your presence here for the next couple of moons."

Othare descends the stairs behind the King, it appears as if he has been here for a while. He rushes over to hug Odimus, and both filled with excitement to see one another. He catches sight of Fuin and Orthalla and quickly moves toward them, ready to embrace. Because she was standing close to Orthalla, he accidentally bumped into Adoria. But she doesn't mind.

Odimus asks Othare if he has been staying here.

"Indeed, for the past few weeks. Getting acquainted with the future in-laws, you know."

Ithilwen declines to make eye contact with Odimus as he looks up at her. He simply then turns his head to talk with his dear friend.

"The energy in this kingdom is truly abundant. It IS the Kingdom of the Energy Tree, but man."

Othare seem to have more energy than usual. Odimus concludes that he has been eating the fruit from the Tree of Energy.

Othare bend down towards Odimus, who stands a few steps lower on the staircase, and proclaims, "This fruit is nothing short of an enormous energy source, packed with immense energy and power." Othare still standing before him, staring directly into his eyes, bouncing slightly and refusing to leave his presence.

Odimus tilts to the side to face the king. "Your majesty, is there a protocol for limiting consumption or at least pulling back on the amount?"

With a booming laugh, King Kyros proclaims, "This fruit has no other effect besides boosting energy, vitality, strength, and power. When first introduced to the fruit, individuals often struggle to control its strong effects. Therefore, it appears to have control over the participant. However, there's no need to worry because he will regain control, and so will each of you as you learn to master the energy fruit as well. Now, come with me inside. We have a lot to discuss."

As they step into the Castle, they are met with a setting that is both fortress-like and captivatingly beautiful, contrasting with the Kingdom of Light, which resembles more of a capital city catering to politicians. Odimus questions reason behind the kingdom's military base-like stature.

Kyros responds while continuing to walk straightforward. "This is where you'll find the greatest military in the world. Despite my brother's possession of the Kingdom of Light and the power of the **Tree of Light**, it is my kingdom that serves as his main military force and protection." At that point, he comes to a stop and directs his attention towards him. "You are Odimus, correct?"

"I am."

Kyros proceeds to go down another hallway. "My daughter has informed me that you are the son of Erastus."

"Yes, your majesty, that is true."

"He and I have both served together on a journey, just as you and Ithilwen will be journeying."

"I am aware, Your Majesty, but my father did not inform me of your mission years ago. It was King Kyon."

"So, Erastus is still hiding behind all his secrets, is he?"

"Indeed, Your Majesty, that appears to be the case."

"Odimus, as you will soon find out, we do not live in secrecy here. If there's anything you want to know, just ask." Upon entering, they discover a magnificent room containing a sizable table capable of seating fifty people. In a chair at the table's end, the Queen sits beside another chair. Sitting to her, right around the corner of the table, is another woman and a man. "On my right side is my wife, Lithanya. Next, you'll find my daughter Mivanya, and her husband Titus."

Odimus and the others all begin to bow, and Kyros halts them. "We do not do that here. It is only appropriate when you ask for permission for things, receiving a gift or, during a leave from a room or farewell from the Kingdom. This is my kingdom, not my brothers'. I disagree with these customs, but I agree with some particulars here and when we attend to his affairs. So, while here, a gentle bow for permission, farewell, and gratitude of a gift will suffice." Kyros now instructs them all to sit. Everyone is seated, and he carries on. "Everything has been relayed to me by my brother. Therefore, discussing why you're here and what you're doing is unnecessary. I believe my daughter is an excellent choice to accompany you and your team on this mission and journey. Tomorrow marks the start of our training."

Othare look to the King and say, "Your majesty, may I ask what it is that we must do to pass your training?"

King Kyros, staring down and pointing at Odimus, says, "When I decide he is no longer a boy."

Odimus is caught off guard and embarrassed by what is said. Unaware of the cause of his provocation.

Mezlikied interjects, "Why, your majesty, are you so harsh and quick in judgment?"

Then, Ithilwen, seated next to him to his left, interrupts and quietly asks her father what he is doing.

Kyros maintains his unwavering gaze at Odimus and declares "Until Odimus can demonstrate his maturity and prove himself as a man, your journey will never commence and will inevitably fail before it even begins."

Standing up, the King beckons Mezlikied to follow. Mezlikied quickly obeys and disappears from everyone's view as he turns the corner. Kyros turns abruptly towards Mezlikied and asks, "Do you have knowledge of the boy?"

"Kyros, in what manner are you referring? There have been multiple occurrences with the boy."

"Enough with the wordplay, you wise old coot. Do you have knowledge of his Shadow and Light potential manifestations?"

"Oh, the medallion."

"Yes, I already know about the manifestations, Mezlikied. You act like you've forgotten my medallion, but I know you remember. Your face gives you away." The King laughs and playfully bumps Mezlikied in the sternum, remarking that it's good to see him.

Mezlikied acknowledges, "It is good to see you as well. Since his youth, I have had my suspicions."

Kyros inquires, "Has he yielded to the shadow manifestations?"
"I believe I saw him surrendering to a shadow manifestation when he was fourteen years of age after being bullied by another boy."

Kyros sighs, "We can't really hold it against him considering his young age."

Mezlikied then inquires about the number of manifestations.

The king cautiously peeks around the corner at Odimus, then glances at Mezlikied. "I've never witnessed someone with so many." Peeking around the corner again, Kyros catches sight of a couple of leaves of shadow and a few leaves of light twirling in the room, then quickly hides back.

Mezlikied now tells Kyros, "I have wondered all these years but needed to be sure before I ever asked for your assistance. As fortune would have it, we have ended up here in your home to train, and now you can fill me in on everything the boy sees. Now tell me, Kyros, was it really necessary for you to label him as a boy?"

"I wanted to see if it had any effect on his manifestations or caused him to give heed to any. Despite their abundance, he hardly gives them a glance. Not even the slightest glance. It's astounding!"

Mezlikied asks if he can explain the meaning of this.

"I believe the boy possesses the greatest potential for both light and shadow. Despite their presence, his gaze remains fixated on her." Both of them cautiously glance around the corner and spot Odimus gazing at Ithilwen.

Mezlikied admits to Kyros, "He cares for her of course."

Kyros tells him, "It appears that he still has feelings."

Mezlikied argues, "What makes you assume there are feelings?"

"The boy is openly staring at my daughter; he should learn to be more discreet. Also, tell me, how are things between him and Othare? Mixed feelings should not be allowed to interfere while embarking on this journey, particularly considering his numerous shadow manifestations."

"Kyros, the boy, possesses a uniqueness that sets him apart from anyone I've encountered. He displays meticulous obedience, exemplifies boundless charity, and possesses an unparalleled level of honor. Odimus would never dishonor Othare. They are the closest of friends, and he has a strong loyalty to them. I've noticed that the boy tends to dwell on loss a lot, like with his mother."

With sincerity, Kyros turns his attention to Mezlikied, "Yes, how is our old friend Erastus?"

"Since losing his precious Adelphia, his spirit has been broken, and he is no longer the same man he once was."

"Back to Odimus, are you suggesting that he finds it challenging to accept loss?"

"Yes, he does, so I'm suggesting he feels he lost Ithilwen. He briefly courted her but withdrew when Othare asked him to. So, there's nothing for you to worry about."

"Mezlikied, don't make such proclamations. We can't control what will happen." Kyros now begins to tell Mezlikied his plan; "while training the boy, I'll assess his ability to reject shadow manifestations under immense pressure. Calling him a boy was the perfect way to stir the pot."

"So, you're still enjoying stirring the pot?"

"Yes, and you still enjoy meddling, you old coot!"

"Please refrain from calling me an old coot, and no, I do not meddle."

"Fine, youngish coot, and yes, you do."

Mezlikied pushes him, causing him to stumble into view of the group, but he plays it off as simply walking back into the room. Mezlikied follows' walking back into the room. Mezlikied acts as if they had a very serious conversation.

Othare ask Odimus, "What is it like having Mezlikied as your master?"

"He possesses the qualities of kindness and selflessness. Always prioritizes others over himself. He possesses great wisdom, yet there's a hint of arrogance and self-righteousness in his demeanor. He is never wrong, even though it may be irritating. He never talks unless he is certain about what he is saying. In summary; an awesome, charitable, know-it-all uncle."

Othare gives a slightly amused smile and leans back. Mezlikied and Kyros approach and take a seat at the table. Kyros commands everyone's attention and proceeds to deliver his message. "Once this meeting is over, we will accompany you to your respective accommodations. A curfew is going to be implemented."

"Um, Curfew?

"Yes Ithilwen, there's a curfew. In the *Kingdom of Energy*, it is mandatory for all citizens to serve two years in the military once they turn Twenty-one years of age. Once again, this kingdom is the dominant military power on Luxtenebri, with the only equal being the *Kingdom of Light* followed by the *Kingdom of Ludaea*, where Othare is the crowned prince. Therefore, as you are be trained for this mission, King Kyron has summoned you. I will be ensuring you meet the same standard as the *Kingdom of Energies* military."

The people in the room no longer worry about a curfew, but they begin to worry about the challenging training they are about to endure.

"At the waking hour, we will commence. You are dismissed."
The following morning, Odimus is awakened by a room filled with soldiers. They appear to be overly enthusiastic and full of energy. They are waking him up in a rush and yelling so many instructions that he can hardly comprehend them all. As they hurry into the hall, he barely has time to put on his clothes. Orthalla, half asleep, meets him while Othare stands straight and serious, unfazed by the chaos. Fuin, struggling to leave the room, seems unaffected as well but is quite clumsy upon waking. Mezlikied does not appear to be in his room, but suddenly, a soldier is forcefully ejected from the room via gravity powers, causing a commanding officer to chuckle at the soldier and remind him that Mezlikied was not to be disturbed or to raise their voice at him.

"Apologies, sir, but I didn't recall which room he was in," replies the soldier.

Orthalla begins to belly laugh when the commander whips around, showing no fear of his size; though Orthalla towers over him, he still proceeds to yell, "Did I ask you to speak sasquatch." The commander turns around, and Orthalla attempts to hit the commander, but Othare intervenes by seizing his arms and pleading for him to stay composed. Odimus now realizes the upcoming challenge will require significant effort. During the upcoming weeks, they are informed the focus will be exercises and fight training with the staff Saita. They have been informed that their relics will only be used at designated times during this training, as the Staff of Saita can perfectly shapeshift into any weapon. However, Odimus still believes it cannot replicate the Sword of Valiance and frequently experiences a profound sense of loss for his relic. Ithilwen and Adoria have been training side by side with them every single day. He reflects on his pride in his sister and her strengths and skills. Noticing his gaze fixed on her, she smirks and proceeds without interruption. He glances at his friend Othare, watching him train in arms with Fuin. He admires Othare's skill and how effortless it seems to him. He feels grateful that Othare will be by his side on this mission.

A soldier interrupts, "It's your turn, daydreamer."

Before they begin, the soldier says he is free to obtain his personal relic for this exercise. As they train together, he feels a surge of power and begins to notice he can anticipate the soldier's every move. He starts to feel captivated by this sensation and then musters all his strength to retaliate, delivering a powerful blow to the soldier's sternum, sending him flying several feet and crashing onto the ground. Odimus becomes self-conscious upon realizing everyone's attention is now on him. He notices King Kyros on the balcony, walking back inside, he glances back with disappointment, then vanishes.

Gathering his bearings, "This is not strike training, so control yourself." The soldier then commands Odimus to run fifteen miles around the castle, to which he reluctantly agrees.

It is now the one-month mark of training, and Kyros is giving instructions. "After one month of training, all of you have shown exceptional growth and natural talent, even the boy."

While slumping down at his desk, a couple of them offer Odimus a comforting look amidst the insult given by the King.

"Our agenda today includes a lesson on the Mother Moons and Bremium armor, followed by elite soldier training. I believe you all surpass the average soldier and require more advanced training."
Everyone sits up excitedly except Odimus, who remains slumped in embarrassment. However, he lifts his head and smirks at Othare.

"Ithilwen, can you provide an overview of each Tree of Power and the *Mother Moon* in which they belong for us?"

Ithilwen goes on to explain the properties of the Trees of Power fruit and their Mother Moons. "The Fire Tree, belonging to Othare's bloodline, is one of the strongest fruits. It provides both strength and fire abilities to the user. Moving on, we have the Earth tree, which empowers the user with control over the earth and stone. Bremium is the only thing from underground that earth users cannot manipulate.

"The Water Fruit Tree is capable of purifying water and keeping you hydrated for up to seventy hours without drinking. The Water Tribe can live underwater, breathe, and defy the effects of water as if they were on land. Adoria, like her mother, belongs to the bloodline of the Wind Tree, which grants the ability to control wind and make crafts fly. Users of the Elastic Fruit can stretch and bounce when falling from far distances. If you ask me, the effects of the Elastic Tree are quite gross to look at." Everyone agrees with Ithilwen in laughter.

"The powerful Void Tree has no presence of either light or shadow within it. It grants the user teleportation capabilities and a protective shield. The user appears to float above the ground due to the shield enveloping their entire body. Due to the absence of light and shadow, they can spawn reflective shields that camouflage them from enemies; Fuin is the bloodline of this tree. Healing powers are bestowed upon Orthalla's bloodline by the Aura tree. Our bloodline father bestowed upon us the plant and animal fruit, granting us dominion over plants and animals alike. The next is the Gravity Fruit, which gives the user control over gravity except for the allowance of flight. It is basically telekinesis; this is possibly and arguably the most powerful fruit. Mezlikied and Odimus's bloodlines belong to this tree.

Next are the trees capable of duplication, generating electricity, and creating ice. The user has the ability to duplicate themselves, creating up to four copies. However, this skill is exceptionally uncommon, and only a select few have truly mastered it, resulting in usually only two or three duplicates. Additionally, they can create duplicates of items or non-living objects, but only one copy can be made that is not in contact with their body. The only way to recognize a copy is if it shatters like glass.

Electricity Tree grants users the ability to manipulate and control electricity. This fruit requires more control than any other, which is why only the Monks of Levkaetus use it. The peaceful people of their bloodline are the only ones who dare to try this fruit. They primarily reside on their moon and avoid involvement in the military, government, or any kind of war. Furthermore, they do not have any form of government. This is because of the incredible self-control needed to wield this fruit for centuries, as these Monks have chosen to live in peace on their moon. Military force is not required as the moon's fruit emits dangerous electrical strikes. It remains a mystery how they managed to colonize the moon and gain bloodline control over the fruit. No one bothers them because anyone who is not from their bloodline dies when they try to eat the fruit. The Electricity Fruit's main purpose in society is to power Bremium vessels used by Monks for travel between Luxtenebri and the Mother Moons. Allowing them to peacefully be a part of society and for them to receive substantial wages to provide for the entire people of Levkaetus.

Due to the Harvest Wars, the Ichassarae tribe has forbidden the sight of any Ice Tree, making the Ice Fruit of Ichassarae the only part of the tree from the moon allowed into society. It is also forbidden for any member of the Ichassarae tribe to draw or describe the tree. None have ever broken that vow. Although they distribute the fruit in large quantities. Users can remain unaffected by freezing temperatures and can summon ice from their hands with an exceptional amount of power."

"Ithilwen mentioned bloodlines multiple times. Can anyone explain why?"

Adoria responds, "Because there was no knowledge of each other's existence on the other Mother Moons prior to the Harvest Wars. We all lived centuries unaware of one another, and when we all discovered the existence of each tribe on the moons, the Harvest Wars began to try to harvest as many of the other trees of power for themselves. Each of the other tribes soon discovered that they couldn't utilize the fruit from a different mother moon in the same way as the tribe that belonged to that mother moon. This led to what is known as the tribal wars, which were to gain power over one another.

For example, Fire Fruit, for any other tribe, only allows you to start a small fire, nothing else. While wind can generate an underwater or polluted air oxygen mask, controlling the wind is not possible. The Flight Fruit only enables non-bloodline users to jump to great heights but not to fly. The Aura Fruit has healing properties for those who consume it, but it doesn't grant the ability to heal others. The full potential of all other fruits can only be unlocked by those from the bloodline, while others can only possess certain characteristics of the fruit's power."

"Adoria, can you consume multiple fruits of power at once?"

Adoria states the rules; "Every tribe of their respective bloodline fruit can be used together, only consuming one additional fruit. A third would cause you to not be able to use any ability any longer, and it is potentially fatal depending on if you consumed too much. No matter how strong the user is, more than two is physically impossible. There is, however, only one exception to this rule pertaining to fruits from the Mother Moon. That is the Water Fruit. Since water is the substance of life and essential to all creatures, it does not interfere. However, it gives no abilities to someone who is not of the bloodline. It allows you not to need water for seventy hours. The Energy Fruit can be used independently of the rule since it belongs to Luxtenebri and not the Mother Moons."

"Now, what about the *Tree of Light*?"

"The fruit grants immortality, which means only immortals are permitted to eat it. After the *King of Shadow* consumed the fruit and turned to the **Tree of Shadow**, the **Tree of Light** was the only one who selected those who are permitted to partake of its fruit. His actions resulted in the construction of the *Kingdom of Light* and *Kingdom of Energy*, ensuring the proper use of the trees and preventing corruption by shadow potential."

"Lastly, pertaining to bloodlines, does this mean a bloodline or a tribe consists of only one specific race of people?"

Odimus answers, "No, there are dozens of races amongst all the tribes. We have reason to believe that before total bloodline control of a Mother Moon, many of different races came together to colonize their individual Mother Moon. This is another reason, besides the ancient ruins, that we have reason to believe we were once one people. Therefore, we do not distinguish our civilization based on race; we live by the need of the Trees of Power and the Bloodlines that use them. Our civilization is beyond the foolish distinguishing judgments of inequality for race. Male and female, we are all equal."

"Kyros moves forward from there in the classroom instructions, "Now, let's discuss the Bremium coin of armor in our final lesson before moving forward."

Odimus raises his hand, and Kyros asks, "Yes, boy, what is a Coin of Armor?"

"Through the power of will, all armor can be turned into a coin, giving its name; A Coin of Armor."

Kyros proceeds to ask, "Where is the Coin of Armor placed on a person's body?"

"The chest and shoulder are encased by a strap crafted from the bark of the elastic tree. A circular section about 3 inches in diameter is located in the center of the left chest. When activated, the coin transforms into a full suit of armor. The elastic strap stretches with the armor, providing a comfortable barrier between the body and Bremium metal to prevent skin wear or discomfort."

"Exactly. See you all tomorrow."

Tomorrow comes, King Kyros has gathered everyone in the courtyard for a final lesson, marking the end of the last month of training. When they enter the courtyard, all they see is King Kyros shirtless, wearing his Coin of Armor and holding a Staff of Saita. "Today, you will engage in group combat against me. With the training you've received, a group like this should have the power to make me submit to them……should be able to."

Mezlikied respectfully, "Your majesty, please, this is unnecessary."

Kyros tells Mezlikied, "In order to pass my test and gain the trust of my daughter with the group, this is my requirement. This mission cannot proceed without my approval; therefore, I also require this to gain my permission. You have to complete this task."

Mezlikied appears afraid and asks Ithilwen if her father is joking. When Ithilwen looks into her father's eyes, and then at Mezlikied, she declares that he is in fact, not.

"Can you reason with him?"

"I can't be certain, but questioning him doesn't seem like a wise choice."

Others is standing, feeling fearful as well. Curiously, Adoria leans over to the group and asks, "Why is everyone all scared."

Odimus then turns to the group and states, "There has never been a warrior greater than King Kyros in over five thousand years. Only the Shadow King has managed to defeat him. Notice the scar running from his trapezius to half of his pectoral muscle. No scarring occurs with the use of Aura. The user utilized shadow abilities to imbue a Bremium weapon, resulting in that kind of wound. Complete healing after a wound like that from shadow abilities is not possible."

Orthalla looks to Fuin and says, "I'm guessing we are the shields as they attack?"

Fuin nods his head yes.

Mezlikied goes to the King and asks the reason behind his actions. Kyros ignores and declares, "The boy becomes a man today; he needs my trust, and I believe he will rise to the occasion. Fight alongside him, make his safety your top priority, and allow him to be the point man." With a smile, he looks over at Mezlikied and says, "Don't worry, I'll go easy on you ancient one."

Mezlikied is aware that Kyros has grown feelings of care for Odimus and is teaching the lesson of wisdom rather than humiliating him further.

"In this engagement, everyone must wear Training Bremium Armor and the only use of the Staff of Saita is permitted. Individual relics are not allowed. However, the staff can only be used to imitate your personal relic. Mezlikied your gauntlets, Ithilwen, sword-like your sword of power, Othare your cavalry saber, Orthalla the battle axe. Now Fuin, you are of the Void Tribe. Therefore, you do not use a Staff. Just use your master of defense abilities, which we all know is sufficient. Adoria uses the whip from your father, and Odimus, the falchion sword like your Sword of Valiance. Using the staff, I will imitate my shield."

Startled, Ithilwen turns to Othare, who also shows signs of alarm. But they have no time to speak. "Begin," says Kyros.

Mezlikied summons the heart stone of Erayiphim, which materializes out of nowhere and starts orbiting around him like a moon around a planet. A wave is cast towards Kyros, throwing him back several feet, but he quickly bounces back and returns to his starting point.

He raises his shield and staff taunting, "Anyone else?"

Ithilwen and Othare launch an attack from both sides, giving Kyros a tough time before being knocked to the ground. Adoria and Orthalla team up and attack together, putting up a good fight against Kyros, but ending up knocked down as well. Mezlikied, Fuin, and Odimus are now working as a team. Both Odimus and Mezlikied are using gravity to fling objects at Kyros, yet he summons vines to intercept. Kyros initiates his initial assault on Mezlikied, only to encounter a shield conjured by Fuin. Realizing the significance of eliminating a void master, Kyros immediately targets Fuin. Before reaching him, Odimus meets Kyros, and a battle ensues between the two, sword clashing against the shield. Odimus is astonished by Kyros's ability to wield a shield as a blunt weapon. His amazement grows as he witnesses the skillful manipulation of the shield between both his hands to attack. Odimus is perplexed and struggles greatly as the shield's usage is unlike a typical shield, leaving him unsure of how to block and defend, unlike his heightened focused experience with the soldier. He becomes extremely confused, and then, out of nowhere, the shield smacks his face, causing intense pain and leaving him on the ground with ringing ears. He needs a moment to gather himself and recover, but when he does, he glances up and witnesses everyone converging on Kyros in an all-out assault. Objects are flying through the air, and fire is being cast.

Adoria summons wind at the king, trying to slow him down. As he lunges towards her, she begins to cast her whip into the wind current to attack him as he is charging. He skillfully defends against all her whip strikes in the wind. Orthalla suddenly appears and delivers a powerful blow to Kyros, sending him flying across the room and crashing through a nearby wall.

Now shapeshifted as a Manticore, Kyros comes flying from behind the wall, causing Ithilwen to transform into a Cipactli to match her father. Odimus stands up and joins in the attack. Now, the entire team is attacking in complete harmony. Kyros appears to be overwhelmed as he takes hit after hit without any chance to bounce back. Odimus starts to believe they might actually win, but suddenly, an endless number of vines appear out of thin air and begin to entangle and immobilize Adoria. In a surprising turn of events, Kyros anchors himself and effortlessly wards off every attack. He grabs an unused staff nearby and directs it to turn into a long rod, and begins wrapping it around Fuin while whispering a command to prevent him from gaining power over the Bremium, preventing him from setting himself free. While Kyros was whispering the command, Othare attempts an attack to save Fuin, but Kyros's tail whipped Othare's legs out from under him. Kyros aims his focus on Othare and begins to beat him mercilessly on the ground. Othare raises his hand in submission to indicate his injury, but Kyros continues to attack. Orthalla attempts to rescue Othare. Kyros, however, throws Othare at Orthalla and knocks them both down. He quickly catches up to Othare's body and removes Orthalla from under him, leaving Othare on the ground.

He snatches Orathalla's axe and tosses it aside. The two are engaged in a boxing match, each punch landing with a thunderous impact. Orthalla begins to show his immense strength, proving he has greater hand-to-hand combat abilities. Mezlikied currently struggling to rescue Adoria from the vines while Ithilwen ensures Othare's safety. Odimus attempts an attack to assist Orthalla but is knocked back instantly by Kyros's tail. Kyros eventually conquers Orthalla, causing him to approach Adoria and exchange positions with Mezlikied. Mezlikied and Ithilwen have taken Cipactli form, they and Odimus are the last ones standing against Kyros. United in their assault, they overpower him. Just like Ithilwen, Kyros also becomes a Cipactli and viciously bites her neck, rolling like a gator and almost rendering her unconscious. Kyros initially appears ruthless but eventually forfeits as Ithilwen loses her capacity to fight. She is knocked out of her Cipactli form and starts crawling towards Othare. Now, Mezlikied and Odimus are the ones left to fight.

Kyros questions Mezlikied, "Is this boy truly your great student!?" Then turns and begins to talk as if talking to the *Tree of Light* in a reverent tone, *"Tree of Light,* this your chosen warrior?" With a snarl on his Cipactli form snout, he whips his head towards Odimus, "What a bad choice."

Mezlikied unleashes a battle cry and engages Kyros in an unprecedented display of strength, as if he had been holding back all along. Mezlikied and Odimus are both utilizing gravity to ensnare the King, but his shield strikes them every time they try, preventing them from concentrating. Kyros and his shield are now engaged in separate battles as if the shield is being controlled by an unseen adversary. Kyros alone seemed impossible, but now the shield was fighting alongside him. The shield overwhelms Mezlikied, causing him to be knocked to consciousness.

Kyros turns to address Odimus, "It's just you and me now, boy."

Spotting a shadow feather near his relic, without thinking, Odimus swiftly calls upon gravity to bring his sword to his hands and initiates an attack.

Kyros laughs, "Anger is a sign of weakness."

With a strong elbow strike to the back of his head, Odimus is brought down forcefully. He feels the familiar power within, regains his balance, inhales deeply, and assumes a meditative stance as he stands upright.

"Finally" Kyros whispers and calls forth the Shield of Light, using it as his actual relic to attack, on par with the Sword of Valiance.

They engage in a fierce battle, but neither can successfully strike the other. Kyros transforms into his most powerful form, the manticore, and becomes an even more formidable opponent for Odimus. Odimus discovers himself in a state of control far surpassing his previous feelings. Each breath brings rejuvenation. Instead of exhaustion, muscles growing stronger, and weakness vanishes. Every part of him feels an increase in strength, speed, and ability.

A beautiful light catches his attention from the corner of his eye, emanating from his sword's hilt. He notices it as the spiral cylinder he saw around Ithilwen, and it seems identical, except for the absence of a shadow and the light resembling that of the ***Tree of Light***. It's coiling around his hand and seems to be entering his wrist. Odimus has come to realize the sword's true abilities. It revitalizes the owner and grants them the power of valor. He harnesses this emotion to land an attack against Kyros's protective Shield of Light. The impact knocks him across the floor and through a wall and is strong enough to force him out of his Manticore form. Despite being hit hard, he emerges from the debris in human form, with only a few scratches and chuckles

"It has been more than a millennium since I last experienced a blow like that from another warrior."

The speech is short as he launches himself at Odimus in a burst of incredible speed, only for Odimus to counter with gravity, immobilizing him and launching him across the room. Vines sprout from the ground, ensnaring both arms and legs, preventing him from being thrown. Odimus harnesses gravity to create a force that compresses Kyros in an attempt to crush him. Kyros cries out in pain, but vines ensnare Odimus's hands, preventing him from continuing his attack.

Freeing himself, Kyros snarls "Now, I finish this!"

Odimus is being hit repeatedly, unable to see his attacker. The frequency and intensity of the hits make his body feel useless. Suddenly, he loses his grip on the sword of valiance, and the subsequent blows begin to hurt and injure him. Odimus is in such a state of injury that his mobility is severely limited. The hits stop, and he turns to see Kyros standing over him… "Do you yield?" Odimus attempts to retrieve his sword from a distance with gravity, but Kyros intercepts it with his shield and knocks it far out of the courtyard. Using the shield's momentum, Kyros strikes Odimus in the face. Then asks once more, "Do you yield!?" Odimus makes an effort to get up and successfully stands on his own, with Kyros granting him permission. He takes hold of a Staff of Saita and continues his fight. Kyros triumphs over Odimus by knocking him down and unleashing a barrage of punches. Despite Ithilwen's weak voice pleading for her father to stop, Kyros continues, relentless. Odimus reaches for the shoulder of Kyros, and taps.

He pulls back and instructs people in the courtyard to bring Aura vials. Kyros, breathless, points to a medallion around his neck and tells Odimus to look, "Can you make out what is on it?"

Weakly, Odimus glances and observes a rune In the center of the medallion.

"Do you have any idea what this rune is?"

"I do not, Your Majesty." Fuin then speaks up to help Odimus. "Your majesty, if you would allow me to answer, for I know what that rune is. This rune's power is unique in its ability to reveal the potential manifestations of others. It's not about sharing them but rather about seeing things from others' perspectives. In essence, you behold the Potential Manifestations of others."

"Correct." Kyros now bends down on one knee to reach Odimus's level. "I have observed the countless number of potential manifestations of yours, for both shadow and light, over the course of the past two moons. Depending on their adherence and progress, most have one or two a week. An individual who is dedicated, progressing in life, driven and making strides can expect to have one or two per day. Odimus, I've observed that you have dozens daily. Yet you have not given heed to the shadow but once, when you called for your sword, despite my instructions not to. I carry this medallion to detect if my soldiers yield to shadow manifestations, and if they do, they are unfit for my ranks. Carrying this helps me as a leader identify the weakness of temptation for shadow power. Shadow may not always be evil, but it still carries dark consequences."

In Kyros's words, Odimus is reminded of Amulius and the consequences of fighting him.

"I have been creating immense stress for you every day. Then, the one time you gave into a shadow potential, it was not for harm or evil-doing but to summon your sword to gain the point. That person is not a boy, but a man, who has my respect and is welcome among my ranks upon his return, if he so chooses."

Odimus is marveling at what the King has just said to him.

"I lose respect for those who have few manifestations but are still tempted by the Shadow Potential. We may not be perfect, but we have the power to reject shadow potentials. Odimus, it appears that a Potential Manifestation is a recurring element in almost all of your daily decisions. So, I cannot hold your everyday decisions against you. Just like some individuals simply make errors. I perceive every decision you make has potential for greatness. Odimus, I never thought of you as a boy. I've been testing your determination to fight the shadow all along. I needed to see if you succumb to their influences frequently, but you have consistently avoided making bad choices. You and your abilities have my utmost respect. You can count the seeds within a fruit. However, you cannot count the fruits within a seed. Odimus, you can count your actions, but you cannot count your consequences, both good and bad. Remember these words as you see your potential manifestations, for they both have consequences. Choose wisely the path that will have good consequences for not only yourself but for others. I think you are an exceptional man, and you have my trust with my daughter and the leader of this team for this mission."

Kyros, the great warrior, demonstrates his superiority by leaving Odimus on the ground, ensuring he understands his defeat yet manages to uplift him with his words.

While Kyros walks away, he tells Odimus, "Do not consume the Aura; instead, command your sword to come to you."

Crawling in attempt to stand he grunts, "You knocked it out of the courtyard."

"Ah yes, but I believe it has the same qualities as my brother's sword and can be summoned from any place."

Odimus attempts to connect with the sword, commanding it to come to him, when suddenly, a faint glimmer of light materializes, and the sword is now in his possession.

Kyros chuckles. "Your ability to will Bremium is astounding. I'm quite curious to see the effects of that sword on you."

A rejuvenation of Odimus begins but at a much slower rate compared to the effects of the Aura fruit, which are instant. While Odimus observes the slow progress of the sword healing him, he is astounded as he watches every scratch, cut and bruise heal.

Kyros spots Fuin still in his Bremium bar wrap, apologizes and offers assistance. Like a young child, he sprints over and whispers to the Bremium to set free him.

"Your Majesty," Fuin asks. "How were you able to do that?"

Kyros claims that "Bremium's response depends on the strength of one's will. Therefore, Bremium will only respond to the person with the strongest will.

Fuin's reaction leans more towards amazement than offense.

Suddenly, the mighty cry of the great Volantuiva resounds in the air. Everyone looks up as they spot one a short distance off in the sky. The creature from the Mother Moon Nathlaphane is not causing alarm to anyone, as it is benevolent. They see Anniphus the wise riding on the back of the Volantuiva. Orthalla becomes very happy, and upon his landing, asks why he has come to the Kingdom of Energy.

Anniphus dismounts, hugs his son, and says, "Kyros told me today was the final day of your training! My purpose for coming here is not to see you though, my son, although we will sit and talk, as I want to hear everything" He grins proudly at his son and then turns, "I have come specifically for Fuin."

"Come," Orthalla says to Fuin, "He is here for you."

Fuin is approached by Anniphus, who retrieves the Book of Knowledge from his bag and gives it to him. "You are authorized by the Kaleidoscope Council to take this on your mission, and we offer you membership upon your return."

Mezlikied appears concerned at his knowledge of their upcoming mission. Anniphus turns to him and remarks, "When will you realize I know everything?" smirking sarcastically and raising an eyebrow. He laughs and says, "No, King Kyron has informed me of the situation and only on a need-to-know basis, not all the details."

Turning towards Fuin, he reveals that he is aware that one aspect of the mission involves collecting and finding runes. "Understand that many attempts have been made to fuse a rune to the Book of Knowledge, but it never works. So, this is a relic that won't accept a rune. The Book of Knowledge grants power to its possessor or caretaker, unlike any other relic. The power is wisdom. Its knowledge will only be revealed if you give it your power of will and willingness to receive wisdom since a person can only have the power of one relic and one set of Bremium armor at a time. Seeing that you are of the Void Tribe, having sworn to only defend and never attack, this Book of Knowledge will be your weapon. Inside the book, you'll find a complete roster of ancient runes, along with the historical accounts of the Relic and Rune Wars." Anniphus is overwhelmed with gratitude as Fuin offers him the Bow of Honor. The group stands in awe, and even Kyros stands with reverence. Anniphus then proceeds to raise him the proper way to raise someone during this sacred bow. Following, they all proceed to the dining hall.

The next day, Kyros awaits Odimus and his team's departure with a legion. Kyros is in his full armor, and a military ceremony sash is attached to the armor. He walks over to Odimus "When my brother King Kyron and I set out with Erastus, Mezlikied and our team, we decided to call ourselves the Guard of Light. After careful consideration and council with Kyron, Mezlikied and even your father, Odimus and Adoria, we have decided that this team too, shall be called the Guard of Light." A thunderous cheer reverberates from the legion, making the ground quake. Standing at attention, they each receive Coins of Armor. Each armor is created for the highest-ranking individuals. Kyros then tells them "Each one has its own unique design, and it so happens that they were all designed and prepared by Erastus himself. Kyron summoned him to the grand forge in the City of Light, providing him a place to stay during your absence." Kyros leans closer to Odimus and Adoria, "I believe my old friend shouldn't have to be alone and should have a purpose to distract him." He leans back and then proceeds to the group, "Each unique armor was made for each unique person. May these Coins of Armor serve you on your journey." Kyros beckons soldiers to bring something as eight Volantuiva swoop down and land in front of them. "Considering the challenging nature of flying Bremium ships and their limited use to being only used as passenger ships, I believe it is appropriate to provide each of you with your own Volantuiva for the journey."

Odimus is overjoyed to have the opportunity to ride a Volantuiva... without being half-conscious. Knowing that Drilgom can no longer stay by his side, he beckons Drilgom to approach and asks Kyros if she can remain here with him.

"Of course, I've always wanted to spend time with a Ngawboves. They are fascinating creatures; I've never had the privilege, though." Kyros looks into Drillgom's eyes, and both of their eyes flicker a green light. He looks up at Odimus and says, "And don't worry, she is happy to stay here with me."

Odimus shows gratitude to him, and everyone proceeds to mount their respective Volantuiva. Kyros walks over to Odimus's side and suggests that he begin his journey by seeking out a master of duplication. "They may not be well-regarded by Orthalla due to their lack of honor. However, they are highly adept thieves and truly exceptional fighters. I recommend traveling to Sohmencharis, the *Mother Moon* of the duplication tree. Collecting runes would benefit from the expertise of a skilled thief, particularly when dealing with traps. Once on the *Mother Moon,* Sohmencharis inquired about a man named Vartula. His father, Thinius, accompanied us on our runes' journey in the past. Now, Vartula is not the man you are looking for; he has a son who is known to be a master of the Duplication fruit and can create four duplicates, which is a very rare ability among their people. The man's name is Trenidus, but be careful, he is a squirrely one. Years ago, I came across him as a mischievous little lad, and his troublesome nature was apparent. A humorous trickster with a penchant for mischief. After that, head towards the grand island kingdom of Naphdali, the twin moons kingdom located here on Luxtenebri. They have prepared a rune for you and your team. Make the decision on who receives each rune wisely, remembering only one per relic and one per armor. Lastly, here is a Coin of Armor for Trenidus and the reason why eight Volantuiva were brought forth. The moment I heard Kyron's plan for this mission, I knew I had to choose Trenidus for this team."

Kyros moves away and expresses his love to Ithilwen, commanding her to depart. Ithilwen did not require a Volantuiva since she could transform into a manticore, but the long distances made it impractical for her to remain in that form constantly. Thus, she traveled on a Volantuiva, too. She heels the Volantuiva and flies off into the air. Odimus starts to feel an overwhelming sense of adventure and joy. He heels his Volantuiva to take off and begins soaring through the air. As he ascends into the sky, he looks down to see the *Kingdom of Energy* begin to fade in the distance. Seeing them leave it behind, he lets out a cheer, and all the members of The Guard of Light join him.

Chapter 8

TRENIDUS AND THE START OF A COLLECTION

The Volantuiva are the sole creatures with the ability to fly between Luxtenebri and the Mother Moons. Many centuries ago, people discovered one another thanks to this mighty creature. One day, a brave man decided to ride the Volantuiva on its migrating path from Naphlaphane to Dalanias. This young man, brave and daring, was the first to uncover a whole new civilization. He also discovered the moons are in Luxtenebri's Atmospheres so he could breathe when leaving his mother moon's atmosphere. He was curious about more than just the twin moons. Gathering a small group of fearless men, he embarked on a journey to the nearest moon in search of other possible civilizations. He found that the nearest moon to the twin moons was Ludaea, the Fire Moon.

As the years went by, the many discovered civilizations became increasingly curious. Eventually, all thirteen mother moon tribes were discovered. For twenty-five years, the tribes of the moons started interacting peacefully but soon desired to rule each other and control the Trees of Power. For the next hundred years, Tribe was against the tribe and at first, the cause was the Harvest Wars. These wars were about gaining possession of each other's Trees of Power, but they discovered the Trees of Power could only be truly unlocked by the bloodlines of the Mother Moons. This realization then led to the wars known as the Tribal Wars, whose purpose was to decide which tribe would rule. In the end, peace was discovered. The tribes had learned to fly between the moons, had spread the trees of power throughout each other's Mother Moons and established a government.

Following the establishment of a government and the ability to travel between moons, many began to be curious about the planet Luxtenebri and its possible inhabitants. However, no records or evidence of any population on Luxtenebri were found. The people found identical ruins and symbols on each of the thirteen moons, providing evidence that they were once one people. There are no records that have been found as to how they were separated and how they were unaware of one another's presence prior to the Harvest Wars.

Odimus and his team are now departing Luxtenebri on the mighty Volantuiva, heading towards Sohmencharis. The size difference between Luxtenebri and the mother moons is astounding. As they enter Sohmencharis's atmosphere, the gravitational shift felt strange for everyone except Mezlikied and Odimus due to their Erayiphim heritage and gravitational fruit abilities. All tribes consume their fruit every seventy hours to counteract the diminishing effects. Each member of a tribe always consumed the fruit of their mother moon without exception, for it was the way of each tribe to always have the ability of their Mother Moon's tree to be a part of their everyday existence. The effects won't get stronger with increased consumption. The usage of abilities was determined by time. The individual who consumed the fruit had the choice to master its abilities or not. Once seventy-two hours have passed, and you haven't eaten the fruit, the effects will wear off, and you'll be without abilities. No one was born with abilities or powers. The only sources of abilities and powers were from Bremium and the Trees of Power's fruit.

Fuin's body reacts to the gravitational shift, making him feel nauseous, he vomits.

Laughter erupts from the crowd as Orthalla tosses him a small vial of Aura. As he laughed, he shouts, "Here, this will help counteract motion sickness."

They now arrive at the city where Kyros had suggested going to find Trenidus. The Volantuiva are placed in nearby stables as they move forward into the city. Adoria notices a tree nearby and points it out as they walk up to the gates. Harvesters near a Duplication Tree touch the fruit, causing it to vibrate and duplicate like cells in a body. Whenever the harvester touches the fruit, it generates additional ones without the need to be plucked from the tree. Odimus is astonished as he makes his way to the gates. Four soldiers stand as the Guard of Light approaches, and then the gate was suddenly covered with twelve soldiers. They have replicated themselves, creating two more indistinguishable copies of themselves. Leaning down, Orthalla pokes one of the duplicates and receives a command from the soldier to back off. Orthalla steps back, and the team looks at him with judgmental eyes and pursed lips.

"I'm curious about your reasoning behind that."

"Can you blame me?"

Odimus greets Othare with a smile, then directs his attention to the soldiers, "Our purpose is to seek out a man named Vartula. Do you have any idea where we can locate him?"

The soldier questions their reason for seeking Vartula.

"We have been sent here by King Kyros."

The soldier immediately waves for the gates opened and steps aside.

Odimus turns to the Ithilwen "Is it always this easy for you?

She casually yet confidently shrugs to agree.

Following her, Othare chimes in "You have no idea."

In an attempt to provoke Othare, Odimus shakes his head sarcastically at him. As Othare passes by, he delivers a blow to his stomach, leaving him breathless. Reacting swiftly, he jumps and places Othare's head into a headlock.

Adoria, right behind them pushes past "Alright children, break it up."

Now, they are at a tavern, per the soldier's instructions. They step inside the tavern and quickly notice its popularity, with a sizable dining area, spacious bar, and a vast area dedicated to table games. They are amazed at the size of the tavern and how exciting it is inside. They attempt to disperse and enjoy themselves, but Odimus instructs them to wait until they locate Vartula.

"You got this, oh fearless leader!" Othare states, grabbing Ithilwen's hand and leading her into the tavern. She shrugs at Odimus and goes along with Othare.

Adoria takes Orthalla's hand with a smile, "Let's go play the table games."

Odimus asks Orthalla and Adoria to wait, but they ignore him. With a touch on his shoulder, Mezlikied suggests allowing them to take a break, "Let them play; it's been a while, and they deserve it."

He realizes it's been quite some time since they've simply relaxed and enjoyed themselves. Mezlikied now bids farewell, and Fuin accompanies him. Odimus wishes to find Vartula instead of following his group.

Within only a few seconds, as he begins to approach a nearby bar stool, he hears a deep voice, "Are you Odimus?"

Upon turning, he discovers a burly man with a full beard dressed in the most fashionable attire. The material was not of high quality but rather made of animal fur. In his entire life, he had never witnessed such exquisite craftsmanship of fur. The style had the appearance of a sophisticated businessman but with rugged animal fur.

He responds in a tone sounding more like a question, "Yes, sir.. I am Odimus."

"I received a message from King Kyros a few weeks ago, and he informed me about your appearance. He was completely accurate."

Odimus's curiosity was now focused on Kyros's depiction of him. "You must be Vartula."

"Yes, I am the proprietor of this tavern and respected establishment."

Odimus felt a slight worry about the necessity of proving his establishment's respectability, but he was the man Kyros had instructed him to locate. "I'm in search of your son, Trenidus."

"I am completely aware of the reason for your presence, and I requested his just a few weeks ago. By now, he should have arrived, as I received a reply letter stating his intention to return, but unfortunately, I am unaware of his whereabouts. He cannot be far behind you and your party." Vartula motions towards his friends at the tables and then shifts his focus back to Odimus. "Why don't you go and join them, and tonight stay in the hotel upstairs. I have an abundance of rooms, enjoy complimentary services for you and your friends. I consider anyone who is a friend of Kyros a friend of mine, even though we often disagree, and he doesn't always approve of what I do, we are still very good friends."

Odimus was now certain why he had emphasized the significance of a respectable establishment. "Yes, sir, tonight I will join them. However, we need to locate your son tomorrow."

"Well, I see you are more business than pleasure. Kyros said as much. While I respect how you think, tonight is the perfect opportunity to treat yourself to a night of pleasure while we wait for my son."

Odimus joins his friends, and they have a good night of healthy fun. For a moment, it seemed as though they were back at the institutions without a care in the world.

Upon the waking hour, Odimus rises slowly, feeling groggy from the late night before and finds a man sitting at the hotel kitchen room table.

"Um, pardon me, who are you?"

The man disappears, and another emerges from the bathroom. "Hi, I'm Trenidus. Looks like someone's still a little sleepy sleep. Was it a rough night? Or just late one?"

Odimus is primarily focused on this intrusion now rather than anything else. "Trenidus, explain this intrusion and why you're wearing my cloak."

The man vanishes once more, and a fresh presence emerges right next to his bed. "I was just trying it on! No need to worry."

Odimus jumps out of bed and exclaims. "This situation has to come to an end! Tell me why you're in my room."

In the living room, four of them suddenly appear and simultaneously say, "I'm doing my homework." Then, a fifth emerges "I need to observe the man I'm about to follow into a potentially certain death." Now, there are no longer four others in the room.

Odimus staring forcefully, "You may go while I get myself ready, and I will see you downstairs in the mess hall."

Downstairs, Trenidus is seated at the bar, enjoying his breakfast. "That was definitely a breach of someone's privacy, don't you agree?"

"Meh, it's always better to be safe than sorry." Another Trenidus emerges from behind the counter and serves Odimus breakfast, who quickly notices yet another as the cook.

Odimus glances at him, perplexed, and questions, "Is this your usual behavior?"

With a smirk on his face, Trenidus looks sideways at him and nods. He then becomes the sole individual. "My duplicates are capable of doing everything I can do. Except eating does not provide any benefits to a duplicate. I consume food, and all my duplicates take care of the challenging work."

Odimus surveys his surroundings as Trenidus playfully shares, "I usually only duplicate in meal prep, fighting, distraction and well, dealing with nagging women."

Turning his chair straight as he begins eating, Odimus poses the question, "Are you planning on joining us?"

"I do intend to join you. Both King Kyron and King Kyros have told me everything, so there is no need to fill me in."

A look of surprise appears on Odimus' face.

"The fact that both kings of the sister kingdoms are aware of a petty thief and the son of a tavern owner surprises you?"

"Not in the slightest. Despite their disclosure, you still made the choice to join us, that, is what surprises me. The rest of us were united through the sharing of a potential manifestation. Despite being the odd man out, you choose to stand with us."

Trenidus ceases eating, rotates the bar stool towards him, "My grandfather and your father were friends and fought together in many of the battles for the **Tree of Energy** and the **Tree of Light**. Until his passing, my grandfather always spoke of Erastus, and I loved my grandfather deeply. Because of that, as my grandfather stood with your father, I would proudly stand by your side." Following that, Trenidus states, "There are my sticky fingers."

He presents Odimus with a Bremium coin bag, causing Odimus to pat himself down and smile at Trenidus. "It's becoming clear to me why Kyros mentioned a thief being helpful on this journey." They exchange handshakes and depart to gather the remaining people.

The entire team is now boarding their Volantuivas while Orthalla looks at Trenidus with complete disgust. Trenidus rides over to Odimus inquiring the issue.

"Who Orthalla, He is an honorable man who finds those without honor distasteful and disagrees with you on this journey."

"Seriously? He's huge! He's not going to sit on me and squeeze me into jelly, is he?"

Odimus just laughs, heels his Volantuiva and takes off. Othare, having heard Trenidus, charges past and in a monotone voice, "Nah, just grind your bones for his bread," and takes off into the air.

Adoria comes charging past as well and with a wink she says "Don't worry, he is a teddy bear inside, mostly." and begins to fly.

Trenidus sends his Volantuiva flying into the air to avoid Orthalla approaching. After traveling for a while, they catch sight of the grand Kingdom of Naphdali over the horizon. Odimus points to it for Othare, and Othare throws a little pebble he finds in his pocket at Fuin, who is very much asleep, causing him to wake.

Odimus then flies over to Orthalla, who is flying right next to Adoria and interrupts their conversation, "Its Naphdali."

The excitement builds as they begin preparations for landing. As they land, Mezlikied dismounts first and is greeted by local representatives and is instructed to stabilize the Volantuiva and follow them to the throne room. The team gazes down a hill and sees the great orchard of the Wind Trees and the Flight Trees.

Odimus proudly proclaims, "I know this island originated from the tribal wars. When the orchard was planted, the tree roots lifted the land from Luxtenebri. Naphlaphane and Dalanias decided to make this island the ruling kingdom of the twin moons, but why didn't the twin kingdoms stay on the **Mother Moons**?"
The guide proceeds to ask, "Are you aware of Dalanias and how treacherous the moon is?"

Ithilwen leaps forward and confirms, "Most of the moon is uninhabited due to its rapid rotation, making it difficult for life to thrive. The moon's rotation created a massive mountain range larger than any found on Luxtenebri or the mother moons. The mountain range formed a massive bowl in the center of the mountain formation, containing a breathtaking oasis where the tribe civilization thrived. Apart from that, the moon is extremely hazardous, and the tribe known as Dalanias possesses exceptional strength due to the intense gravitational pull."

Adoria leans forward, flexes her arms, "You know it!"

The guide comes to a stop and asks "Are you connected to Dalanias' bloodline?"

"I am from my mother's side. My father is Erayiphim, but I was born with my mother's bloodline. My brother Odimus is of Erayiphim bloodline."

Continuing on, the guide remarks. "Oh, how wonderful it is to have a member of our tribe on this mission. Tell me what you know about Naphlaphane, the moon of flight?"

Trenidus interrupts, "They are all airheads, which is the sole reason for their ability to fly."

"You be quiet," Orthalla barks to Trenidus in a hushed tone.

Ithilwen apologizes to the guide, "The moon is covered in floating islands, and they often crash into each other. This causes new soil to be lifted as the roots of the trees from destroyed islands create another island. The rain soaks into the islands to give them nourishment. As a result, the ground below becomes a muddy and barren wasteland. The islands are beautiful and teeming with life as the plant roots enable them to "walk" from one destroyed island to a new one, always following the Flight Trees. Due to the moon's treacherous nature, tribes reside in flexible cities made of tents and frequently change locations. Because living on these two moons was challenging, the twin moon kingdoms agreed to designate Naphdali as their joint kingdom and residence. While a few reside on the mother moons, the majority live here on the great island of Naphdali."
Odimus asks about the size of the island in acres.

The guide proceeds to inform the group that "The island's size is 2 billion acres."

The entire group reacts with astonishment and gasps. Odimus proceeds to ask, "The islands on Naphlaphane have resulted in mud and dirt dripping onto the earth below; how does this island not do that?"

"Over the centuries, we built wooden frames beneath the island to prevent the earth from collapsing. The maintenance seemed never-ending, and the laborer frequently worked in awful, dirty conditions. It was your grandmother and father who created the remarkable Bremium bowl that holds the island in place. The orchard doesn't experience any depletion of earth or water. The water measurement during rainfall is precise, and any excess is drained to the underground water reserve beneath the lake where the island once stood. Below in the water reserve, a water tree orchard has been planted to clean and filter drained water. Creating the ultimate recycling system. We can now dedicate all our abilities and talents to keeping our kingdom thriving aboveground, without anyone having to toil below."

They arrive in the Great Hall where the King and Queen were sitting, eagerly awaiting their arrival. "The Guard of Light!" Proclaims the Queen. They are welcomed. Odimus tried to speak with the King, but the Queen, with a gentle touch on his shoulder, asserted her role as the supreme ruler.

Odimus apologizes and admits, I am not accustomed to the Queen being the supreme leader."

"Believe it or not, there are four kingdoms where the Queen rules with absolute authority. Our kingdom, the water kingdom, the earth kingdom and the elastic kingdom. Rehnburan and Levkaetus, the Void Moon and Electricity Moon, have no kingdom or government. They pledge loyalty to the *Kingdom of Light*. Erayiphim stands out as the only republic among the others. Oh, I do have a strong passion for politics", declares the Queen.

Odimus, in his head, says, "That makes one of us."

Othare then steps forward and says, "It is an honor to finally meet you, my queen. My mother speaks highly of you."

The queen turns "Oh, my young Othare, how you have grown; last time I saw you, you were but four years old. How is your mother doing?"

"She is doing well, your majesty."

"Oh wow," she says looking to Mezlikied, "You've aged, haven't you?! Yet still as handsome as ever!"

"Your Majesty, or shall I say, my dear Ophelia, it has been a long time, indeed. Perhaps too long."

She blushes. Odimus casts a glance at Mezlikied, aiming to make him feel guilty and embarrassed by flirting with the Queen. Mezlikied then caters to the glance, blushing himself.

Queen Ophelia turned to Ithilwen and smiled, "You, my dear, are unmistaken, for you have the bearing of your father but your mother's eyes and beauty." Ithilwen smiles and gently nods to the Queen.

"Now Odimus, follow me over here. The rest of you stay put a moment." Odimus follows Queen Ophelia, and they move a short distance before she presents the rune. "Odimus this rune, when fused to Bremium armor, can bestow the ability to fly, similar to the fruit. Flying is possible as long as they have the Coin of Armor or fully activated armor on them. I've just learned that there's a bloodline descendant of the Dalanias among the Guard of Light. Is this correct?"

"Yes your Majesty, my sister, from our mother's side."

Moving closer, she speaks in a hushed tone into his ear. "I understand it's your choice to choose whom each rune is given to, would you consider honoring our people and giving it to her?"

Odimus nods respectfully, Queen Ophelia now takes a step back and makes an announcement to everyone in the great hall. "Odimuvalere has been granted the Rune of Flight, but after deliberation, it has been determined that Adoria is to possess the rune of our people. She is a descendant of Dalanias! Therefore, the twin kingdoms of Naphlaphane, the Kingdom of Flight and Dalanias, the Kingdom of Wind, have made our decision, and as ruler of the kingdom of Naphdali, I see fit that Adoria becomes the rightful heir and guardian of the rune of our people." Adoria completely speechless walks toward the Queen who hands her the rune, and everyone in the great hall claps and cheers, and with over a thousand people in attendance, it creates a loud and marvelous roar. Adoria fights back tears, concealing her emotions, and gives a slight wave to everyone present.

Queen Ophelia now addresses the Guard of Light, "King Kyron has instructed me to inform you that the next rune is located in the buried city ruins in the Ocean of Arthiatus on Manekaizah, the Water Moon. To have the ability to breathe underwater, the Wind Fruit is essential. It will produce an oxygen mask that can sustain you for seventy hours. Seeing how you are only going down there for a couple of days, I suggest eating the fruit moments before descending below. Understand that there's a reason nobody has gone down there to obtain the rune. According to legend, it is protected by the beast that destroyed the city. No one has ever laid eyes on it, only catching glimpses of its magnificent tail and the aftermath it leaves, so be swift, or you will have no chance of survival in those depths. Before setting off, make sure to pluck the necessary amount of fruit you will need for your journey."

The Guard of Light departs and picks from the trees, especially Adoria since she is in the Wind Tribe, so she picks significantly more for her constant need to partake. After putting the rune into her armor, she pivots towards her Volantuiva and playfully pretends to send her Volantuiva back to the Kingdom of Energy.

Orthalla notices "You can't sustain the flight time and speed the Volantuiva are able to maintain, so don't send your Volantuiva away." Adoria turns to him, giggling, and he realizes she was playing a joke on him.

Many days later, the Guard of Light experiences a rainstorm as they land on Manekaizah. A man comes running up; "You Odimus!?" He yells through the sound of the storm. Odimus confirms he is, "Come with me," instructs the man. They all run to a building but stable the Volantuiva on the way in. "I understand you're tired and hungry, but it's best to go underwater now during the storm. It seems luck is on your side. When there are storms, the great beast of the deep stays away from the city ruins below." Urgently, he ushers the team outside and assumes the Queen had already informed them about needing the fruit to breathe underwater. "If you happen to have any Energy Tree fruit, it would be in your best interest to take a bite since you will be searching for the great hall for over fifty hours."

Odimus widens his eyes, "fifty hours!?"

Laughing, the man estimates, "You'll spend ten hours going there and another ten coming back." Just the travel itself takes twenty.

Odimus inquires, "What is the depth of the ruins?"

"Oh, one of the deepest parts of the ocean," the gentleman responds. "These water suits have been carefully made using the bark of the Water Tree, exclusively for you. They will keep you dry; the pressure of the ocean will have no effect on you, and it will insulate you from the cold-water depths."

Othare walks over to Odimus and expresses, "I am more than willing to follow you anywhere, but I truly have a fear of drowning. You know, being a member of the Fire Tribe poses a challenge. My fire fruit ability will be of no use to you down there."

The man chuckles, "Yep! you're pretty much useless here, aren't you?"

"Shut your mouth, watered-down garbage!"

The man raises his hands, signaling he will step back. Othare calls back to the gentleman and expresses apologies for his actions.

The gentleman says, "I should not have said anything. It wasn't my place."

Odimus rests his hands on Othares shoulder "You will be okay. You possess both a relic and Bremium armor. You will have the wind fruit as well, so you can't drown. It will have your lungs filled with air the whole time. It's just a matter of searching and finding, then returning to the surface." Othare nods, displaying his trust in him.

After laughing at Othare, Ithilwen states, "I don't need a Wind Tree fruit," and suddenly she changes into her water creature form, a Cipactli, an ability that the plant and animal fruit of Zequiberus offers. "I possess the capability to breathe underwater while in this form. Communication is a challenge, but hey, I can breathe."

Their faces fill with amazement as they look at her. Trenidus chimes in, "How does she manage to still look ravishing as a humanoid water creature with a snout?"

Othare throws a rock at him "No sir!"

Next, the gentleman says "One final thing" and then proceeds to give a loud whistle. Multiple water creatures surge out of the waves of the ocean. Odimus identifies them as the powerful Equuselko, The Dominant creature of Manekaizah. He walks over and delicately glides his hand down the Equuselko's side. It has the feel of a fish, but it walks on land on all fours like a land creature.

The gentleman instructs, "You will ride these Equuselko down to the ruins. Make haste while the storm persists, it allows you safety before the great beast returns. Here on Manekaizah, it goes by the name Liviathidus." The man warns the team that they won't be able to communicate underwater due to their lack of water tribe bloodline, so they must rely on hand signals and maintain eye contact.

The Guard of Light now starts their descent into the depths of the ocean. As lightning flashes overhead, everything falls into silence. Several feet down, they becomes engulfed in a dark and ominous presence, prompting them to pause and tether themselves together. Into the depths of darkness, they descend for several hours until suddenly Odimus is captivated by a radiant glow in the distance. As his eyes adjust, bioluminescent plants and animals illuminate their surroundings as if it were daytime on the surface. The beauty leaves them amazed as they look around the ocean floor. The underwater garden of the Manekaizah rivals the gardens of the fire moon Ludaea. Despite being called the Fire Moon, Ludaea is not actually on fire. The moon is recognized as the most beautiful garden in all of Luxtenebri and the Mother Moons. This occurs because its orbit is always directed towards the sun. Ludaea, located closest to the sun Klibous, has the shortest nighttime of just one hour. Because Klibous is not a fiery or gaseous sun but a sun made of pure energy, nothing on Ludaea burns; instead, it is transformed into the most stunning garden imaginable. Despite being raised in such a beautiful Mother Moon as Ludaea, Othare was amazed by the breathtaking underwater gardens of Manekaizah. Since the gentleman on the surface had given them directions, the party continues to follow his instructions. After several hours, they finally come across a massive ancient city submerged deep in a canyon. Odimus is amazed by the vast canyon and the ruins of an ancient city below. They start their descent until they reach their final destination. Odimus had already distributed group partners to everyone, and the search commences.

A few more hours pass and Orthalla unexpectedly emerges, startling Odimus. He waves eagerly for him to come and notices Adoria with him, raising an eyebrow in curiosity as to why she's there since he had instructed her to go a different way with Fuin. While following them, Mezlikied is by Odimus's side and gestures for him to look. Fuin and Trenidus are seen emerging from a grand hallway. They motion for them to approach and join the group. Thoughts of Ithilwen and Othare cause Odimus to worry since they are nowhere to be seen. A door of immense size appears, with the inscription "The Great Hall" overhead. Odimus gives Orthalla a pat on the back to show appreciation for a good job. No matter how hard they try to tug and pull, it is useless. Odimus suddenly realizes the door has more of an ancient appearance to it but bears a resemblance to the doors in the Kingdom of Energy. Adoria notices as well and immediately taps on the door. He slightly pulls back his Equuselko and commands the Bremium to open.

As it opens, they are instantly pulled into the door while bubbles pour out. Once they have all been pulled into the door and come together, they realize they're in a room filled with air. Odimus springs up and commands the door to close. Everyone gathers themselves, and help calm their individual Equuselko and are now able to talk to one another. The great hall is bigger than the one in the Kingdom of Lights, and the concrete walls are unbelievably intricate.

"It's an air pocket," Mezlikied says, then he urgently instructs, "But we need to hurry. Ithilwen and Othare are still searching outside."

In the middle of the room, they spot the stand where the rune was supposed to be, but it's missing. They survey their surroundings, searching high and low for the rune. Trenidus notices a potential manifestation; he follows it, and it leads him to its location. From behind a pillar, he reveals a rune, and they all quickly gather around.

Mezlikied turns to Fuin, "Can you enlighten us on what the Book of Knowledge claims this rune can do?"

Reading from the book out loud, Fuin states, "It is said to gain control over the effects of water and land. They never feel thirsty, exhibit heightened strength and agility, and can jump long distances. It goes by the name of the Rune of Resilience."

Taking a moment to ponder, Odimus makes up his mind to give it to Ithilwen. All of a sudden, the group remembers that Ithilwen and Othare are not present.

"We must hurry," says Mezlikied, "We have been down here too long. Our fruit is going to lose its effect in just enough time to make it to the surface."

Suddenly, the walls of the great hall are hit by a tremendous crash, shaking the ground and creating cracks through which water infiltrates. The group quickly moves towards the door and gets ready by mounting their individual Equuselko, preparing for Odimus to open the door. As the door opens, water starts rushing in. The Equuselko defies the laws of water, walking on it as if it were solid ground, and approaches the door. In the same spot as before, another powerful crash hits the wall, causing the cracks to open more. A massive pillar is displaced and starts descending, seemingly on a path to crush Adoria. Despite Odimus using his full strength to utilize gravity and stop the pillar, it only slightly decelerates. All of a sudden, he can see a dim gray light shining, and the pillar hovering only inches above her. Upon looking toward Mezlikied, Odimus observes the heart stone orbiting around him. They nod and together, proceed to cast the pillar aside.

All members of the group enter the water and start their mission to leave the ruined city. They search intensely for Ithilwen and Othare along the way, but they cannot find them anywhere. As they make their way out of the city walls, the Liviathidus comes into view. A creature of enormous proportions. Odimus witnesses Ithilwen and Othare maneuvering to escape capture. He motions for the group to tie themselves together and go up to the surface. They all follow instructions without any hesitation. Rushing in with valor, Odimus confronts the Liviathidus, parrying its claw to save Othare from capture. He signals for them to head for the surface, and they all begin to flee. In a fierce struggle, they swim for hours with the utmost determination, channeling the energy of the Equuselko to swim with all its might. Their charging resembles a battle rather than an escape, always in a state of readiness for combat. Returning to the wall of darkness, fear begins to consume them, and it feels like an eternity as they climb through the darkness. However, the light eventually breaks through, and they see the surface.

Having weathered the storm, Odimus takes a moment to rest and enjoys the comforting sensation of the sun on his face. The remaining team members are only a few hundred yards off. Othare and Odimus motion for them to come closer, but Odimus quickly reacts as he hears Othare inquire about Ithilwen's whereabouts. Without hesitation, Odimus dives underwater, spotting Ithilwen being pulled towards the dark wall just a few feet away. He charges after her knowing she will be lost if she reaches the darkness. He catches up and notices the Liviathidus's claw wrapped around her Equuselko. It appears the beast only wanted the Equuselko. He sees her foot trapped in its grip. Despite having to fight to be freed, she shows no signs of fear. Odimus realizes she can't escape.

By now, they've spent seventy hours underwater. It took a long time to find the great hall and then ascend. The fruit cannot be eaten while the effects of another fruit are still present. Odimus is now experiencing fear as he aids her in the struggle for freedom. The wall of darkness was mere moments from them and soon, they began to enter the darkness. Odimus and Ithilwen are starting to grasp the severity of their situation as the Liviathidus descends quicker than they can ascend. Odimus fastens a rope around her waist, then lets go of his Equuselko and embraces her tightly. He gives his Equuselko a slap on the rear to make it rise. This manages to pull her foot out. Clinging to each other, they endure the darkness for what feels like hours. Suddenly, Ithilwen transforms from her Cipactli form back to human form, and Odimus feels her warmth in his arms, reminding him of his mother's embrace on the night of her death. The warmth of Ithilwen's grasp provides him with comfort, but then he quickly turns to fear as he realizes what this means. Suddenly, they broke through the dark wall. The Fruit of Zequiberus effects no longer work for Ithilwen. Without the water tree suit, she begins to grow cold, and she is forced to hold her breath. Filled with fear seeing how great the distance was. In a desperate attempt to breathe, she began to drown. In order to save her life, Odimus, still having the abilities of the wind fruit, began to blow air into her lungs with his own. With every breath, Odimus retreats, enabling her to exhale. She locks eyes with him and feels a sense of safety, causing her fear to fade. Odimus repeats this action several times, intensifying Ithilwen's newly found longing, for his lips to return to hers.

As the water rushes over them, break through the water to the surface. Othare, seeing them do so, begins to ride his Equuselko to her aid. Ithilwen, coughing and struggling to breathe, watches as Odimus rode off on his Equuselko. Othare lifts her onto his, and holds her tightly. Realizing that Othare was holding her, she embraces him instead of looking towards Odimus, riding away towards Mezlikied. A sense of uneasiness creeps over her regarding the feelings she had felt for him under the water.

Chapter 9

REHNBURAN THEN TO TERTHIATH

The Rune of Resilience is now in Ithilwen's possession, and the team is soon to be landing on the Void moon Rehnburan. Having been raised in the Mountain Kingdom near the City of Light and never being able to see his Mother Moon, Fuin's joy became immeasurable. They land in the first city his people constructed after being liberated from the Mines a century and a half ago. After being set free, they promised to serve as the royal guards to protect and refrain from attacking. The people he belonged to were masters of defense. A kingdom was constructed within Luxtenebri's largest mountain, just outside the city gates of Light. Digging beneath the earth, they built a grand city within but ultimately destroyed the underground passage. Only those from the Void had the ability to teleport in or out of the kingdom. The mountain had no entry, so outsiders weren't allowed to see inside, nor could they teleport into the Kingdom within. In lieu of that, they established a grand city beyond the Mount Walls to facilitate trade and offer refuge to people from various tribes. Upon landing in the city on Rehnburan, Orthalla's excitement grew as he realized that this was where his mother had relocated to since their last encounter.

As they land, a faint trembling sensation is felt beneath their feet. Orthalla, full of excitement, starts walking towards the rumble like a child filled with wonder. The rest of the group are more concerned. Suddenly, his mother appears from behind a wall. Except for Mezlikied, no one else in the group has encountered a behemoth tribe member. So, they are all slightly frightened. Laughing, Mezlikied passes by them and positions himself directly behind Orthalla, with Adoria following suit. Hayleta's action of picking up Orthalla is a surprise as he looks just like a normal-sized man in her arms.

"Hello, mother!"

"Hello, my little joy! I received your Anohail notifying me of your arrival."

"Yes, we have arrived to meet with the elder Monks."

With folded arms, Trenidus, next to Orthalla, is looking suspicious. Looking at him, Orthalla asks, "Is there something amusing?"

"I'll be honest with you, I've always been curious to see a behemoth woman, besides her few mutations she is still insanely beautiful! Would you give me your blessing to ask your mother on a date?"

Orthalla in response to the question, swings with all his might, and the powerful swing strikes Trenidus, but the duplicate vanishes instantly. Frantically, he scans the area for him, catches sight of another, and swiftly jumps to land on him. Then, another vanishes as well. The impact of his landing on the ground is quite rough.

Trenidus then sets one foot on his back, "You really think I wouldn't dupe more of myself after duping on you?" Then he suddenly vanishes. Orthalla searches for him and discovers Trenidus with a triumphant expression as he is leaning on the door frame eating a fruit, overfilled with pride and arrogance.

"Just wait, I'll get you when you least expect it, you conceited imbecile!"

"Eh, we will see," says Trenidus as he makes a swift exit around the corner, leaving Orthalla to follow after him.

Adoria yells at Trenidus, "Just give him a break!" as the two-run past.

The team reaches a modest yet spacious home equipped with everything one would need for comfort. The door lacks any special material or fine craftsmanship and is simply made of wood. There are no cracks or flaws; everything is well constructed. When they scan the other homes, it became evident that all of them looked the same, except for this home, which was the only one with a door.

Then Hayleta states, "My home stands out because it has a door, unlike others, as they can teleport in and out of their homes."

Opening the door, they proceed to sit in the living quarters. Without warning, four men materialize out of nowhere. The refreshments slip from Hayleta's hands as she is startled. "I'm still getting accustomed to that."

"We are so sorry, our sweet Hayleta." Then, all four elders walk over to her and have a group hug. She seems happy and opens her arms. The four of them are so small they look like children in a mother's arms. Observing the kindness and love bestowed upon her by the people, Orthalla becomes teary-eyed.

"Are you seriously crying?"

"Are you seriously talking, Trenidus?" Adoria scoffs as she grabs a tissue to hand to Orthalla.

"I'm simply happy because she is happy, you know?"

Adoria handing it over "Ya big love bug"

"More like a big wimp," says Trenidus, while cautiously checking for onlookers before sneaking over and embracing Hayleta with the four elders. She responds with a smile, but Orthalla interrupts by yanking him away. In the midst of laughter, Trenidus inquires, "What!?"

Orthalla smacks him on the back of his head and says, "Knock it off!"

Adoria asks chuckling softly, "What is the matter with you!?"

Trenidus shrugging his shoulders, "You know what, I have no idea."

Mezlikied rolls his eyes and declares, "We have come to obtain a rune."

The Monks release their embrace with Hayleta and face Mezlikied, and pulling from ones robes, presents it to them. The peculiar thing about this rune is that it gives off a dim blue light.

"Is that really the Guarding rune!?" Fuin gasps. Then he proclaims its abilities, "A shield is created around the user that cannot be penetrated, almost indestructible, but if hit too many times, it loses its power."

Odimus points to Trenidus; "Me?" Trenidus points to himself, questioning? Orthalla seems offended, yet remains silent. The rune is passed to Trenidus. After he integrates it with his armor, the rune activates, causing a blue shield to surround him. "Now I have the freedom to do anything to you, Orthalla, without consequences."

Immediately, Odimus questions if he has made a mistake. Standing up, "Trenidus, simple fun is acceptable, but the condition to you having that shield is to let off Orthalla a bit big guy."

"Ugh, fine. Thank you, Odimus, for the rune." Trenidus now seems calmer, grateful, and surprisingly humble.

Mezlikied graciously thanks the Monks, "It is time to take our leave, for our next voyage will be quite treacherous."

They stand, Orthalla hugs his mother before they leave. As they exit the door, Hayleta quietly asks her son, "Have you discovered the purpose of the rune on the axe?"

"No, not yet, mother but I will keep trying." she nods, and he leaves.

They make their heading and ride their Volantuiva following Mezlikied. Through the wind Odimus hollers, "Where were you thinking we go next?" Mezlikied's voice becomes a deep and serious tone filled with dread, "Terthiath."

They share a fearful glance, and Orthalla's words break the silence; "My Mother Moon"

The party descends near the Atmosphere of Terthiath, Odimus instructs them all to take a bite of a Wind Fruit. The moon's thin air and lack of oxygen are a result of the destruction of all life during the battle against the Terelaviathons. He gives the instructions to double-check that they have recorded the time of their last Water Fruit consumption. Upon landing, the Volantuiva grow increasingly frantic and uneasy. Mezlikied whispers to his Volantuiva and gives it a slap on the rear, prompting it to head back towards Rehnburan.

Odimus turns to him "What are you doing?"

"This is the furthest they can go, so we must now send them on their way."

"If we send off the Volantuiva, how will we get off the moon, Mezlikied?"

"Over there, you can see the old Bremium passenger ships."

"We do not have any electricity fruit or Levkaetus monks here."

"Odimus, these are ancient. We can use our will to bring us back to Rehnburan. Sure will is how Bremium ships were once controlled. We found that the speed significantly increased when we added fire to the vessel, which was previously very slow. We then realized that utilizing electricity on the vessel resulted in increased speed and reduced the need for a will to control the vessels. It's our only option, no matter how hard it may be."

Looking around his Mother Moon, Orthalla collapses to his knees, overwhelmed by a deep feeling of loss. With hands covering his face, he begins to shed a few tears. Adoria walks over, gently rubbing his back, and he pulls her in. He seems to completely engulf her, but she doesn't mind. In this moment, Trenidus surprisingly, refrains from speaking. The ground starts shaking violently, as though it's on the verge of splitting. Every individual brings out their relics, activates their Bremium armor, and readies themselves. It appears as though the earth is heaping up as if something is ascending from below. They all begin to distance themselves, fearing a creature will emerge from the ground. Gravel falls off a stone, slowly and gently, revealing a magnificent stone that emits a brighter aura than the fruit. The stone seems hollow as the light inside dims and becomes visible. Inside seems to have a glimmer of aura, a rainbow-like fire emanating from inside. Mezlikied nearly topples Fuin while forcefully making his way toward the stone, also bumping into Odimus. He approaches the stone, and shows his respect by kneeling before it. Odimus commences to kneel as well, and the group follows suit.

Trenidus breaks the silence, "So yeah, why are we kneeling to a rock?"

Mezlikied, for the first time, stops Trenidus from speaking and urges him to remain silent. No further sound escapes Trenidus due to his profound respect for Mezlikied. Mezlikied summons the Heart stone of Erayiphim, and the two stones begin to orbit around one another, like a dance. He gasps, "This affirms my suspicions. Behold, the heart stone of Terthiath. It has been here the entire time." He reaches out to grab it, but it hops away and gradually makes its way to Orthalla. Orthalla's tearful eyes are locked onto the stone, and his concentration is unwavering. It reaches him and hovers in front of him, completely still.

Mezlikied quietly instructs, "Place your hands out."

Orthalla reaches out, and it comes to rest in his hands. In an instant, he finds himself surrounded by a vibrant ball of fire, displaying every color imaginable.

"Has anyone else noticed Orthalla is on fire?"

They all simultaneously hush Trenidus once more. The fire dissipates, and a loud rumble from deep within the earth momentarily shakes before ceasing. Orthalla seems to be mourning, "The Moon no longer is able to sustain any life. Terthiath's final life resides within the Heart Stone, the Aura Trees, and the Terthiath tribe."

Mezlikied and the others slowly rise to their feet. He approaches Orthalla, and lends a hand, "Orthalla, do you understand the significance of this?"

He shakes his head in confusion "I apologize, but I am uncertain."

"Orthalla, you are the guardian of Terthiath and the caretaker of the Heart Stone of Aura."

Adoria now inching closer, her eyes fixated on the stone's mesmerizing beauty. The core of a Mother Moon, also known as the Heart Stone, is composed entirely of Bremium. It is also of pure energy, holding all properties and only the properties of Aura. It is beautiful.

"You can enhance your aura abilities by tenfold and eliminate the need to consume fruit for aura abilities" Mezlikied informs.

Odimus approaches and sarcastically congratulates him, "You are now a know it all."

Everyone laughs, and Mezlikied attempts to Odimus, failing. Mezlikied demonstrates how to make it disappear into the heart and reappear as needed. the stone does just that. "See, it is relatively easy."

Suddenly, Orthalla's Heart stone of Terthiath disappears, and he lets out an uncomfortable grunt. "Ah, that feels so strange."

"Yes, it is, you'll get accustomed. You can't utilize its ability until you summon it, at which point it will begin orbiting around you like a moon. Everyone, come with me. Let's get a move on!"

They begin their journey towards a mountain off in the distance. Mezlikied points at one and says, "That's our destination. Fuin, Odimus has been designated you to be the receiver of this rune. It is the rune of reflection," while they walk, Mezlikied continues to share details about the rune with them. "If someone were to strike you while wearing the rune fused into Bremium armor, the impact would reflect back on the attacker and harm them in the same way their attack was intended. We found this to be the perfect solution for Fuin, as the rune will defend him against attackers without him needing to attack anyone."

Fuin's sudden laughter causes everyone to stop and watch as he moves from the back to the front of the line. Fuin, who was known for his seriousness, had never been heard laughing before, so all of them were unexpectedly shocked. Then Fuin stopped laughing and said one simple word, "Perfect!"

The party has now been in the lifeless wasteland for several days and is now feeling weary. It feels like the air is thick and heavy, even with the Wind Fruit activated. They find their every movement to be tiring. Everyone is exhausted, and a few are starting to feel the effects so much that they request Odimus to turn back. Odimus turns to Orthalla and requests that he use the Heart Stone for rejuvenation. Despite Orthalla's attempts, it doesn't have a significant effect on them. The lack of life all around in this baron land is just wearing on them too fast to maintain a constant rejuvenation. Due to having the sword of valiance, Odimus isn't as worn down as all the others. He tells them to rotate the sword among themselves to help each gain a little relief at a time. From this point on, the team rotates between themselves, healing them little by little. Yet the effects are still heavy and difficult on every member of the Guard of Light. Finally, they reach the front gates of a castle situated at the base of a mountain. A very large, destroyed city with thousands of ruined buildings is visible in the distance. It's evident to all that this was once a formidable and mighty kingdom.

Othare asks, engulfed in exhaustion "Mezlikied, can you tell us where we are?

"Before it was rebuilt on Luxtenebri, this was the kingdom of Aura."

Orthalla slowly maneuvers through the team and positions himself in front of Mezlikied. "Are you saying that this is the castle where the benevolent king and his son lived? The one who brought about the destruction of Terthiath?"

"The very same."

Without hesitation, Orthalla burst through the gates and sprints towards the castle doors. Adoria cries out to Orthalla to halt, then swiftly flies next to him charging towards the doors. He proceeds to enter the castle's entrance. With a fierce gaze, Orthalla surveys the surroundings and roars loudly. All individuals have caught up at this point.

Trenidus comes through the door and asks. "What's he going on about now?"

"Can you, just for once, show some respect!" yells Orthalla. Then, his axe brings about a surge of energy, causing a lightning bolt to strike right in the middle of the place where they all were standing. Everyone is propelled away by the blast. Nearby pipes are ignited by a surge of electricity, causing energy to flow throughout the building. The noise of a generator begins, with lights starting to glow. Although slightly pained, the team recovers and witnesses Orthalla's Axe releasing these bursts of electricity. Observing his Axe, he mutters, "Oh, so that's what it does. Is everyone alright?"

"What was that?" inquires Odimus.

"My Axe is ancient and already had a rune fused into the hilt, but my mother couldn't decipher its purpose. I couldn't either, until I stepped foot in this castle."

Mezlikied appears unfazed by the Axe or being thrown by the blast as he is fixated on the lights with amazement. "So the stories are true"

Odimus asks, "What stories are you referring to?"

Mezlikied turns and shares that the son of the great king supposedly created bizarre machines that operated using electricity and could even create light. Rather than torches or fire, we employ Bremium lanterns for light generation. There were rumors about machines with the ability to generate light instead of Bremium lanterns. Mezlikied then suggests, "There was a power source" pointing to the Axe "That could possibly have been said source."

"My mother said it was her great-grandmother's."

"Yes, that may be true, but I'm thinking it came from here."

Orthalla wonders if the Axe has exclusive use in this location. Mezlikied suggests "The only way to know is to wait and see if it still works after we leave Terthiath. However, our current priority is to locate the rune of reflection. It was reported to be in a facility called a 'laboratory'."

The team starts their search for this laboratory. Around an hour's time has passed when they hear a shout "Over here!"

Upon entering the room, they discover the east wall completely missing and rubble scattered everywhere, giving the impression that the castle had once extended far in that direction but had collapsed entirely. Their attention shifts to the west wall, where the majority of the lab remained undamaged. They discover a desk that had been untouched, except for some touches of dust, for centuries. Bremium was the only metal found on Luxtenebri and the Mother Moons, making it the only material of choice for all metal objects, such as the desk. Upon opening the drawer, they discover a rune positioned neatly in the center, surrounded by what appeared to be strange tools. It looks like the King had been studying the rune, but the Terelaviathon's destruction interrupted him.

Odimus begins to reach for the rune when suddenly Trenidus interrupts. "Proceed only if you're prepared to meet your maker or be foolish enough to realize it too late." Odimus stops and glances up at Trenidus signaling towards the trap sitting just inches from his fingers. At the bottom of the drawer, he spots a pressure switch that is set to ignite a vial made from Fire Fruit juice. "That stuff is extremely dangerous, and sitting here this long will have become increasingly powerful and significantly less stable."
Odimus cautiously moves away, grinning at Trenidus "It appears you have finally found your purpose in the group, outside of annoying Orthalla."

Trenidus places his hand on Odimus's back and confidently answers, "Yep, that and my good looks."

Adoria scoffs.

Othare says, "Good looks aren't everything."

Mezlikied finally chimes in, "Trenidus, do you have the ability to disable the device?"

"Yes, I'm capable of it, but it's an old and extremely unusual trap. I haven't encountered something this old before. The workmanship is intriguing and undoubtedly the creation of an intelligent individual." he continues to evaluate.

During their conversation, Odimus spots an ancient journal crafted from Aura Tree bark paper and binding. As a result, this book would be resistant to aging. It looks almost brand new. He picks it up and begins to read. This journal was written by the account of the Son of the great King. The story that everyone was familiar with. He begins reading out loud, and all pay attention except Trenidus, who is still working on the trap. The King's account is being read by him until he comes across the part where the Shadow King orders fifty Terelaviathon. In the account, he asserts his belief that this force would be capable of conquering everything and be invincible. The fear was so intense that he made multiple attempts to halt his work, but the Shadow King's presence scared him too much.

Odimus looks up to Orthalla shouting "COWARD! Terthiath's destruction could have been avoided if he had refused to create the monsters."

Mezlikied turns "This was an expected occurrence for the Shadow King. It all makes sense. Over the course of thousands of years, Aura has been the cause of all viruses and illnesses being completely eradicated. No one from the tribes of Luxtenebri is subject to disease, and we can heal wounds almost instantly except in a few rare cases when the wound is just too extensive. The people of our civilization live hundreds of years, Immortals live forever. However, if the Aura Tree were to go extinct, then Illnesses, diseases, injuries, and infections would all be reintroduced into a civilization that has no ability to fight them because we have been without them for thousands of years. That is why your fever was so irregular, scary, and strange, Odimus. No one has seen a fever in thousands of years. Not even Immortals could survive illnesses and diseases because immortality only allows you to live forever when healthy, but wounds, disease and infections could still take their lives. This was the Shadow King's design, and he did not want those beasts. He wanted to destroy the Aura Trees."

Orthalla proceeds to say, "If I wasn't a healer, I would seek vengeance upon him."

Mezlikied then lifts his gaze, appearing perplexed. "Rebuilding the Aura Orchards after the destruction of Terthiath was painstakingly slow, and an endless army emerged out of nowhere, attempting to conquer everything. Using this endless military force, a new kingdom was established, and they frequently launched attacks on the Aura kingdom. For many years, the Aura kingdom protected themselves, and then the Light and Energy Kingdoms came to their aid. Over the next several centuries, the twin kingdoms became involved and eventually kept the defiant kingdom from the newly built Terthiath. This led the defiant kingdom to shift its focus to the Kingdom of Light and Energy, sparking the Light and Energy Tree wars. Kyron, Kyros, Erastus, and I united in the same war to vanquish the powerful kingdom of Othkule by setting out on a quest just like this one. Daily, many people were drawn to them for their seemingly boundless strength. I'm afraid the Shadow King may have been responsible for this as well because of the growth time required for the Aura Tree's orchards. Due to the scarcity of supply, we often lost men to infections as there wasn't enough Aura to go around. There seems to be a connection between all of these things. I must send word to Kyron, Kyros, and the Kaleidoscope Council."

Mezlikied retrieves The Orb of Anohail from his hip pouch. Now, the Anohail was a Bremium orb, and everyone from the twelve tribes of Luxtenebri was given it at the age of sixteen. It was a small sphere, small enough to be held in your hand. By willing the Bremium Sphere to guide you, the ball could act as a compass, leading you to any location. It can also be sent as a messenger to anyone you choose. When you let go of the ball, it instantly changes into a plate that matches the size and shape of a piece of parchment. It transcribes your message on the plate and records your voice as you spoke. It then reverts to its spherical shape and flies off. The sphere has the ability to travel anywhere on Luxtenebri or the Mother Moons as per your instructions. The Anohail transforms into a plate again once it reached the intended recipient of the message. If you wish, you can use the Anohail to project your voice, especially if you want a large audience to hear the message. Once the message is received, you can tap your Anohail to theirs to record it on yours. The Anohail promptly returns to the owner upon delivering the message. The Anohail emits light and forms a glowing sphere. It is not very bright, but sufficient in very dark places to lead you the way to where you need to go. Since it is a compass, this is an important ability for it to have in darker places of travel. Mezlikied instructs his Anohail to send word to several people and tells it not to return until all he listed have received the message. The Anohail wisps off, straight for Luxtenebri.

Trenidus announces, "I have possessed the vial!" and he slowly positions it between two rocks, ensuring it remains stationary. "Safety is guaranteed if you all stay away from that spot."

Odimus seizes the rune, "We must depart, we've spent too much time on this baron and lifeless moon. We all feel the effects."

All nod in agreement and begin to leave. The group fail to notice Orthalla approaching a peculiar machine. Odimus then hears Adoria questioning Orthalla's actions, expressing concern about meddling with it. He believes he has identified the shape of his axe etched out of the counter next to a large machine.

He is about to place the axe when Trenidus shouts, "No!" From the strange machine, he notices cords leading up to a massive bowl brimming with liquid.

The axe suddenly releases a surge of electricity, traveling down the cords and reaching the glass bowl of liquid. The liquid begins bubbling, and there's activity within. The glass shatters, revealing a colossal beast as it fell and hit the ground. This beast was larger than any land-dwelling creature anyone had ever seen.

"The king of Shadow requested fifty to be made, whereas the King of Aura only fought against forty-nine."

Mezlikied shouts with vigor "RUN!"

It is a Terelaviathon, the creature of myth that destroyed Terthiath. As the team entered the hallway, the ground rumbles. They persist in running at full speed, understanding that this is a creature to evade, not confront. They step into a ginormous dining hall and the sound of an explosion rings out. They instantly recognize it as the Fire Fruit vile. Suddenly, the Terelaviathon unleashes a roar that reverberates through the walls and pillars surrounding the dining hall. Dust is scattered all around, and everyone is coated in it.

Trenidus exclaims loudly, "It is quite ironic of us to be running through a dining hall as we are all about to be eaten!"

Othare yells back, amused "Not the time as always, Trenidus!"

As they head towards the entrance, the Terelviathon breaks through the wall and lands on the thrones of the ancient King and Queen that sat in the great hall, letting out a terrifying roar. Orthalla turns and swings his axe, sending a slash at the beast, but this time, he adds a bolt of lightning to it. The beast is hit but becomes even angrier and begins to chase them.

Trenidus remarks, "Great, you had to show off your fancy axe, and now it's chasing us."

Odimus yells at Fuin to initiate teleportation, prioritizing the women as the beast charges them, Fuin quickly takes hold of Ithilwen and disappears, then reappears and takes Adoria. Once he snatches Adoria, the beast springs into the air, prepared to pounce on all of them. Fuin makes a sudden reappearance, with only seconds to seize Mezlikied. Trenidus duplicates four more of himself, and moments before the beast lands, he is able to pick up Orthalla with all his duplicates and pulls him to safety. Right behind Othare and Odimus, the beast lands and creates a huge hole in the ground before falling into it. Othare and Odimus fall in after the beast. Falling several hundred feet, Odimus breaks his fall by landing on the beast. His injuries are severe and Odimus is unaware that he did not fall alone. With tremendous force, a cement block crushed the head of the beast, resulting in its death. Looking up, Odimus notices a hole that is so deep he can hardly see its top. He shouts upwards but realizes the distance might be too great. Odimus scans his surroundings, searching for signs of a cave, but finds none. It seems there is now no way to enter or exit. Then, with the very faint light, he is able to make out a door. He pulls his Anohail from his belt pouch and wills it to produce light. Due to the darkness, the Anohail proved able to emit enough light to illuminate the vault door, allowing him to see it clearly. The words "For those who want a life of misery" are written on the top of the vault. Without any superstition or fear, Odimus searches for a latch to open the vault. Finding none, he notices the door's intriguing craftsmanship. Stepping back, he uses his willpower to open the Bremium vault door. In the room's center, a stand with a rune sits as the door creaks open slowly. Another Aura binding journal sits right in front of the rune on the stand, where Odimus walks over and sits. This time, the journal had a more feminine look. Odimus opened the bindings and proceeded to read.

"Today, Prince Orthalla came to my window and invited me to go outside. The thought of seeing him again excites me."

Odimus flips a few pages.

"Orthalla will become the crowned Prince tomorrow, making him the heir to the throne, and he has invited me to the ceremony. I'm struggling to choose the perfect outfit for when I meet his father. I really want to make a good impression."

Odimus continues flipping pages and concludes that Orthalla is a popular name among the Aura people, and then he begins to read further.

"Orthalla proposed to me today, and his parents blessed our union. I am about to become a princess, feeling a mix of excitement and fear, as I love him wholeheartedly and believe he will make a great King with me as his Queen."

Now aware that it's the Queen's journal, Odimus is intrigued.

"Today, Orthalla brought back a rune from the Pit of Anglishes that was unlike any other. He ventured to that awful place in order to safeguard his people and establish an unprecedented empire, which he named the Aura Dynasty. I have faith in his ability to achieve such a remarkable accomplishment."

He skips ahead, "I wish he had never found that rune, for we have been at war many times against those that desire to hold the power of Time Observance."

Time Observance, can this really be the rune that slows down time upon being attacked? A rune of myth is that when fused to armor, and if an attacker made a strike, it would allow the user to see the move slowly and give them the ability to dodge the attack. Odimus interrupts his reading to examine the rune positioned on the stand. Out of curiosity's sake, he opens to the last few pages.

"Today, the King has fallen during the last battle of our great and terrible war. At great cost, peace will finally be achieved. I hope my son can restore what has been taken from Orthalla as he assumes power over the Kingdom. The intention behind creating this vault is to restrict access to only those who possess knowledge of its location and only be able to get down here through teleportation. I pray that today and for eternity, I am the sole keeper of this information. I write upon the vault door a warning if an unfortunate soul happens upon this vault, for those who desire a life of misery".

Odimus deciphers the last words as a cautionary message about the rune, which attracted numerous people after King Orthalla's discovery. During this period, there were no established laws regarding the use of runes. Since these days, the sister kingdoms established laws for authorities and regulations to be placed that runes have to be reported and recorded, and many are deemed unsuitable for civilian use. Looking up at the rune, Odimus takes it off the stand, "I'm leaving the decision in the hands of the party." Remembering his situation, Odimus scans his surroundings from the deep well for an exit strategy. He sees a tiny box with the words "In case of emergency." He opens the box to find it full of some kind of jelly. It smells wonderful but is very sticky and stretchy. He thinks to himself, this might be Elastic Fruit jelly, for it is known to stretch and preserve the life of all foods. Then, inside, he sees a Void fruit, "Ah, teleport in or out, got it." He thinks back on how long it has been since he has eaten a Gravity fruit since he had to have the Wind Fruit active here to breathe. He realizes it may be close to time for it to have run out. He raises his hands and tries to lift a nearby rock, but it remains immovable. He is now aware of his ability to eat the Void Fruit. Odimus gazes upwards, contemplating his non-void bloodline and the limitations of teleportation for those like him, knowing he can only teleport a few yards at a time and not for long, for it will exhaust the fruits' ability. However, Void Bloodline is able to teleport a mile at a time and for the course of seventy-two hours, so basically, as much as they want. Leaning against the wall, he notices brick ledges sticking out. After eating the fruit, he starts teleporting from ledge to ledge. When one of the ledges breaks, he grabs on. The fall would undoubtedly be fatal for him since the beast is not directly beneath him to break the fall. From his vantage point, he notices a human hand protruding from beneath the creature's arm. He thinks to himself, knowing deep in his heart, "Please don't be him." He teleports back down and raises the beast's arm to retrieve the body, which turns out to be Othare. He has a terrible wound to the back of his head that no one could have survived. With Othare in his arms, he begins to wail. Odimus stays at the bottom of the well, holding his dear friend and crying into Othare's chest.

"We should go down there."

"But wait, Ithilwen, we need to make sure we have everything and confirm it is safe. It's possible that the Terelaviathon is still alive down there."

"Then we must act quickly. Otherwise, it will result in their demise."

"Fuin, is it possible for you to teleport down there?"
"No, the bottom is out of my sight."

"Ithilwen, could you fly down there by shapeshifting into a manticore?"

"I can try," Ithilwen shapeshifts, takes off into the air and descends. As she reaches the bottom, she hears Odimus sniffling. In his arms, she observes him rocking Othare. She lets out a whimper, and changes back from the Manticore as she does not have the strength to stay in her form. Instead of the usual graceful shapeshifting, it appears to fall and peel off her flesh. On her knees, she crawls towards her fiancé, and gently touches his cheek with a trembling hand. She pulls Othare into her lap, and both Odimus and Ithilwen grieve for him.

A sweet voice calls out to Odimus, saying, "We need to leave." Adoria suddenly appears and flies down to assist Ithilwen. She gazes upwards and finds the beast lifeless, then shifts her attention to the vault but does not inquire about the vault. "Odimus," she repeats herself, "We need to leave." Casting a glance at Ithilwen, she chokes back feelings, making an effort to stay composed for their sake. With a gentle touch, she takes Othare from Ithilwen's arms and requests assistance in moving him. They fly out with Ithilwen, she is struggling to fly not from a broken wing, but a broken heart. Odimus rises to his feet and initiates teleportation to ascend the ledges. All of them reach the top simultaneously.

Orthalla hurriedly exclaims, "Oh no," before rushing over. Upon summoning the Heart Stone, he starts producing fire that has a rainbow-like appearance from his hands. None of his attempts yield any results.

Mezlikied softly places his hands on top of Orthalla's hands, "You cannot minister healing to the dead."

Orthalla pulls back and makes a second attempt. With tenderness, Trenidus pulls Orthalla close, allowing him to sob. They all mourn as they hover over his body. Mezlikied requests that Fuin teleport them back to the place they landed so they can find a passenger ship to fly back together. Mezlikied and Fuin arrive shortly after and gather all things and people before flying off into the atmosphere.

All are silent when Odimus says to Mezlikied, now standing at the stern next to him, "We need to change course to Ludaea. He needs to be taken to his Mother and Father immediately."
Mezlikied looks into his eyes briefly and notices his young stagiaire, tears welling and assures him without hesitation. Mezlikied looks to Adoria "I will swing by Rehnburan, fly to the Volantuiva, and catch quickly as they are faster than this current vessel."

Adoria readies herself to leave the ship and takes off in the direction of Rehnburan. It doesn't take long for Volantuiva and her to arrive at the Bremium ship. They all transfer to the Volantuiva, and Mezlikied wills the Bremium ship to the closest location on a nearby Mother Moon to touch down. They see the Bremium ship fly off like it has an invisible captain at the helm, and disappear. It takes several days, but they eventually see Ludaea's Atmosphere on the horizon. Odimus always dreamed of visiting the stunning Kingdom and gardens of Ludaea with Othare. However, as he gazes at the Mother Moon, he starts to fear the task of delivering the King and Queen their deceased son.

Chapter 10

WOUNDS HEAL AND HEARTS MEND

In the ceremony, Odimus is sitting in the front row. The Fire Tribe in Ludaea honors their dead through the sacred practice of cremation. On a large hill, there is a place where the deceased is taken, featuring a massive circular pavement and a cremation chamber at its center. You can find seating for thousands of people. It has been a very long time since a funeral of this magnitude has taken place, yet the ceremony remains the same. In the eyes of the Fire Tribe, all individuals die as equals. Othare is lying on a floating bed made of Bremium, which is meant to float into the chamber and then float out. A symbol of starting fresh or beginning anew. The bed makes its way into the chamber. Thirteen men and women in robes now proceed to the chamber, which has six holes on one side, six holes on another side, and one hole at the head. At the head of the chamber, the man is dressed in a robe bearing the Fire Tribe's national colors, with the national emblem displayed on the right side over the chest. Every tribe possesses a national color and a national emblem. The emblem is a circle symbolizing the moon, with a tree shape inside of the distinct Tree of Power belonging to the Mother Moon of the Kingdom of Luxtenebri. Every Tree of Power has its own distinct shape, unlike any other. All except Ichassarae have their tree symbol inside the national emblem, because it is forbidden among the Ichassarae tribe to show the tree, so their emblem is the shape of their distinct fruit. All the Power Fruit shapes are also very different and distinct.

Now, the other twelve individuals are all in robes and colors of each of the different tribes. The chamber is made up of men and women who are all from the Fire Tribe. Wearing each individual tribe's robes is a way for the Fire Kingdom to demonstrate their service to all Luxtenebri tribes. Fire doesn't only die for the Fire Tribe but for all tribes. At the foot of the chamber, there is a man wearing a white robe, which is the national color of Luxtenebri. On his chest, there is a circle with two trees inside, The **Tree of Light** and the **Tree of Energy**. The Twin Kingdoms trees are side by side, symbolizing their equality.

Both men and women now reveal a Fire Fruit from their robes. Everyone begins by taking a bite simultaneously. They cover the chamber hole with their left hand and place their right hand on the shoulder of the person beside them. The last in the line have their right arm on the shoulder of the Luxtenebri representative, who has their arms folded in reverence. They all say together, "In life and in death, let the power of Fire Burn within you." From their hands, they activate fire that emits such intense heat that it can be felt from twenty feet away. Non-fire bloodline individuals have to raise their hands or move away a bit because of the heat. No member of the Fire Tribe moves or shows any signs of being affected. The extreme heat causes the body to incinerate within a minute, preventing any odor. With their hands, the men and women stop the fire, then turn and leave respectfully. The man in Luxtenebri robes will open the chamber doors, and the Bremium bed hovers out, slowly lifting and resting on top of the chamber.

Kyros is now standing before the team, who are all seated. With the exception of Ithilwen, who sits in the chair adjacent to the King and Queen, reserved for a spouse or, in this scenario, a fiancé. Everyone else took their seats elsewhere. "I kindly request that all of you stay at my home on Luxtenebri during the time of mourning." The duration of mourning was seven weeks or forty-nine days, and typically, this was reserved for relatives. Othares mother and father invited The Guard of Light to take part in the time of mourning, as they were often referred to as family in his messages. "After the funeral, please gather your belongings and come stay at my home for the next seven weeks. While you observe the time of mourning, King Kyron has put the mission on hold."

In a reverent manner, they all bow at the hip and join the crowds. After the funeral, the team gathers their things and leaves for The Kingdom of Energy.

Now, during the next few weeks, Ithilwen is rarely visible as she follows the tradition of seeking solitude, meditating, and finding solace in her loss. After fifteen days, she reintegrates into society and begins to grow with loved ones. Despite what some may think, Luxtenebri and her Mother Moon civilization prioritize progression and healing, even during times of mourning. This civilization does not experience issues with depression and mental illness.

This is due to the Aura Tree possessing healing properties for both the body and mind. Therefore, those in solitude drink tea leaves of the Aura Tree, which have slightly different properties than the fruit. They have more healing properties for the mind. The leaves are not boiled in water from natural springs but rather in water from the water fruit. The tea isn't boiled in a kettle; instead, drops of juice from a Fire Fruit are used. This helps warm the body and supports the muscles, bones, and marrow within the bones. Then, a drop of juice from the Energy Fruit to give them strength and energy, a drop of juice from the Aura Fruit to bring healing and rejuvenation properties for the hormones in the body to regulate, and a drop of Void Fruit juice to help the feeling of a void within their hearts to be filled. Last is a drop of Gravity Fruit, and this is for a different purpose. It is to intensify the weight upon them so that they can fully grasp the weight of the things they are going through. This helps them feel the burden but have the ability to lift up their head even when they are feeling weighed down. They utilize this tonic as a meditative practice to heal their body, heart, and mind. The ritual is challenging, but it results in complete healing and enables them to progress. Still holding the memory but no longer burdened and able to forever move past the loss. Although it's a fast process, everyone knows they can progress afterward.

Everyone is sitting and having dinner in the dining hall when Ithilwen walks in. All of them had experienced and completed a condensed and easier Mourning ritual. Their laughter fills the room as they reminisce about Othare and the memories they made with him. During this time, they continue to consume the tonic of mourning and loss to foster a collective healing experience as more of a group therapy setting. Adoria bumps Orthalla's shoulder, and he welcomes Ithilwen motioning her to join them. Kyros stands and escorts her inside. She is comfortable and happy to join. Walking towards the table, she wears a smile. Odimus remains seated, not bothering to turn around and acknowledge her. This is not out of disrespect. Instead, Odimus just can't bring himself to look at the woman he has come to love yet. Confused, she sits beside her father as her mother and sister initiate a conversation with her. Despite her many attempts at looking at him, he avoids eye contact and carries on talking to the party.

Leaning in, Mezlikied whispers, "She is finished with the ritual of mourning, for your information." It's entirely acceptable to have a conversation with her at this moment if you understand my implication." He nudges his shoulder.

Odimus gazes at him with a bewildered expression and murmurs, "I can't do it right now. Be patient."

Surprised by his reaction, Mezlikied leans in and asked if he performed the mourning ritual.

Odimus shakes his head.

"Odimus, this goes against proper customs and etiquette and is disrespectful in Othares' name. Rather than sorrow, he would want you to find joy in his life after a period of mourning. You did this same thing with your mother, and I thought you were past this."

Odimus confesses to Mezlikied that he shares the same thoughts for Othare but can't explain his reluctance to perform the ritual, "It just feels wrong."

"Well Odimus, it isn't. You are just looking to berate and inflict punishment on yourself for your loss. It's right to find healing and joy in our loved ones rather than succumbing to darkness and despair. This path leads to the Tree of Shadow."

Odimus stands up and prepares to leave due to his comments about the Tree of Shadow. "I will commence my ritual and undertake ten days of solitude."

"Odimus, I think that is a good idea. I'll make sure the others are informed."

Ithilwen notices him departing and starts to rise, intending to speak with Mezlikied about Odimus because she wants to talk to him. Having completed the ten days of mourning, Odimus now walks out into the castle ground gardens. Feeling healed and joyful about his dear friend Othare, he can finally breathe with the acceptance of his death. He explores the gardens and admires various plants from all the Mother Moons. Even large fountains have plants from the Water Moon under the water. Seeing such a garden in the military Kingdom of Energy, he can't help but be amazed.

Suddenly, a Surulac, the dominant creature from the moon of Zequiberus, comes skipping around, plants bloom and spawn from under its feet everywhere it steps. Odimus then sees the Drilgom hopping around with the Surulac, playing and wrestling one another. Catching a whiff of the air, the Drilgom spots Odimus, runs toward him and settles down next to him. The Surulac acts as if it knows Odimus well, following the Drilgom and sitting beside him. As Odimus pets it, he realizes that the creature's fur has a texture similar to that of a plant, giving the impression that it is part plant and part mammal.

This creature has Odimus completely intrigued, and just as he is pondering it, Ithilwen arrives, "There you are, I see you are finished with the ritual."

Looking up, Odimus notices two leaves of light on either side of Ithilwen's feet instead of the usual one leaf of shadow and one leaf of light. The dance they are performing is the same as the one they did many years ago when Odimus first met Ithilwen at the gates of the *Tree of Light* castle. Slowly, he observes this alluring array of potential manifestations dancing around her until they align with her eyes, revealing her breathtaking beauty. When he thinks of how beautiful she is, he immediately breaks free from the trance. Ithilwen observes him gazing at her with the same intensity as when they first met, and this time, she feels a slight sense of shyness and flattery instead of embarrassment. "How are you, Odimus?" She gives him no time to answer, and proceeds to talk all about the past twenty-five days and all that she has felt and experienced through the ritual. Odimus silently accompanies her for hours, attentively listening as they stroll through the garden. Mivanya, Ithilwen's elder sister, arrives in the garden and inform them that supper is ready. Together, they make their way to the dining hall, sitting side by side and conversing for hours on end. The others simply let them interact without interference.

For the next ten days, it is all the same. Ithilwen will discuss the academy and everything she's learned, her desires, wishes, interests, and what she cares about most. Odimus remains silent, letting her speak, and only speaks when she prompts him with questions. Odimus likes hearing her talk, him being one who likes to listen more than talk. The mourning period has now reached its forty-fifth day. Odimus and Ithilwen have been inseparable, spending every waking hour together walking, talking, and studying. When it began raining one night, they hurried to an outdoor hall near the castle entrance for cover. Ithilwen looks intensely into Odimus' eyes while they share a laugh. The air thickens around Odimus as he recognizes the intensity in Ithilwen's eyes. He leans in to kiss her. Ithilwen has been anticipating this moment for days and now is filled with joy in this moment. Just as their lips are about to make contact, he looks down, turns around, and walks away. Ithilwen accepts this with sadness, just as she he had done did years ago. Odimus steps into the castle halls, only to leave Ithilwen standing alone outside, and the door closes behind him.

Ithilwen stands there a moment and says, "Not again, not this time." As she enters the castle, she confronts Odimus and demands him to cease. "I'm curious why, on our first date years ago, you almost kissed me just like tonight but never pursued it or asked me out again. That's why I pursued Othare. Yes, I was interested in both of you for a time, but after your rejection and my pursuing Othare, I did come to love him dearly, although my feelings for you never ceased. Can you explain why you chose to not be with me now?"

Odimus reveals, "Othare sought my approval to be with you and for me to step aside. He expressed the opinion that a Prince and Princess should be together. He also informed me that the union of Ludaea and the Kingdom of Energy would be beneficial for everyone in Luxtenebri and the Mother Moons. While he respected me, he believed I wouldn't be as useful to the entire population. Besides that, Ithilwen, he wasn't just my best friend, but more of a brother, which is why I stepped aside."

Ithilwen now states, "Despite both of us completing the Mourning ritual and being completely acceptable for us to now be together," she steps closer, "why are you stepping aside now?"

Odimus now completely redirects his position to face her. "I lost two people I loved the most, and they were killed while with me. In the Ocean of Arthiatus, I came close to losing you. Despite the fact that you were never mine to lose, I still couldn't believe the fear I had of losing you. Ithilwen, if we both belong to each other, losing you would be unbearable."

Ithilwen takes hold of his shirt, brings him in, and gives him a kiss. As their lips remain sealed, Odimus finds solace in her embrace, holding her tightly.

Amidst their embracing, they hear a familiar voice, "Finally! The tension was becoming unbearable." Their guest's arrival interrupts them, causing them to look up and discover Trenidus there, casually eating from a bowl. Turning at a leisurely pace, staring at them to make them feel uncomfortable, he proceeds to climb the stairs. They share a quiet laugh as Odimus pulls Ithilwen into his arms, planting a gentle kiss on her forehead and holding her for a moment.

She whispers a confession to him, "In the Ocean of Arthiatus, I realized after our lips touched, I was not afraid to die but realized I was afraid that we would have to live, never to be together."

He grabs her hands and proceeds to follow Trenidus up the stairs. Hand in hand, he then confesses to her, "I was afraid of the same thing. Although I would've lived forever in silence, rather than betray Othare."

"Myself as well, I loved him too."

They have reached the seven-week mark, which is forty-nine days of mourning. Everyone is summoned to the great hall by Kyros. As they enter, Odimus and Ithilwen are holding hands and are surprised to see King Kyron sitting on King Kyros's throne. When Kyron stands, everyone bows down in reverence.

Kyron rejects them and reminds them that they are in Kyros's kingdom, not his. "My brother doesn't follow those traditions. I respect his customs in his kingdom, just as he respects mine."

Everyone stands, and he starts speaking. Initially, he directs his attention towards Odimus and Ithilwen, remarking, "I am pleased to see things are in order."

Ithilwen knows what he is referring to as she blushes. Odimus leans in and asks, "Is there something you want to tell me?"

"I will, later."

"The time of mourning is at an end, and I fear our time is running out. According to my spies, my cousin is amassing his forces and preparing for an imminent attack. Per our laws, we cannot initiate the first strike, so we must wait for him to make the first move. I have been informed that it is more fearful than we initially believed, and we have come to understand that he has legions at his disposal. Almost equal in number to the Kingdom of Energy's forces."

Shock and uneasiness are evident among them all. He continues, "Day and night, I've been preparing my forces and withholding this news to give you the time to heal from your loss. I am hesitant to make a request and would not ask this unless it was absolutely crucial. Each of you has obtained a rune for your Bremium armor. Orthalla, you do not have one for your armor, but you do for your axe. With a few sparks, Orthalla makes his axe glow to showcase his rune. None of the rest of this party has a rune for their weapon, and it has taken several months to obtain the runes you now possess. Continuing on this path won't lead to success but to utter failure, so I recommend going to the Pit of Anglishes to acquire a rune for each of you collectively in one mission."

Fear and desire to not follow through with such instructions overpower them as they look at each other. "Your majesties, may I have a moment to speak? Mezlikied steps forward.

Kyron reluctantly grants permission despite Kyros's initial objection. He directs his gaze toward his brother and reminds him, "Mezlikied has a justifiable reason to be fearful of going to the pit." Kyros now exhibits remembrance and understanding towards Mezlikied.

"Your Majesties, the most dangerous place on Luxtenebri and the Mother Moons is the Pit of Anglishes. Asking this could potentially lead to another lost life."

"It is understandable to be afraid, but if we don't take action, millions of lives could be lost if my cousin attack us without our elite team, The Guard of Light, fully prepared. Abilities and power can be acquired through relics and Trees of Power. However, they are nowhere near the relics and runes this team holds. Apart from The Guard of Light, there are only a few relics, runes, and warriors with similar capabilities. This mission will not only give some of you two runes but also grant the team more abilities and powers than many combined legions. The team's preparation in this manner is crucial for our victory. Each of you was brought together and chosen by the *Tree of Light*. We have chosen the right individuals to put our trust and faith in. Othares death has left this team heartbroken, lost, and afraid of losing one another. Nonetheless, you were aware of your duty before this assignment and the potential dangers of this mission. Odimus, I believe this is the right course of action. What are your thoughts?"

Odimus takes a step forward and acknowledges King Kyron but stresses the importance of having a plan. "Both you and Kyros, as well as Mezlikied, have been to the Pit of Anglishes. I request your assistance on our journey. Kyros, the King and great warrior of the Energy Kingdom, is skilled and able to ward off early offensives. Your majesty, your reputation as a skilled warrior is well-known, and again, you have ventured into the pit yourself. We are currently missing one member of our team. What say ye?"

Without delay, King Kyros addresses Odimus, demanding he remember his place. Kyron raises his hand towards Kyros, causing a look of surprise on his brothers face as if he has never witnessed a dismissal before. Without breaking eye contact with Odimus, he speaks to Kyros, "Don't answer for me, brother. I do not say this as your King but as your elder. Hold your tongue." With eyes brimming with curiosity and a yearning for adventure, he instructs nearby military guards to notify the Queen and request his Bremium armor and travel bag as he embarks on an adventure. The team is surprised and begins to feel a surge of excitement. Odimus, having observed multiple potential manifestations around the king, shows no surprise at his response. Without breaking eye contact with Odimus, King Kyron approaches, "I have wanted to get off my royal behind ever since I adventured with your father. Thank you, my friend, for recognizing where my heart truly resides." Odimus places his hands out toward the King, and they grab forearms. The King informs the Guard of Light that Odimus is their leader, not him, and expresses willingness to follow.

Chapter 11

THE PIT OF ANGLISHES

The Guard of Light rises earlier than the waking hour. There is a loud disturbance in the hall, causing this. Everyone heads to the hallway. Fuin observes that the voices are not in the hallway itself but emanating from around the corner. It sounds like people are in the midst of a fight. All members of the team draw their relics and secure their Coins of Armor as a precaution. Upon turning the corner, they observe Kyron and Kyros engaging in a dueling match, with one portraying the villain, the other as the hero. Engaging as children in destructive behavior such as knocking over decoration plates, paintings, and throwing each other into bookshelves. Everyone stores their relics and eagerly observes the comical showdown between hero and villain. Odimus gazes upwards and sees Ithilwen leaning on the balcony, laughing at her father and uncle behaving in such a manner. Mivanya and the Queen are in the room, leaning against the wall and giggling together. Odimus smiles as the scene is fun and joyful. Looking at Adoria laughing, his heart fills with warmth. Watching her, he recalls a time when they were young, before they lost their mother, they were not so different from Ithilwen's family. It brings him happiness to see her family enjoying themselves. Unexpectedly, Kyron takes down Kyros, who is portraying the antagonist. His intention was to fall onto the nearby couch, but he miscalculates and hits the ground instead. Kyros remains in character, and everyone can't help but laugh. Kyron raises his sword, signaling his triumph. Kyros sweeps his brothers legs, sending him crashing to the ground. Laughing, they both jump up and bow. Everyone claps in appreciation and enjoyment, then departs to ready themselves for the journey ahead. Odimus looks up at Ithilwen again, she is wearing her night garments. She looks stunning in her cute nightwear. Looking down at him, she simply smiles. Odimus senses this might be the last time for a while that things feel so normal and that he and Ithilwen can feel young and full of passion. Odimus wishes for life to stay the same, allowing him and Ithilwen to enjoy life together. She has returned to her room, prompting Odimus to prepare for what lies ahead.

The whole military force is assembled outside the Castle for the departure of The Guard of Light once again. With the presence of the reigning King, this ceremony is much more formal compared to the last, and there is a larger crowd of civilians. King Kyron delivers a brief speech about the upcoming journey, being cautious of spies. He summons his Anohail, It can not only amplify ones voice but can also connect to everyone else's Anohail in the crowd, ensuring that everyone can hear the speaker's announcement, regardless of their distance from the speaker.

"On this day, I, a grateful King, stand before you, ready to embark on a crucial mission alongside our Guard of Light. I have an opportunity to demonstrate that as your King, I serve both as ruler and servant to this kingdom. I have handpicked this small group to become the force we require in order to confront the increasingly powerful Shadow, which seeks to dismantle the Light. We, as the Kingdom of Light and the Kingdom of Energy, refuse to let darkness overshadow us, our lands, our people, or our Mother Moons. We will be victorious and prevail over the ever-growing darkness. Our goal is to spread light and shine brighter, using our inner energy to prevent darkness from overtaking us. Light cancels darkness, and so that is what we shall do."

The king's words elicit cheers from the crowd. Turning around, he puts on a show of being embarrassed. Odimus acknowledges his dissimilarity to his brother. Kyros is significantly more serious, while Kyron is more carefree. Kyron approaches, taking hold of Odimus and Ithilwen's hands, and tosses them into the air, prompting the crowd to cheer once again.

Kyros asserts, "He is destined for politics, and it is evident that I am meant for the military."

Kyron ensures his elbow connects with Kyros's sternum as he brings his arms down. He needs to move behind Orthalla, who is slightly in front of him on the opposite side of Odimus, to conceal his reaction from the crowd, then says, "Good hit."

Afterward, Kyron takes a step forward to mount his Volantuiva. He approaches with professionalism and grace, mounting the great creature and performing stunts that only a Volantuiva can do. Then, with a sword in hand, he charges forward as if going into battle. He takes off, gracefully stands up and turns around on the creature's saddle, bowing charmingly before flipping back around and landing flawlessly as he continues to ascend.

Trenidus comments on his dramatic showmanship, "I like him."

Kyros notices Odimus expressing some doubt. "He is dedicated to playing for his people, so don't worry. Through his actions, he shows he is fully capable, making them feel at ease and confident in their King. The people are scared, we have few secrets here in my kingdom. He recognizes the significance of providing moments of fun and joy, and he excels at captivating both the masses and the politicians. He is a valuable asset to you and your team, being both a good king and a formidable warrior. On the battlefield, he will show a different personality. Don't regret inviting him along, as I am confident that this mission will succeed with him by your side. I guarantee that he will be of great service to you." Odimus and the rest of the group take off towards the Pit of Anglishes.

The Pit of Anglishes is near the north pole of Luxtenebri. The Kingdom of Light is on the West Pole since the planet orbits in a rolling spin motion as it orbits the great sun Klibous. Therefore, the city of Light always faces Klibous. The Tree of Shadow also always faces outwards but never sees the sun, which hints at the Shadowlands. You can find the Pit of Anglishes just a little beyond the North Pole, towards the East Pole of the Planet. Luxtenebri's size makes the distance between its West and North Pole approximately two hundred thousand miles. The Volantuiva's exceptional speed enables a five-day journey from Luxtenebri to the nearest Mother Moon. Roughly three days are needed to travel from the West to the North Pole. Bremium helmets must be worn when flying the Volantuiva as the creatures gain speed. While in the air, the Volantuiva can repel wind and create an invisible protective barrier, shielding you from the wind currents. Odimus observes Ithilwen sleep on her Volantuiva and reflects on her less-than-appealing sleeping appearance. He realizes he can get over it because she is so beautiful. As he completes his thought, she tumbles off her Volantuiva, causing him to panic and search frantically for her, shouting her name as he searches, looking down towards the planet. Suddenly, she swoops up, almost causing him to lose balance on his ride. Landing on her Creature, she chuckles in her Manticore form.

Everyone else is laughing now, and Kyron jokes, "She takes after her uncle more than her father."

Odimus rolls his eyes and sarcastically, "Great!"

As the Guard of Light approaches, they notice a massive fissure in the earth, the largest they've ever encountered. The entire team assumes a serious demeanor, putting an end to all jokes and silliness. Mezlikied flies alongside Odimus and warns, "This will be our most perilous endeavor yet. Are you certain this is your desired course of action?" Odimus remembers King Kyros' words, gazes at Kyron, then shifts his gaze back to Mezlikied and nods in agreement. "Okay, then we will proceed."

They descend and make their way towards a few remaining buildings at the top of the pit, which had not been pulled down along with the rest of the city, most are severely damaged and barely standing. Nevertheless, the most distant building remained intact and spacious enough for everyone to camp overnight. The concept of sunsets does not exist on Luxtenebri; instead, the planet has different light intensities across its locations. The pit of Anglishes is located on the planet with moderate lighting, as it sits just beyond the horizon, causing a quarter of the sun to be lost. So, to sleep during the sleeping hours, they provide tent equipment that can block out the sun entirely. Odimus lies awake in his tent for a considerable amount of time during the time of rest. He is unable to find sleep. A shuffling noise comes from outside his tent, causing him to brace himself for an intruder. To his surprise, it's Ithilwen.

She is unfazed by him having his sword and tells him, "It's just me, there's no need for that."

She, jumps on him, knocking the breath out of him. Laughing, she cozies up, making this the first time they're resting closely and the first time they fall asleep together. In the beginning, he's uncertain about what to do. He feels uneasy and self-conscious, causing him to lie on his back. With a kick of her heel to his foot, she orders him to hold her. He complies, feeling a profound sense of comfort and newfound revelation. "I love you."

She softly responds, "Mhm, go to sleep."

Odimus becomes embarrassed, lowers his head, and attempts to fall asleep. Holding her in his arms makes him feel sleepy, and he eventually succumbs.

"Odimus, wake up! We need to hurry." Kyron has opened the tent door and is urging him wake. Upon seeing Ithilwen, he shows no concern and casually responds with, "You too, we have to hurry."
The tents and belongings have been packed, and everyone is standing near the large crack in the earth. It looks never ending, as the bottom remains unseen. Many homes were partially submerged in the pit, stopping at various ledges along the way down. There were countless buildings everywhere, yet this was only the outskirts, not even the heart of the Kingdom.

Odimus inquires King Kyron, who stands on a ledge peering into the pit, "Why have you awakened us?" Kyron slightly turns towards him and points downward. Curious, Odimus leans over to get a better look. Kyron playfully grabs him and pretends to push him in. Despite being startled, Odimus is both slightly amused and embarrassed.

"I woke you because it's the time when the creatures down there rest. These creatures sleep deeply and are unaffected by moderate noise. It's too dangerous to go down there with them roaming around. If we were to awaken one, this still would not be too dreadful because they don't pack together unless they are drawn to the power of the rune's relics, but if they discover a mutual enemy, they unite and fight against us. Runes and relics provide them with power, granting extended life and strength without the need for nourishment. Outside of that, they are mindless creatures. Don't you think it'll be better to fight only due to our mistakes of waking one or two rather than hundreds or thousands just because they hear or see us?"

Odimus acknowledges this approach and wonders about their destination. He describes how the runes they made would be kept in vaults scattered across the city. Vaults seven and thirteen are the ones we're after. "Fuin, will you bring forth the Bremium plates?" Fuin handed him the book, and Kyron whispers to it, and it unbound itself and levitates one plate of Bremium into the air. The plate rolls like a scroll and lands in the King's hand's hand. He softly utters something else, resulting in the book lighting up and being sucked into a ball of light, vanishing instantly.

Respectfully, Fuin inquires, "Where did the plates go, King Kyron?"

"The Kaleidoscope Council usually selects a holder of a Scroll of Knowledge from the plates, so I have sent it back to Anniphus." Subsequently, he reaches out his hand, and another scroll of Bremium materializes. "I was chosen a long time ago to be a holder. Now, the scroll has all the capabilities of the book. As we have reached the destination, the book has chosen you rather than the council. Following careful consideration, we decided the Plates should return to the possession of Anniphus. So, I am bestowing upon you, to be a keeper of a scroll of the Bremium plates of Knowledge and Wisdom. May it serve you well. Now, we're looking for a rune for Odimus's sword of valiance and his Bremium armor, Adoria's relic weapon, Ithilwen's sword of power, and Orthalla's armor. In vault seven, there is a unique rune for each of you."

In a school-like manner, Adoria raises her hand and waits to be chosen.

"Adoria, we are not back at the Academy of Achaicus. You can interject."

"On Terthiath, Odimus stumbled upon a rune inside a vault; I know this because I went through his bag."

Since Othare's passing and while courting Ithilwen, Odimus had completely forgotten about the rune. After giving Adoria a mischievous smirk, he opens his bag and confirms, "Yes, I did." He reveals the contents of the journal he read and discloses the identity of the rune's owner to them.

Quickly, Kyron walks up and snatches the rune from his hands, examining it with great curiosity. "This time observance rune is truly unique. There are very few like it." He marches over and, without warning, fuses it into Odimus's Coin of Armor on his chest. Turns and says, "Take care of your armor,

"It is time to go." The King's assertive behavior confuses Odimus, but everyone else remains unaffected.

Mezlikied walks over and quietly says, "It would've been yours anyway."

With her relic in hand, Adoria directs it towards a few houses on a cliff in the pit and sends the chain flying across the pit to create a zip line. Each person goes down one at a time, except for Adoria and Ithilwen, who can fly. It takes hours for them to reach the bottom. As they descend into the pit, they repeat the process level by level. With everyone now standing at the bottom, they survey the darkness. Kyron moves towards a pole and touches it with his hand. Then suddenly, every building, balcony, and window bank that remains intact starts to light up. Pointing behind him, he says, "Bremium lanterns. While we're down here, they should light the way the entire time, even though they will eventually go out. The creatures can see in both light and darkness, so light doesn't wake them." The ruins of the ancient Kingdom of Anglishes are of an indescribable size, Odimus notices. Only Kyron and Mezlikied have witnessed something so grand.

Kyron faces the Kingdom and claims, "There never was before and never has been a place like it, but unfortunately, its King was a power-hungry fool." They head towards a massive building in the distance, where Kyron instructs, "Take out your Anohails and make them glow. These lights will be necessary in areas where the outer lights won't be useful." Subsequently, he begins behaving like a tour guide, pointing at different objects and sharing his knowledge about them. He also summoned his scroll and read facts about various things as they journey.

Odimus walks up to Mezlikied and states his concern with Kyron, "He seems untroubled by the possibility of waking the creatures, based on his calm demeanor and talkative nature."
Mezlikied proceeds to inform Odimus, "We descended into this area, the farthest from the vaults, because they're not here in this section of the city. The vaults are where most creatures will be found, and a location marker will notify us when we need to be alert."

"Why is there a marker down here, how did it get here?"

"The marker was placed shortly after the city first sank, and many tried to obtain the runes from the vaults, as well as many armies during the relic and rune wars. It was placed to show areas that were always safe and others that never were. Despite their efforts, they were unable to succeed in large groups; and learned that smaller groups were more advantageous. Despite this, the creatures remain highly dangerous, and few can withstand their power."

"What was your experience like the last time you came down here?" Odimus asks."

Pausing, Mezlikied looks at him and reveals, "We lost a cherished and beloved friend in this place."

With a face filled with sorrow, Kyron stops and faces Mezlikied. Ithilwen inquires about the person who was lost.

Continuing to walk forward, Mezlikied answers, "My sister." Odimus has never heard him mention a sister, and no one chooses to ask any further questions.

As they reach the marker, Kyron instructs everyone to prepare their armor and relics. The team deploys their armor and arms themselves. "Orthalla, make sure your Heart Stone is summoned and I'll do the same." Odimus finds it intriguing how Orthalla and Mezlikied have their Anohail floating above their right shoulders and the Heart Stones orbiting them like a moon

Trenidus seems to share the same sentiment, "Show Offs!"

Kyron summons his Anohail, and it forms a 3D map of the Kingdom of Anglishes in his hands. He unveils the location of vault seven and points to a building on the map. "Vault thirteen is right over here. Fuin, please pull out your scroll and provide us with information about the Runes of Intent, Agility, Influence, and Strength."

"The Rune of Intent, when combined with a relic weapon, enables the holder to release the relic, which will then defend them regardless of control or anticipation of an attack. It shares abilities with the Sword of Light and Shield of Light. When using the Agility Rune, the user becomes incredibly fast during attacks, making it nearly impossible for defenders to anticipate the strikes. With the Rune of Influence, a weapon can duplicate and fire at incredible speeds. This attack can be recharged and used repeatedly. When the Rune of Strength combined with armor, the user gains the strength of one hundred men."

Kyron turns to Odimus and grants him leadership by inquiring, "What are your thoughts?"

"Adoria's whip should have the Rune of Intent, Ithilwen's Sword of Power needs the Rune of Agility, Orthalla's armor should have the Rune of Strength. The Rune of Influence on Trenidus's knife is ideal. It will enable him, as a duplication master, to create weapon copies without them breaking."

"Now, all these are in vault seven, Odimus, your rune. I carefully searched for and studied, and it was the Rune of Energy. It gives the user energy like the energy fruit but multiplies, with no need to partake of Energy Fruit, then granting heightened focus and endurance in battle. The Sword of Valiance provides nearly all the abilities necessary for battlefield domination, except against my cousin and his First General. The Absorption Tree is the sister kingdom of the Shadowlands. If you let the First General get too close, he can absorb any power, and only relics and runes can save you from its draining effects. When he depletes your energy, it becomes his and increases his abilities. Both of these runes will help you resist being drained and will help you recover quickly if you're hit or harmed by him." Odimus agrees, and they set off to explore the city's depths. King Kyron gives a final warning before embarking on their journey: "We have to stick together, no splitting up. Separation would mean certain death."

The Guard of Light continues deeper into the pit and encounters their first creature within an hour. Leaning closer, Kyron discloses the existence of three creature varieties in this place. "Big, medium, and small - that's all there is to know."

They move away from the sleeping creature and continue walking for hours. Encountering one after the other and these creatures are terrifying. They have yet to come close enough to one to really see a lot of details and they haven't seen a big creature, either. They reach a corner and spot the building that houses Vault Seven. With caution and silence, they approach and enter. Surprisingly, the building appears to be remarkably intact, with doors still in place. They open the doors and enter; it is quite dark. The light emitted by their Anohail provides sufficient illumination for the group in close proximity. Kyron suggests embarking on a search to find traces of Bremium lanterns and activate them. After searching in vain, the lights suddenly come on, and Trenidus appears across the room, holding a Bremium wall lantern. He has willed them to light up the entire building. It appears devoid of any creature, so they make their way to the vault, which is both massive and made of solid Bremium. The doors this time have a unique design, very different from previous ones. The method to open this vault door is the same as all other Bremium doors though. Kyron stands in front of the door, and using his willpower, opens it. Upon opening, the vault reveals numerous runes adorning the walls, with Bremium bricks stored inside. Kyron glances at the Bremium Bricks, not the runes, and expresses disappointment at its wastefulness.

"What's the deal with all these runes?" Trenidus asks.

Kyron warns, "Excessive gathering will lead to our demise in this place, so do not concern yourselves with the other runes. It's important to collect and possess only two each, as gathering more will draw the creatures towards us. Fuin, open your scroll and search for the specific rune symbols that match the ones we're seeking."

Within minutes, each is discovered, and as they go to leave, they encounter a small snarling creature from the pit at the door. The creature had been nearby and could feel the influence of the vault once it was opened. It springs into the vault and latches onto the hilt of Kyron's sword. Odimus is quickly instructed to close them all into the vault, or it will attract more. King Kyron forces the creature to retreat slightly by shooting a blast of ice from his hands. The door seals shut, and the only light that can be seen is coming from an individual Anohail. The vault is very large, so it is quite dark, and the creatures happen to be covered in black fur, which makes them appear as a shadow on all fours. Despite being the smaller species among the creatures of the pit, yet still quite large compared to humans.

The creature attacks Ithilwen, but Fuin's shield protects her, keeping it just inches away. Ithilwen watches in terror as the creature desperately tries to reach her. Adoria takes advantage of this opportunity to wrap her whip around its waist, shooting one end to latch itself to the ceiling, lifting it off the ground and swinging it through the air. While swinging, Orthalla keeps his Axe with the blade facing the creature, but rather than swinging it, he releases a blast that merely cuts the creature on the shoulder. It shows no signs of being bothered. Using its teeth, it grabs the chains of the whip, yanking it down from the ceiling, and proceeds to attack them relentlessly without difficulty. Odimus takes advantage of the situation and employs gravity to keep the creature airborne. He shouts at Mezlikied to hold it there, then unsheathes his sword and drives it with all his strength, into the creature's belly until the blade's tip breaks through the top of its spine. The creature still having its strength, continues fighting. Ithilwen unsheathes her sword, and decapitates the creature.

Of no surprise to any of the party, Trenidus is the first to speak "Oh, just one small one, eh? I need a nap."

Kyron picks himself up after being knocked down during the altercation, "This is the very reason for our urgency while these creatures slumber and why we must remain united, acquiring only the necessary runes."

The group is injured, and Orthalla is healing each member individually. Odimus directs his gaze toward Kyron and questions, "The bloodline of Ichassarae, huh? I remember you telling me you had never seen someone from the Ichassarae tribe in battle."

Kyron chuckles "Yes, it is useful in battle. Now, after we gather ourselves, let us open the vault doors. In the absence of a creature, we should promptly seal the vault and distance ourselves from it. As it seems the energy within has the power to awaken the creatures from their sleep." Kyron opens the door, and to their relief, no more creatures.

They exit and close the vault door quickly. Vacating the premises quickly, they make their way to another nearby building for refuge. There is no other creature to be found inside. "Let's examine the map to determine our next destination. It shows that we need to reach vault thirteen, which is several miles away. We must hurry in order to surpass the creatures' sleeping schedule, which is around is around fifteen hours a day, we've only been here for half that time."

Ithilwen, displeased and frustrated with being hit so many times, transforms into a Cipactli for added strength and tail for attacking. Despite being a Cipactli, Odimus is surprised at how good she still looks.

"Did you just check her out in her Cipactli form? Dude, gross."

Odimus scoffs, "Oh? And what exactly were you thinking while staring at her in this form on Manekaizah, Trenidus"

Adoria walks by and silently chuckles at the two, shaking her head. At the same time Ithilwen passes and encourages Odimus, "I like it when you check me out. Keep it up" caressing his chin with her tail, she continues on.

The building that houses Vault thirteen is now only a few feet away, but it is extremely unstable and damaged. Nevertheless, there is an open entrance leading to the vault door from outside. The problem is that there's a lot of rubble in the way, and opening it will make too much noise, and will absolutely result in waking up some of the nearby creatures. Gravity could be used, but repeatedly harnessing fruit abilities would make this task extremely challenging. Moving the rubble would take too long, and some pieces would be too heavy. They realize the noise is inevitable. They gather closely and unanimously agree to open the vault, defend themselves until they can enter, and quickly close the door. Then, wait inside until probable creatures lose interest, and attempt to escape. Kyron walks toward and wills the door open, only to be startled by a louder sound than anticipated, awakening multiple creatures. Kyron had earlier instructed them not to fuse the runes until they had all left the pit because fusing a rune sends out a large amount of the rune's energy. The individuals with their new runes are unable to utilize their new abilities, and this makes the team just as unable as they had been in their last confrontation. Finally, the door is open, but there are three medium-sized creatures and one small one, creeping towards them.

With a look of terror, Kyron tells Mezlikied, "Victory is impossible."

Odimus decides the last rune is not worth risking their lives for and orders Fuin to teleport them back to safety on the other side of the marker. There are no arguments. Grabbing Orthalla, he quickly disappears. Odimus instructs Adoria to fly straight out of the pit without looking back. The creatures move in a side-to-side motion as if stalking their prey. The creatures are patient to strike until the perfect opportunity arises. The team have time to give instructions to flee, but quickly sense an imminent attack. Ithilwen transforms into a manticore, grabs Trenidus but while attempting to grab Kyron, a creature attempts to attack. Kyron orders her to leave and she does so swiftly. Odimus and Mezlikied utilize gravity to create distance between them and the two creatures that have begun to charge. The small one approaches Kyron, prompting him to conjure a massive wave of ice forming a protective wall. He then begins spreading the wall in front of Mezlikied and Odimus as they use gravity to push the creatures away one by one, allowing Kyron to build a barrier between them. Now, in a bowl of ice, Fuin has returned and assures that Orthalla is safely beyond the marker. He grabs the King and disappears.

Mezlikied moves close to Odimus, "I guess it is just you and me."

Nearby, a creature has climbed over a wall and found its way into the ice bowl. This creature is of medium size and stands out as it is able to lift itself on its hind legs and attack with its front paws. Mezlikied is attacked by the creature, and Odimus's rune activates for the first time. The attack appears slow, allowing him to adjust his sword and execute an uppercut that cleanly severs the creature's arm. Mezlikied uses his Gravity abilities to send the creature into the ice wall, causing it to withdraw. The creature displays minimal hinderance from the loss of its limb, remaining strong. It lets out a terrifying roar and swiftly attacks Mezlikied with great speed. Odimus's rune can grant him time observance, but its effectiveness is inconsistent due to the imperfect nature of runes and their reliance on the activation of Bremium through willpower. Without enough focus and strength in one's will, the rune won't be effective.

The creature's power and speed captivate Odimus, causing him lose concentration. He is overpowered by fear, causing his Time Observance Rune to functioning incorrectly, he is battling the creature solely with gravity and his sword. Mezlikied displays his great skill and strength as they stand firmly against the creature. Never before had they encountered a battle as intense as this. However, they have gained extensive experience and improved their ability to fight together with flawless coordination and communication. Odimus is attacked by the creature, but Mezlikied swiftly counterattacks, delivering a powerful uppercut to the creature's jaw, causing it to crack, rendering it unable to close its mouth. The creature is stunned by this, and it begins whimpering. It retreats, but Mezlikied uses gravity to seize and draw it towards him. It appears that his gauntlets are charging with energy, forming a ball, and upon reaching the creature's proximity, he delivers a powerful punch to its side, shattering every bone his gauntlet lands on. It looks as if its folded in half before suddenly snapping back open and falling to the ground. Its heart instantly stopped, immediate death.

Odimus glances at him wide eyed and breathless, "I have never seen that before."

Mezlikied claims, "The Gauntlets of Truth and the Charging Rune make for a highly difficult combination. By being honest and upright, the user of the Gauntlets can always achieve perfect aim with the Charging Rune. Taking the time to gain full power is useful… if you have time to charge it up. Hitting your target with enough force, nothing can survive. However, it is very challenging to execute, and I've only managed a few perfect hits. I am impressed with myself."

A huge creature bursts through the ice. Mezlikied turns to Odimus, "Run, my boy, run for your life!" Mezlikied, suddenly in Fuin's grasp, utters a futile plea to save Odimus first, before disappearing.

In search of safety, Odimus turns to the vault door and rushes inside. Two medium-sized, one large, and one small creature are rushing towards the vault door as Odimus commands it to close. Ithilwen appears suddenly and swiftly flies into the vault, her tail fending off a medium-sized creature trying to enter. Nevertheless, a single small and single medium-sized creature successfully infiltrate the vault. As the large one relentlessly beats at the door, the whole vault trembles.

Ithilwen confronts the small creature, while Odimus takes on the medium-sized one. In her defense, she swings her sword at each attack from the creature yet fails to land a damaging blow. Odimus and the medium-sized creature are in a similar standoff. He shouts at her to duck as the small one jumps toward her neck. His swing connects, and the sword slices through the side of its face, splitting it from mouth to neck. Without hesitation, they stand side by side, ready to confront the other creature. This one surpasses the strength, size, and speed of the one Mezlikied and Odimus had encountered. The creature strikes him, propelling him several feet back and causing him to collide with the vault wall, hitting his head forcefully. He experiences a sudden and mysterious sensation in his forearm. Despite the impact, he tries his best to stand quickly but struggles. He exerts all of his strength to come to Ithilwen's rescue, witnessing the creature strike her down and preparing to deliver a fatal blow with its paw. With a battle cry, his forearm illuminates and his hand instinctively raises, unleashing a burst of light that sends the creature flying. He attacks, driving his elbow and shoulder into the creature, smashing it against the wall, and another burst of light flashes from the impact. With both hands, he seizes the creature's mouth, and a bright white light beams from his hands, allowing him to tear the creature's mouth and head apart. He collapses, completely depleted of energy and strength.

Rushing over, Ithilwen lifts his sword from the ground to help him heal and places it in his hand, "How were you able to accomplish that!?"

"I have no idea. I could just feel the ability to do so." Odimus gradually recovers and reveals to Ithilwen, "I sensed a power within my arm, not through a relic or armor."

She beckons her Anohail to come closer to see what's happening. The light approaches, revealing a rune symbol on his forearm. "How is this possible?" she starts to rub the symbol as if trying to get it off of his forearm.

Odimus replies, "I have no clue. I have never seen a rune on someone's body, but I feel its power within me, and I believe it has somehow altered me."

Ithilwen assists him in standing and suggests they search for the Energy Rune to enhance his armor and escape. While searching, Odimus is able to recall the symbol that King Kyron showed him. Within minutes, they discover the rune, and Odimus wastes no time combining it with his sword. The sword fills him with a surge of power as he approaches the vault door, he questions Ithilwen's preparedness.

From her bag, Ithilwen retrieves the Rune of Agility, fuses it with her sword, and proclaims, "I am now."

Standing behind Odimus, she grabs hold of him into her manticore form and then tells Odimus to open the vault. The door starts to swing open, and creatures are scratching at the vault's crack as it opens. She takes flight, carrying Odimus with her, there is just enough room for a single creature to pass through. Odimus's feet narrowly escape the creatures. Now heading straight to the big one, he draws his sword, swings it and hits the creature's paw, deflecting it from hitting them. They climb higher and higher up the pit, then fly out in search for the group.

From a distance, they observe their party standing at the edge of the cliffs where they had all entered. They all gather and start recounting the events they just experienced. Before revealing the rune on his forearm, the King interrupts and walks towards Odimus, grabbing his arm and summoning his scroll to read. After a few minutes, he mentions, "This rune was believed to have been lost long before the city was destroyed, and there is no record of it being stored in a vault. Odimus, the rune you have is called the Rune of Light, and you have no idea how significant this is. The holder can shoot blasts of light from their hands and summon a damaging wave of energy upon hitting an enemy. Odimus, you now possess immortality as this is the only rune that fuses to the body and grants eternal life."

Odimus gazes sadly at Ithilwen, who now shares his concern as she is not immortal. They choose not to let this affect them now and decide to address it later.

"In addition to holding one of the most powerful runes ever created, were you also successful in acquiring the Rune of Energy?"

Odimus confirms and displays the hilt of his sword with the embedded symbol.

Kyron exclaims, "How fortunate it is that you now possess the power of energy and light!"

An Anohail suddenly appears and begins delivering a message to Kyron.

"Odimus's vision and Mezlikied's message of the King of Shadow's intentions and treacheries many years ago have been confirmed, he has, in fact, begun his attack on cities outside of the Shadowlands. There are rumors that he has legions of newly mutated tribes, but no confirmation has been found on a battlefield." The recording playing is out loud for all to hear and reveals that "the Shadow King is unstoppable, as none of the Fire Tribes' forces have managed to impede his progress. He is proving to be equipped with a very powerful and well-trained military force. The Kingdom needs you to return so that you can summon all the tribes and call upon them to join forces against the Shadow Kingdom; Odimus's vision is becoming reality, and we are in serious circumstances."

Kyron packs his things and informs the team of the next mission he requires. "Demonstrating your strength on the battlefield with the Shadow King would be unwise. Instead, I request that you travel to the sister kingdom of Shadow, the Absorption Kingdom, and defeat the First General of the King of Shadow before he calls to his aid at the Valley of Yurthalla, located outside the Kingdom of Light. Assuredly, my cousin will have kept the First General behind in preparation before making an attack on the Kingdom of Light. Preventing the First General and his forces from aiding the Shadow King would give us significant advantage over my cousin. Since he has officially made his move against my people, we must tactfully move against his forces. I know that taking out his sister kingdom is the greatest advantage we can have over him and his forces." Odimus acknowledges, and Kyron, leaning down from his Volantuiva, declares, "This could be a more formidable challenge than the pit. In order to defeat the military force of the First General, everyone needs to join forces.

You are to first go to the **Inn Between Tavern**. Mezlikied, wait there for a legion of forces to arrive and assist you in the attack. I recommend that you allow Mezlikied to take charge of this, Odimus. You have never been in the military or seen battle of this magnitude. I acknowledge that you have achieved victory in numerous fights. I have never witnessed anyone conquer creatures with such power, strength, and skill as you. But now I ask for your service as one of my soldiers and Captains, and I call upon you to accept this command and rank. Mezlikied, I am reinstating your last rank of General and assigning you back to the service of the Kingdom of Light."

Odimus gazes at Mezlikied with a hint of offense for him not having shared this information prior. "Your majesty, I am and will forever remain at your service," Mezlikied assures.

"All of you remaining, I am giving the ranks of Lieutenant," they simultaneously accept, "Yes, your majesty." He turns, takes off, and directs himself toward the Kingdom of light.

"Oh, a general, are you?"

"Odimus, don't start."

"You never mentioned that you were a general."

"Odimus, that's not typically something one boasts about."

Odimus reluctantly acknowledges this; his attention changes, and frustration grows as he remembers the rune that bestowed immortality upon him. He approaches Ithilwen and attempts to speak, but she quickly dismisses it, "We will discuss it later." Mounting her Volantuiva, she lifts off and heads towards the Shadowlands.

Trenidus, currently riding slowly nearby, remarks, "That woman is as cold as ice. Tough break, my friend."

Odimus looks at him, eyebrows furrowed "Come on, dude.."

With a chuckle, Trenidus lifts off and follows Ithilwen into the air.

"Fuin, would you mind examining the scroll to see if there's any mention of how to remove the rune?"

"I have already consulted with the scroll, it proclaims that it will remain fused, until your existence is no more."

Mezlikied attempts to console Odimus, "You will sort things out with Ithilwen, and I advise you not to be concerned for now. Don't let anything distract you from what's most important at this moment. For what is about to happen is going to require all of your attention and focus."

On their Volantuivas, they ride, and all of their armor and relics are now fused with powerful runes. Each person now has two runes, except Odimus, who has a third one attached to his body. They have all the necessary tools and materials needed for the upcoming battles and struggles. For these upcoming battles will be unparalleled to any that have been known in all of Luxtenebri and the Mother Moons.

Chapter 12

THE BATTLE WITHIN THE SHADOW LANDS

The Guard of Light has now arrived at the **Inn Between Tavern**. The size of this Tavern dominates the small town surrounding it. It has existed since the reign of the Shadow King began. However, its purpose was never to expand or become anything beyond a center for peaceful trade between the Shadowlands and the Lands Of Light. Despite the Shadow King's conquest, this tavern remains just that, a simple, peaceful trade center, even under his command. Peace treaties or truces had only been necessary once between the Shadow Kingdom, the Kingdom of Light, the Kingdom of Energy and the Mother Moons. No one knew until now, just how essential it was to have laid out many laws, treaties and truces with the Shadow Kingdom that could have prevented the Shadow King from being able to gain so much power. However, he had been left to rule freely and without consequence. The Guard enters the Inn Between Tavern, waiting for word from King Kyron's legion. Inside, they observe a multitude of members from various tribes participating in trade with tribes from the Shadowlands. Tribes from the Shadowlands rarely venture out, but find solace at the Inn Between Tavern. Inside, it seems like everyone is observing the truce. The Guard of Light takes a seat at a table while Odimus notices an unusually active potential manifestation in the corner of his eye as if it were attempting to grab his attention and he becomes very curious of this. He looks directly at the manifestation, and sees it is not a leaf but the shape of the **Tree of Lights'** fruit. He knows the **Tree of Light** itself is responsible for this creation, not just a regular potential manifestation. He follows it, which guides him to an unoccupied table. As he sits down, he overhears a conversation between a few men who seem to belong to the sister kingdom's first general army of the Shadow Kingdom. The discussion revolves around shipments, specifically the abundance of Trees of Power coming in from various lands. Many kingdoms have left their lands vulnerable, allowing them to uproot their Trees of Power and replant them in the Shadowlands for mutation. Odimus rises slowly and makes his way to the table where the others are seated. Quietly, he relays what he has experienced and overheard.

Mezlikied whispers, "This is how the Tree of Shadows roots can reach the **Tree of Light**. As other trees mutate and are planted, their underground roots spread, allowing the influence of the Tree of Shadows to work through them."

Odimus declares, "Yes, that's exactly what I'm thinking."

Mezlikied then finishes, "I don't think the King of Shadow has any knowledge of this. Like the Shadow Tree, he acts purely on instinct to conquer and rule. As he becomes more powerful and gains followers, more bloodline trees are brought to the Shadowlands, fueling the spreading power of the Tree of Shadow."

The Guard of Light has determined it is prudent to inform Kyros and instruct all Kingdoms, Governments, and Mother Moons to protect their tree orchards and prevent anyone from disturbing their Mother Moon trees. They aim to halt the growth of underground roots while they fight the influence of the Shadowlands above. Mezlikied brings forth his Anohail and sends word to Kyron, Kyros, and the Kaleidoscope Council.

An Anohail approaches the table and transforms into a plate for Mezlikied to read. He tries to will it to play aloud, but it refuses. Realizing it's a secret message, he grabs the plate and starts reading. Once finished, he stands, "Pay the bill and follow me." They depart from the **Inn Between Tavern**, he points out that the first commander of the seventh legion is just a few miles beyond that large hill, waiting for them. The Guard makes their way to the Volantuiva and departs to meet the seventh legion of the Kingdom of Light. Upon landing, they are is greeted by five soldiers led by the commander of the seventh legion.

She walks up and introduces herself, "My name is Thidora, and I am the First Commander. I assume you're General Mezlikied. Everyone, follow us to my tent, we will bring you up to speed."

The hierarchy goes from a Commander to a General, then Colonel, Major, Captain, and finally Lieutenant. Despite never serving in the armed forces, Odimus was given the rank of Captain due to his formal training and association with the Kingdom of Energy elite training and Ministad Reisling. The others were acceptable as well because they were stagiaires of the Academy of Achaicus. As a result, all members of the military respected their newly bestowed ranks despite their lack of armed forces experience. Their mission brought them numerous accomplishments and encounters with extraordinary creatures and beasts that surpassed the wildest dreams of most military leaders. The first commander herself respected them. The highest rank in the Shadowland military forces was General, followed by Captains and Foot Soldiers.

"Odimus, I've heard of your encounters with the Liviathidus and the Creatures of the Pit."

Trenidus leans over Orthalla and mentions, "Do not forget the Terelaviathon!"

In much disbelief, Thidora looks up from the map on the table in the center of the room and asks, "A Terelaviathon!?"

Mezlikied proceeds to answer, aware that she may doubt his claims about the mythical creature. "Yes, madam, we surely saw and stood against one; there is no fighting a Terelaviathon, but we stood against it until it met its doom."

"Odimus, your reputation as a man of legend precedes you. Your adventures are famous, but the reasons for their necessity remain unclear."

She hands Mezlikied a letter on parchment, and he opens it to read. It was a message from King Kyron. He gazes upwards and declares that discussing our journey is permissible, but only within the confines of this tent. "Thidora, we have been pursuing runes."

She walks towards Mezlikied, standing closely beside him as she poses a question in a serious tone. "Did I hear you correctly? Did you say runes?" She orders the other four commanders, "Exit my tent immediately and keep silent of these matters. Get everyone prepared for tomorrow morning; our journey to the Shadowlands begins." As they exit, she says, "Tell me more."

"Runes are very rare. Bremium armor does not hold abilities as relics do; Bremium armor is powerful and strong, but its only ability is to turn from a coin to full armor. Apart from that, it needs a rune to give it abilities. It is possible to bestow abilities and powers upon relics through forging, although it is a challenging process. Very few relics possess abilities, and even fewer occur to have a powerful ability or have more than one. Runes are necessary to increase or give specific abilities that a relic could never be forged to perform. In a military force, soldiers at different stations possess various relics such as swords, bows, arrows, axes, shields, and more. The usual function of almost all relics is to merge the user's bloodline fruit into it when they use the relic.

Each military force, like the Kingdom of Energy and the Kingdom of Light, has its own unique design for the Bremium armor. In accordance to their respective stations, the relics are all identical. So, the idea of having a rune is somewhat taboo and incomprehensible. The Relic and Rune Wars were horrendous due to the power-hungry individuals seeking various abilities, resulting in an apocalyptic event in which the people of Luxtenebri and the Mother Moon barely managed to survive. The concept of them amassing runes was both fantastic and alarming." Mezlikied proceeds to inform her about each of the runes they have and Odimus reveals the one on his forearm. Upon observation, she notices it resembles a tattoo but is in fact, a rune symbol. She challenges him to demonstrate it. Handing her his sword and Coin of Armor, he shows that the ability will not originate from them. Raising his hand, he attempts to create a small beam of light directed towards a nearby chair.

Trenidus chimes in, "Having performance issues? Because I have heard it is common for men under stress to experience this."

Odimus looks at him and tells him to be quiet. He focuses and sends a blast from his hand at the chair and destroys it. The commander is astonished and seizes his arm to examine the rune symbol. "The idea of a rune fusing with the human body is unfamiliar to me."

Mezlikied speaks, "The only existing records of this rune can be found in the Ministad Reisling, despite its previous belief to be lost."

"Well, with The Guard of Light now possessing runes, it seems we are well-equipped for the battle ahead."

The next morning, Odimus and Mezlikied awaken The Guard of Light. Thousands of soldiers are assembling and appear enthusiastic about a certain matter. Thidora, the First Commander of the Seventh Legion, is joined by another First Commander from a different legion. Mezlikied and Odimus stand before them waiting to be given permission to approach.

They are called over by the other commander, who then introduces himself. "I am Thale, the First Commander of the Second Legion of the Kingdom of Energy. I have been sent here to assist you and the Seventh Legion of the Kingdom of Light. King Kyros believed it was wiser to be present here rather than confronting the Shadow King at this time."

"I am Mezlikied, General of the Kingdom of Light assigned to the Seventh Legion and Commander of the Guard of Light. This is Odimus of Erayiphim, now Captain of the Kingdom of Light and Second Commander of the Guard of Light."

"King Kyros has spoken highly of you both and the Guard of Light. It is an honor. Thidora has informed me that, you all have been collecting runes. This is very good news. Now excuse me, I am going to start preparing for my march on the Kingdom of Absorption,

Thidora declares, "We should start moving. The Kingdom of Light's Seventh Legion will launch a direct assault from the west and, coming from the south will be the Second Legion of Energy. The two fronts will force the First General to deploy all his forces to defend the city. The plan is for the Guard of Light to covertly enter from the east, sneak behind the city walls, and raise the gates for the two legions to conquer the Kingdom of Absorption. There has never been an attack on a Kingdom or city within the Shadowlands borders. Consequently, the terrain holds unknown possibilities. Proceed cautiously during the march."

No one from the two legions or the Guard of Light has ventured into the Shadowlands, and as they consider it, fear and concern consume them. The land and soil here are never touched by the light of Klibous, but the sky is always illuminated by an Aurora Borealis from Klibous' energy. The Aurora Borealis emits a faint glow in shades of blue, orange, and green. Despite the darkness, the stars and Borealis illuminate the lands in a beautiful yet unsettling glow, allowing clear vision once your eyes adapt.

The legions observe the plant life, which consists mainly of dark red, black, and dark blue shades, yet they find it quite beautiful. There are no other colors to be found, and it seems that their bioluminescence emlts at a very low intensity. However, the ground can be observed due to this glow. Although there are no known creatures here, there is a large presence of insects. Reports of insects that are twice the size of the average human although they are neither aggressive nor dangerous. Neither Luxtenebri nor the Mother Moons have any poisonous insects.

As the soldiers march, their main concern now becomes focused on the terrain. Yet, they soon realize it's not as dangerous as they initially believed. They are amazed by the beauty of the Shadowlands and the low light all around, which is completely new to them. They reach the rumored location of the City of Absorption after hours of searching. Thidora brings the march to a halt and instructs everyone to assume their positions and ready themselves for an attack. One of the laws in the Kingdom of Light forbids initiating an attack on an enemy. Lands were swiftly being attacked and conquered by the Shadow King without any resistance, so this attack was now justified. The purpose of this strategy was to dismantle the Shadows Kings second military force, ensuring he had no more support or power. Hence, the objective of the attack was to capture the city quickly and without any forewarning. Thidora commanded that if surrender was offered, it should be respected, and prisoners should be taken. It wasn't an attack to conquer or destroy but to prevent this military force from being able to join forces with the Shadow King. Thidora and Thale have assumed their positions and have commanded the Guard of Light. They directed them to move behind the city walls on the east and wait for the attack. Once the First General sent out his forces, they were to infiltrate the city and open the gates, granting the two legions entry. They are to attack from behind until the opposition surrenders.

Mezlikied guides Odimus and the rest to the wall's east side. Mezlikied tells Adoria to use her relic and shoot her whip at the top of the wall so they could all ascend. He orders her to fly high and keep watch for the attack but remain unseen until it's time to inform them. Once Adoria takes flight, Odimus approaches Ithilwen to finally have a moment to talk. She wastes no time in telling him she doesn't want to talk upon his approach. Odimus refuses her decision, they need to talk about him becoming immortal.

She speaks loudly enough for the entire group to hear, being cautious not to alert any guards on the city walls or the other side. "Odimus now is not the time." She transforms into a Manticore and flies to Adoria to help her and be out of his reach.

Orthalla walks over and, for the first time asks, "Is there anything I can do for you?"

"It's alright, but I want you to know I'm fine with you and Adoria." He responds with a wink.

Orthalla uncrosses his arms in surprise and attempts to feign ignorance, stumbling over his words as he tries to explain himself.

Odimus reiterates, "Orthalla, I have no problem with you and Adoria. You make her feel safe and have consistently defended her throughout our journeys, hardships, and conflicts."

Orthalla inquires, "How did you know?"

He laughs, "The morning after my fever, I noticed that when you woke up she got up roughly from where she would have been lying right next to you. I've noticed you two have been inseparable since, and I think she has made a good decision. I support this."

Orthalla nudges him with his elbow and softly expresses gratitude. Trenidus takes a small step forward and affirms. "She indeed did."

Orthalla glances downward and remarks, "I prefer you pestering me."

"Considering all that has and is about to happen, I think it's best for me to maintain seriousness. Plus, I've grown to like you, big guy."

Orthalla shares the sentiment of feeling honored to be his friend as well.

Fuin, who is typically quiet, declares, "I couldn't have asked for better friends and thank you all for an incredible adventure."

Adoria and Ithilwen appear, declaring that it's time. Mezlikied, who had been gazing at the wall from afar, now seems preoccupied and distressed. Odimus approaches him and informs him that it was time, but he appears to be oblivious to his words. Odimus, filled with concern, looks at Mezlikied and asks, "Are you ok?" Mezlikied gives no answer, and Odimus senses something is off.

Mezlikied now turns and says, "Yes, everything is ok. Let's hurry. Now Adoria and Ithilwen, fly up and scout the wall for any soldiers."

They do as instructed and fly up, very shortly returning, saying it is clear. All of them climb onto the wall and head towards the gates to open them.

Mezlikied suggests, "Something is happening in the city. The First General is no fool, and the city is completely emptied. Unless this is what he desired, he wouldn't deploy all his forces. I am concerned that we are being lured into a trap. What's everyone's opinion? Should we press on, or retreat?"

Orthalla urges everyone to continue, and they all go around the corner towards the gates.

Standing on the castle steps is the First General of the Absorption Kingdom. Mezlikied freezes, and they both stand motionless, staring at one another. The Guard of Light brace for an attack, but Mezlikied instructs them not to fight and instead open the gates. Odimus attempts to stand with him, but he instructs him to assist the others. Even while giving instructions, he and the First General never break eye contact. They all turn and proceed to open the gates. While opening the gates to commence their assault, Odimus witnesses Mezlikied fearlessly approaching the First General. He instructs the team to assist the Seventh and Second Legion from the rear. He tells Adoria to fly out as soon as the gates open and find both Thidora and Thale. She is to inform them that the gates are open and they should claim the city. She accepts, and readies herself to comply with the command.

Ithilwen, for the first time in a few days, asks Odimus, "What is going on, and why are you not going to join us?"

He turns to her, "I think Mezlikied is going to need my help. Please exercise caution and offer assistance to the others—I love you."

Without uttering a word, she turns and readies herself for Orthalla to raise the gates. Odimus rushes to help Mezlikied, who is now casually ascending the stairs, as the First General turns and leisurely enters the castle. Inside, he spots Mezlikied a few feet away and the First General further inside, still walking away.

Mezlikied is now shouting, "Grandfather, please stop." Odimus is in disbelief and halts his advance to hear more. "Please, grandfather, put an end to this madness."

The first general greets his grandson, "You have a striking resemblance to your father, my grandson." He is now completely reversed and confesses, "I dispatched spies to prepare for this assault. We could have surprised the entire military force outside the Shadowlands. When my spies found you among them, I made them swear to secrecy and emptied my entire city, expecting you to come and find me. Have you come to seek justice on me, my boy, for what I did to him?"

"I've come to plead with you, Grandfather, to abandon your allegiance to the King of Shadow and return home. Grandmother misses you and forgives you for killing Father. Your involvement in his death is clear because of the Absorption Fruit's influence and the Shadow King's manipulation."

"Mezlikied, you're mistaken. I killed your father when he tried to bring me home, just like you are doing now. Your father drew his weapon to slay me when he discovered I was a traitor to the King of Light. Are you here to slay me, my boy?"

"No, grandfather I am not here to slay you. I'm sorry Father was quick to anger and attacked you, but I am not quick to anger and will not attack you. I urge you to halt this madness, for obliterating the **Tree of Light** won't grant the Shadow King dominion over Luxtenebri but instead, lead to the destruction of the planet and the loss of all life. Refuse to tolerate this pursuit of the King; I understand you chose power, and that's your decision. I don't believe you'll sacrifice Luxtenebri while remaining loyal to the King of Shadow. Deviate from this course of action and use reason to persuade your King, as he values your advice, of which I am certain."

"Mezlikied, do you truly think me a fool? You come here attempting to deceive me and discourage the King from his plans? I am disappointed, you are weak, just like your father. I had higher expectations for the renowned Mezlikied of Erayiphim. Quite frankly, before now, I was quite proud of you, my boy, but no longer after seeing this weak, groveling coward before me, begging me to fold instead of being brave, as the rumors have said. It seems that today I will lay two sons in the ground."

Unexpectedly, he grabbed his axe and swiftly advances towards Mezlikied. Just as Mezlikied summons the Heart Stone, the First General strikes it with full force, sending it flying across the room and crashing through walls before vanishing. Mezlikied attempts to use gravity, but the First General intercepts and absorbs the power. Odimus charges at him and forcefully knocks him back. With a loud voice, Mezlikied warns against using the powers of the fruit, as he can absorb the abilities of Power Trees to strengthen himself. Absorbing relic or rune abilities is not within his capabilities.

The First General hears this and says, "Ah, so there it is, runes, that was the mission King Kyron had for the Guard of Light." Without delay, he summons his Anohail and commands it, "Send word to the King that the mission of The Guard of Light involved runes."

Mezlikied then replies, "So your intention in clearing the city was not to see me but to uncover our mission, knowing I would come willingly."

"My dear grandson, cunning is greater than wisdom."

"No Grandfather, Cunning resides in the shadow, wisdom resides in the light, and in the end, the superiority of wisdom and light will be revealed."

Mezlikied and Odimus simultaneously attack the First General. They engage in an epic battle. No one is hit directly due to all attacks being blocked by each other's relics. It appears that Mezlikied and Odimus are equal in skills and talents to the First Generals. Two against one indicates that the First general is greater than one alone. Odimus has only witnessed one other person possess the kind of power with which he attacks, it seems like he knows their every move.

Outside the city walls, a vicious battle has commenced. Orthalla dedicates most of his time to healing the wounded on the battlefield. Occasionally, he activates his Rune of Strength to hurl adversaries away from the injured they are assaulting on the ground or trampling upon. Despite having the Heart Stone, active fruit, and medical supplies, Orthalla struggles to make a difference in saving wounded soldiers. Several dozen Aura healing medics on the field spot him with the Heart Stone and cheer together, realizing a Guardian of Terthiath has been called. This rally's the Aura medics, who have now lifted spirits and begin to save more soldiers than before.

Throughout the battle, Fuin stands with Orthalla, safeguarding him as he tends to the wounded. The Reflection Rune has surpassed his expectations by relieving him of all self-concern. Enemy after enemy strikes him, and they quickly become wounded, causing them to flee after hurting themselves repeatedly. He is able to focus on the protection of Orthalla and everyone nearby by blocking and defending against any threats due to his immense protection. Trenidus has replicated himself four times and is now standing together on the battlefield instead of spreading out. If a duplicate is killed, he remains unharmed and only needs to wait half an hour to duplicate again. Nevertheless, when his shield rune is activated, he and his duplicates are enveloped in a small blue shield. His knife rune enables him to shoot multiple duplicate knives at soldiers repeatedly. The Shadowland military forces are no match for him. Nonetheless, he is only taking down a few soldiers at a time while the enemy appears to be never-ending. He is unable to advance in battle, only holding his ground and continuously fighting them off. Adoria is flying around, rotating through the team and helping them each overcome enemy by enemy, and she is using her whip to grab hold of enemies and throw them into the air by using her rune of intent. Employing her Wind Fruit ability, she utilizes it to push back soldiers, making them incapable of attacking her. Ithilwen is shapeshifting between Manticore and Cipactli according to the enemies she is facing. She uses vines, branches, and plant growth to attack enemies and impede their advances. The Absorption Kingdom is proving to be a formidable enemy, unlike any known before, with unparalleled fighting abilities. The Seventh Light and Second Energy legions are engaged in an unprecedented battle showcasing extraordinary skill and ability not witnessed in thousands of years. The battle appears to be at a standstill as countless soldiers from both sides are falling and being revived moments before death, then standing up and re-engaging in battle. Despite lacking Aura Trees, the Absorption Kingdom has an abundant supply of aura vials for healing. Their training is exceptional, making them more powerful and better prepared for this attack than anticipated. As the battle continues, fear creeps over many. Occasionally, individuals lose their lives due to severe wounds or sudden fatal blows. Soldier against soldier, power fruit against power fruit and relic against relic. This battle appears to be impossible to win. The runes are the only thing enabling the Guard of Light to gain the point, but against such a formidable foe, their advantage seems to benefit only themselves.

Orthalla calls out to Ithilwen, asking, "Where is Odimus!? We need him!"

"He is facing the First General, with Mezlikied. It appears that this is only going to be won by cutting the head off the snake, so it is up to them." The First General's attack is stopped by Odimus, just inches away from Mezlikied's head. He attempts gravity force, thinking it would be quick and the First General would not see it coming. However, once he activates the ability, the invisible force transforms into visible black smoke and gets absorbed into the First General's body. Inhaling deeply, he utters the words "Big mistake." Swiveling backward, he smashes his elbow into Odimus's ribs, propelling him several feet away. He is left completely useless after this powerful blow knocks the wind out of him. The First General approaches him quickly, causing Odimus to desperately try to recover before he reaches him. The First General raises his axe as if to strike his abdomen. Odimus, by this point, is unable to defend against the impending attack. Just as it's about to make contact, he hears the sound of metal clashing against metal. He turns to see Mezlikied, who is severely injured and exhausted, catching the axe with his gauntlets and gazing into his eyes as if bidding farewell. At that moment, the First General snatches the axe from his gauntlets and drives it into Mezlikied's back, with a piece of the blade visibly emerging from the front of his rib cage.

Mezlikied's parting words before he falls are, "Odimus, remember that wisdom and light are also acts of charity."

Out of nowhere, the Heart Stone reappears as if he had found it during the battle. The Heart Stone shoots at Odimus's hand, and he feels its power and knows he is the next guardian, his heart shatters. A mighty cry escapes him as he taps into the Heart Stone's gravity abilities, creating a massive wave in every direction that hurls the First General into a pillar and destroys the structure. The destruction of the pillar leads to the weakening and crumbling of the surrounding building. The first general is struggling to get up after hitting the pillar so hard. The building is now collapsing towards the ground. Odimus rushes towards the castle gates to escape. The First General is finally able to stand up and begins to flee as well. Odimus escapes the castle and sees the First General catching up. Just before leaping out of the castle doors, Odimus raises his hand and sends a burst of light to knock him down. The First General gazes upwards and witnesses the imminent collision of the building upon him, only to be crushed at the door's entryway, mere inches away from escaping to safety.

Ithilwen, off to the distance in the air, was flying in her manticore form when she suddenly hears a terrible tumultuous noise. She looks to where the sound was coming from and sees the castle crumbling. She fears that Odimus has been killed, and her heart sinks to the pit of her stomach. She releases a soundless "no" and speeds to his assistance. As she approaches, she witnesses Odimus jumping out of the building and knocking the First General back inside, crushing him. She touches down near him, transforming back into a human before falling to her knees and reaching out to grab him. While embracing him, she whispers a gentle, "I'm sorry."

Odimus gently pulls her forward and reassures her, "There is nothing to apologize for; we will find a solution."

Frantically, she sits up and demands, "Where is Mezlikied?"

Breaking eye contact with her, Odimus somberly discloses, "The First General, he killed him before the building collapsed."

Ithilwen gasps and exclaims, "Oh no!" She then adds, "Odimus, the battle is dreadful and far from over. We need to quickly seek to aid the Seventh of Light and Second of Energy legions."

Wiping his eyes, Odimus stands and declares, "Let's go."

As they rush to the city gates and prepare to fight, they witness the entire Absorption Kingdom forces kneeling. Odimus, having defeated the First General, exposed the weakness of having only one leader in their powerful and well-trained force. So, not knowing whether to strike or flee, they offered themselves up as prisoners. It took them about an hour to search the vast battlefield and locate every member of the Guard of Light, but they finally found each other.

Adoria, who considers Mezlikied to be an uncle, was the first to notice his absence and asks, "Where is Mezlikied?" Odimus pulls her into a hug, and she starts sobbing in his embrace. Orthalla, seeing Odimus struggling to keep himself together, walks over, pulls her to him, and allows her to weep in his arms. He, too, begins to gently weep for his lost friend. Trenidus, collapses to his knees, feeling the heavy burden of Mezlikied's loss. Fuin turns around to leave, adhering to his people's belief in mourning through meditation in solitude. Odimus calls to him and tells Fuin to come to find them at the Kingdom of Light after he finishes his mourning ritual. Fuin doesn't halt or slow down his walk but gently turns his head to nod. Odimus sees his eyes have become red as tears run down his face. Despite his stoic and calm facial expression, Fuin's crying indicates a profound heartbreak.

Thidora has located them and reports, "Thale has died in combat. He fought with courage, and without him, I would have fallen today."

Odimus tells her, "Mezlikied has fallen as well."

She feels the weight of these losses "There were very few men who were greater or kinder than Mezlikied." She then asks how he fell. Odimus shares the story but omits to mention that the Heart Stone had selected him. He will keep the Heart Stone in his heart until he determines the right time to announce his calling. The soldiers are instructed by Thidora to recover Mezlikied's remains. Worried, Odimus fears his body could be completely crushed with no chance of recovery.

Thidora introduces herself as a member of the Glodatri tribe, the Earth moon. "We believe that any remains are worth recovering and putting into the earth. For we are all born of the dust and dust, we shall all return. Though it may be tragic what we find, his remains deserve to be placed back into the ground to find peace in the earth."

Odimus respects her beliefs and acknowledges them. After several hours, a few soldiers came back to report that his body was intact despite the castle's collapse. Despite the massive amount of rubble, he was discovered with no harm or much damage to his body outside of the cause of his death. Odimus inquires about viewing his body, and it is subsequently transported into the tent on a Bremium gurney, just like the one at Othare's funeral. Medic gurneys could be willed by the medic themselves, eliminating the need for carrying.

He walks over to Mezlikied, rests his head on his chest, and says, "Goodbye, my friend." He feels a flicker in his chest and knows the Heart Stone is also saying goodbye. Odimus is slightly startled but grateful to sense the Heart Stone's emotions towards Mezlikied. The Mother Moons, Luxtenebri, and the *Tree of Light* are all sentient beings. Odimus, as the next Guardian of Erayiphim, understands that he is the Guardian of his Mother Moon, with the Heart Stone as its core.

Following the retrieval of the body, Odimus calls for Orthalla to join him in his tent, dismissing everyone except all members of the Guard of Light. Once they have followed the instructions given, Odimus summons the Heart Stone. "It appears that I am the next guardian of Erayiphim."

At first, they are taken back, but then Trenidus confidently states the obvious, "Well, of course you are. Who else would it be? I mean, are we really that surprised?"

"But what does that mean.?" Ithilwen somberly asks.

Odimus states, "Despite being chosen and despite your father's offer, I won't choose the *Kingdom of Light* or *Kingdom of Energy*. My place is among the people of Erayiphim across Luxtenebri and the Mother Moons. Also, since I am now immortal, it appears I am going to be a Guardian for a very long time."

Ithilwen is once again saddened but responds positively, "Erayiphim made an excellent choice for a guardian." Odimus attempts to pull her in for an embrace, but she resists and says, "I'm sorry, I need some time, for I am not ready."

The day after the battle, all the prisoners were transported to the war prison on Ludaea, the moon of the Fire Tribe. The Kingdom of Energy may be the most powerful military force. The largest prison and military force in terms of numbers belongs to the Fire Tribe. This gives them the ability to have numerous guards. It is also among merciful yet a strict and serious people; this means the prisoners are well treated and cared for, but they are under strict schedules and are required to go through education classes, activities, and programs of every kind to help them prepare for a peaceful release after any war comes to an end. After every prisoner has been accounted for and sent on passenger prison ships, Thidora tells her soldiers to report on Shadowland's dead burials. It is reported that all the forces of the Shadowlands that were slain have been properly buried.

"Good, they deserve peace and rest in the ground." She causes a ball of earth to float out of the ground and go into her hand. She then lets the dirt fall to the ground as she says, "From the dust we are born, and to the dust we shall all return." A few soldiers nearby belonging to the Glodatri earth tribe repeat this after she offers up this reverence to the shadowland dead. She inquires if all the bodies of a Seventh of Light and Second of Energy legions have been loaded onto passenger ships for transportation to their respective Mother Moon burial sites. The soldier assures the commander that they are all prepared to depart. Thidora now turns to Odimus and states, "Despite being a Guardian and descendant of Erayiphim, Mezlikied, a general of the *Kingdom of Light*, should be buried in the *Kingdom of Light's* burial grounds to show respect and his station.

Odimus hesitates briefly before saying, "I know he would have agreed with you."

The Guard of Light is now in the Kingdom of Light, getting ready for Mezlikied's burial ceremony. Though he is being buried in the Kingdom of Light, his wife has asked he be buried in the Erayiphim way of the Gravity ceremony. King Kyron has agreed and ordered everyone to prepare for the Gravity burial ceremony instead of the ceremony of Light.

Mezlikied's wife walks up to Odimus and says, "he would have wanted you to perform the gravity ways on his body and place him on the ground."

Odimus, without hesitation, agrees to perform this honorable performance. This performance is usually done only by a Master of Gravity since they must manipulate the body to do certain things, and they must keep the body perfectly held in place as they perform the ceremony. The law of gravity is 'what goes up must come down.' Therefore, the Gravity burial ceremony will be performed to represent this law.

Now, that Kingdom of Light and many from the republic of Erayiphim are found at the burial ground of the Kingdom of Light. Odimus alone walks to stand at the head of Mezlikied, floating on a Bremium bed as Othare did. Mezlikied is only in his undergarments instead of burial robes, for this is an important part of the ceremony. Right before Odimus begins, he can feel the Heart Stone wiggle around in his chest as if to say it yearned to be a part of the ceremony. Odimus summons the Heart Stone without hesitation, and it begins to orbit around him. While the crowd gasps, Odimus remains unphased, maintaining eye contact with Mezlikied as dictated by the ceremony's tradition of stoicism. No expression can be made, not even that of tears. Odimus struggles only a moment but finds his bearing and begins. He lifts Mezlikied's body from the bed, having Mezlikied's arms crossed at the chest, with his feet and knees together perfectly straight in the air. He is standing with his left hand on his chest at all times while the right hand is stretched out towards Mezlikied in the air to show he is using gravity to lift him into the air. Mezlikied reaches about seven feet above Odimus, and he halts him.

He now makes a little circle with his left hand still positioned on his chest and has his right-hand move outwards. The moment his hand begins to move, Mezlikied's arm moves open to bend at the elbow, looking to hold something while his left arm remains in its place. Odimus brings his right arm back and switches his right hand to his chest, and his left-hand stretches out to Mezlikied. He does a small circle with his right hand now and moves his left hand out. Mezlikied, now looking as if standing in the air about to hug someone. He then summons folded robes from off the bed below, and they dress him in burial robes beautifully and carefully, fully clothing him before the crowd. He then does the hand movements backwards, and Mezlikied now has his arms folded again across his chest. He then has Mezlikied in the air and lays back as if lying down. He lowers his body slowly, carefully, respectfully. As his body reaches the bed, it moves with him, almost as if Mezlikied's body never touched it, so smooth and gentle was the contact. Mezlikied's body is lowered into the coffin below, The Bremium bed slides out of a little slit in the coffin, and the slit closes. The coffin is slightly floating above the hole where he is going to be buried. Odimus, still using gravity, has the coffin door closed, latches it and begins to lower the coffin to the ground. One Earth tribe member, with one movement, has all the dirt slide in to cover the grave.

Odimus lifts the headstone that is resting at the feet of his wife with gravity and places it gently at the head of the grave. This represents the loved one is now put to rest from before the feet of the spouse or loved one. The funeral carries on as normal funerals do, and the Guard of Light now stay at the Kingdom of Light to perform the mourning ritual. However, Erayiphim does not have the same seven-week time of mourning as Ludaea. They believe in a single day of mourning ritual only. It has been five days since they were at the battle of the Absorption Kingdom, and they are greatly needed. Though reluctant to take part in the Erayiphim mourning ritual, they are instructed to go ahead and perform the ritual so that they are all prepared for the events to come.

On the last morning of the five days of mourning, Ithilwen is lying in her bed, crying because of the circumstances surrounding her and Odimus. Suddenly, she sees a potential manifestation, and she follows it to the roots of the ***Tree of Light***. The courtyard of the tree is off-limits to most, but the King's niece has special permission. At the base of the tree, she kneels and witnesses a momentary flicker as if fading away. She knows what this means because of Odimus's vision. He saw somewhere deep in the earth the tree was fighting for its life. Suddenly, a tree branch delicately lowers itself towards her. A few guards look with serious curiosity since they were the same guards present as it revealed the Heart Stone. No one has witnessed the tree's branches moving like a limb until this moment when one moved towards her. They are all amazed by what they are seeing. Kyron has been informed of her presence in the courtyard since it was the law he must be. He enters the courtyard to check if she was okay, as she had never done this before. He walks in just as the tree's branch reaches her face and gently brushes the tears from her cheek since she was, at that moment, still crying about Odimus being immortal and she was not. The tree, knowing how she felt, pulled back the same branch that gently brushed her tears from her cheek, grabbed a fruit from another branch, descended down and placed it in her hands. The branch wrapped around her waist and lifted her to her feet. After letting go, it gently taps the bottom of the fruit and pushes it to her lips. The branch returns to its original position and now remains idle.

King Kyron calls for a guard to retrieve her father. He walks up and suggests, "If you agree, I propose waiting for your father to arrive so he can witness your transition into a chosen immortal."

Without realizing he was there, she swiftly turns to him, tears still in her eyes, "That would be wonderful."

Kyron notices that while she was still crying, her tears had transformed from sadness to tears of joy. Kyros rushes around the corner almost irreverently and walks up to her quickly. He now gathers his bearings and asks to confirm that the tree truly had given her a fruit. Kyron confirms by placing his hands on his brothers shoulders. Ithilwen's mother now stands by Kyros, her husband, to witness their daughter's transformation into immortality. Immortality is incredibly rare, making this moment exceptionally wonderful to witness. Pure white light is visible in every vein of Ithilwen's body after she takes a bite. It slowly looks as though the light is absorbed and vanishes under her skin. Ithilwen can feel her body change to a different state, she embraces her parents tenderly.

Her father tells her, "I think there is an exceptional young man who would love to hear the news."

She directs her gaze towards her parents, gives them both a kiss on the cheek, and swiftly heads off to tell Odimus.

Ithilwen barges into Odimus's chambers. He is surprised because this behavior is highly inappropriate. Disregarding customs, she rushes toward him, holding him tightly and kissing him passionately. At first, Odimus was confused and offended by the break in customs. However, he no longer cares because he hasn't kissed her since before The Pit of Anglishes, which was several months ago. The warmth of her skin is almost overwhelming to him. He's indecisive about what he should say or ask afterward, going back and forth in his head. In the end, he realizes it's not important; he should just kiss the girl and deal with everything else later. They stop, and Odimus inquires about the situation, to which Ithilwen explains the recent events. Odimus can only respond by embracing the woman he loves. He releases his grip and again, confesses his love for her.

As a response from Ithilwen, he receives a pat on the shoulder and a "Good to hear it." She leaves the room laughing and skipping to talk to her sister. Feeling embarrassed and confused, he sits awkwardly because he expressed his love once again but didn't get a response.

Chapter 13

ODIMUS AND THE VALLEY OF YURTHALLA

The Guard of Light has been engaged in numerous battles against the Shadow King's military forces since Mezlikied's funeral, which took place several months ago. The Shadow King's main force has not been encountered since King Kyron, and Kyros began sending waves of defense to delay his advances. They are attempting to halt the Shadow King's other forces to buy time for gathering more forces for the Kingdom of Light. In their wisdom, both Kings concluded that it was better to hinder him than risk being defeated by attacking head-on without sufficient numbers. They first gathered the military of every Mother Moon, evacuated civilians in the path of the Shadow King, and drafted as many soldiers as possible before they were going to attack. This had a higher level of importance than just the loss of land.

Now is the time to prepare in The Valley of Yurthalla near The Forest of Caritheus and the Kingdom of Light. King Kyron has commanded that he will stand within the city gates with the First Legion of Light, serving as a final defense for the people inside. King Kyros, on the other hand, will be positioned outside the walls, leading the military forces. Rather than having multiple military forces and commanders, the Kingdom of Energy and the Kingdom of Light combined the Mother Moons all into one entity. The commanding officers from each Mother Moon remained as commanders and leaders but were now under the command of Luxtenebri's sister kingdoms. As they were in a time of great danger and hardship, a law was enacted requiring all tribes to adopt the colors and name of Luxtenebri, uniting them as one people, one government, and one military. Their representation of their Mother Moons consisted of only a waistband, which displayed their national color and emblem as the buckle.

Kyros approaches Odimus and invites him to be his second on the battlefield. "You're not someone I command, but my trusted partner on the battlefield." Realizing the significance, Ithilwen turns to Odimus and instructs him to respond with acceptance.

Odimus, with a confused expression, addresses Kyros and agrees, "Yes, your majesty."

Kyros looks to Ithilwen and gives her a nod, prompting her to provide an explanation. "In the Kingdom of Energy, the King is at the front of the military. He does not stand in the back, cowering behind his forces. In case the King falls, many leaders are ready to step up, and the King of Light will take charge of the Kingdom of Energy until a new heir is crowned. In the battle, he will be in the heart, fighting with his soldiers, leading the attack, and maintaining the line to prevent the opposing forces from advancing. To defend him as he fights for his kingdom, he asks the man he believes to be the greatest and most skilled warrior among his ranks to stand by his side. He's requesting that you ensure his safety."

This request and honorable position leaves Odimus beyond surprised but only momentarily worried. Odimus possesses a heart full of valor and a warrior spirit, refusing to yield to despair or fear. He assures Ithilwen, "I will do everything in my power to protect your father."

Ithilwen holds his hand and confidently says, "I know you will, but don't forget to protect yourself because I've just been blessed with immortality, and I don't want to live for eternity without you."

Through everyone's Anohail, a battle horn is heard. The sound doesn't have the characteristics of an echo or distant origin. The sound envelops them all, a battle horn that strikes both triumph and terror, instilling fear in the hearts of enemies. At the conclusion of the sounds, Odimus goes to Kyros to be at his side near the front gates outside the city walls. Creatures of every kind can be found in almost every Mother Moon of Luxtenebri. Some that Odimus has never seen but only heard of. He is astonished to witness eleven of the thirteen dominant creatures of the Mother Moons together on the battlefield.

Kyros leans over to him and says, "There has not been a battle in this valley since the great King of the Relic and Rune wars laid down his life to save everyone but instead brought an apocalyptic event. I was only eight years old, lying in bed that day. When she was younger, I used to tell Ithilwen that story as a bedtime story. I never thought there would be a day when a battle would take place in this valley once more. Yet here we are, brought on by my own cousin, who was sixteen years old on that great and terrible day. Even though he knows how terrible that day was, he is now here as the opposing force." His words fall silent, and his heartache is evident as he witnesses the actions of the Shadow King.

The Guard of Light is absent from their usual posts, as they have been summoned to lead various legions across the valley. Odimus turns to Kyros and asks if his sister is safe.

Looking at him, he declares, "There is no safe place today, but I guarantee her survival."

Odimus wonders how he can assure her survival if there is nowhere safe. Nevertheless, this offers him a small amount of consolation. Erastus makes a sudden appearance, riding the Monsrumenar from Glodatri, the Earth Moon. The Mother Moon's dominant creature holds the title of the greatest land creature. Seeing his father fully dressed in Bremium armor, Odimus feels a mix of happiness and concern. "It is true, Kyros, that the King of Shadow possesses power stones embedded in his Bremium helmet."

Kyros now has a slightly concerned expression. Erastus seems to be slightly afraid of the power stones, which is why he hasn't acknowledged Odimus.

Odimus inquires. "What is the nature of power stones?"

Erastus grants Kyros permission to explain. "Years ago, he enslaved the Rehnburen tribe to extract power stones from a mine. This was his sole action that caused laws between our kingdoms, and it was to prohibit slavery. For a long time, we were unaware of his enslavement of them. Kyron confronted him, demanding their freedom warning of war if he refused to comply with the prohibition against enslavement. The mine was his birthright from his family's Bremium mine. However, deep within the mines, a stone of power was found. His desire was to dig deeper and wider in order to uncover additional stones in the mine. He discovered five, and now they adorn his crown instead of jewels. Only Bremium, the fruit from Trees of Power, and Heart Stones have been discovered to grant abilities. The power stones don't provide the user with exclusive or defined abilities, but upon discovering these stones, he found they amplified and increased abilities. The King of Shadow possesses amplified abilities and powers at an exponential level. The Shadow Fruit's abilities and a formidable relic are already at his disposal. The only way to defeat him is with runes."

Kyros gazes at Odimus and states, "We could possibly be the only ones capable of withstanding him. Our priority is reaching and defeating him. While this may not be the same as when you defeated the First General, we can still have hope. Since he is the only immortal, his kingdom does not rely on anyone inheriting it. Our greatest likelihood of success is by defeating him, just as it was by killing the first general. Nonetheless, remember that this is merely speculation."

Erastus now speaks to Odimus, expressing, "I am proud of you, my son."

With a smile, Odimus looks at him and questions, "Why are you wearing Bremium armor?"

"Son, I am a warrior, though it's been a hundred years since my last battle. To add to that, I'm still only one hundred and fifty years old. Despite my youth, I hold the rank of general in the *Kingdom of Energy*. I have the responsibility to come back and serve, and I will fight alongside your sister, keeping her safe under my command."

Odimus finally understands Kyros' reference to her survival. Odimus feels comfort for Adoria as he notices Kyros's slight smirk. Another terrifying yet triumphant horn sounds through everyone's Anohail. "Protect the King, my son," Erastus says before riding away.

Then, legions from the Shadow Kingdom emerge from the woods. It appears that this military force is endlessly emerging from the trees. The soldiers surrounding Odimus are becoming increasingly afraid as this enemy continues to appear.

Without flinching, Kyros directs his attention to Odimus and declares "This battle will be both great and terrible. It's crucial that we fight our way to the King and defeat him, or there will be many lives lost..."

As the Shadow Kingdom's full force emerges from the forest and confronts them on the battlefield, they make their way to the center in an attempt to negotiate a truce, as is customary in battle. Both Kyros and Odimus understand that this won't come to pass. Alone, the King of Shadow rides up to the valley's center to meet them.

Odimus, before reaching him, says, "He rides alone. Why not attack and end this."
"That would be considered serious treachery and dishonorable; it goes against our ways and his." Kyros states.

Upon reaching the battlefield, the *King of Shadow* breaks protocol by addressing Odimus first. "So, you are the warrior my cousins have put their faith in. You are nothing but a boy."

Kyros wants to know the reason behind Ethydus actions. "For thousands of years, we have peacefully coexisted, often consulting with you, involving you in trade and supporting you in having your own Kingdom. We even pardoned your betrayal against Rehnburan through the act of slavery due to them requesting us to forgive and move on. We have authorized you to reign in the shadowlands without any intervention from our kingdom or our laws. Why do you feel the need to commit these terrible acts against us?"

Ethydus, who has been staring at Odimus, finally turns to him and declares, "You and Kyron's reign has gone on for too long. It's time for fresh leadership with a new King and new government."

Kyros, recognizing his merciless intentions, warns him, "You may try, but remember that it will be a life for a life and blood for blood if you proceed with your plans."

"Are you referring to this boy, Kyron?" as Ethydus points his spear at Odimus.

"No, Ethydus, it will be by my hand. Odimus is my second on the battlefield, and unless I'm defeated, he will only protect me and won't attack you. He'll keep your soldiers away as we engage in battle."

"Kyros, do you recall our last battle when I first partook of the Shadow Tree fruit, and you believed it to be treason?" Pointing his spear, he draws attention to the formidable scar on his chest. "That was done with your own shield, the one you had before I shamed you, and you weakly sought a more powerful one to protect yourself. Should I shame you further by using your new shiny toy?" Addressing Odimus, "Boy, you stand next to a King who attacked an unarmed man when I returned home after consuming the Shadow Fruit. Without him, I might have stayed in the City of Light forever."

"Ethydus, you know that is a lie. The Shadow Fruit granted you the chance to rule your own Kingdom."

"Although true and amusing, the fact remains that you attacked an unarmed man."

"Yes, I did, Ethydus, and I regret that decision not because you almost killed me but because I was a foolish young prince, arrogant, merciless and chose to attack the family. That day redefined me, ultimately leading to the King I am today."

Odimus now says something, "Our youth is marked by mistakes, but our true character is revealed by our actions afterward. Upon witnessing my mother's death at the hands of your men," he raises the sword of valiance, and Ethydus awakens in anger. "I made a decision to hurt a young boy, which shaped the person I am today, and since then, he has become a close friend. You had the opportunity to be friends with Kyros, just like I became friends with Amulius. You were triumphant over him, yet you still embraced power and hatred."

Ethydus takes a firm stance, proclaiming, "Life for life and blood for blood it is," and then departs.

Kyros inquires of Odimus, "Will you still stand by me even after discovering the wrongdoings of my youth?"

With a smirk, Odimus replies, "He seems perfectly fine, and it appears you're the one who learned the lesson. There's no reason for you to be punished any further, considering he almost killed you."

While returning to the line, Odimus asks Kyros about the capabilities of the powerful spear relic.

"The spear is called the Spear of Immobilization. Whether it's Bremium armor or flesh, it makes no difference. A single blow to your body can render a significant portion of it useless or paralyzed for over five minutes. The moment his spear touches you, your life is in danger because that is all the time he needs to strike you down."

"If your shield isn't a weapon, how does it keep you safe?"

"The shield was crafted by your father to be both a weapon and a protective shield, allowing me to be shielded from the spears powers."

They have arrived back at the Kingdom, where light and energy forces reside. Kyros signals to prepare for a charge, and everyone gets ready to advance on foot or on their creature. The forces of the King of Shadow rally as they simultaneously shout and clash their relics or shields together. The thunderous sound echoes across the battlefield, shaking the ground beneath their feet. This is intended to instill fear in them, and for some, it works. Raising his arm, Kyros waits to give the signal the charge by lowering it. The Shadowlands military force starts to charge as soon as Ethydus gives the advance signal. Kyros lowers his hand to signal the charge, and the Kingdom of Light and Kingdom of Energy rush forward to face their enemy on the battlefield. The valley's vastness seems to make the charge endless. Odimus notices the approaching forces and start preparing to defend the King on his way to Ethydus. The Shadowland army is suddenly encountered, leading to a fierce and epic battle.

Trees of Power from Luxtenebri and the Mother Moons allowed the roots of the Tree of Shadows to grow under the earth. In this mighty military force, one can find legions of tribes belonging to mutated trees of power that possess unique power mutations, like the aura tree, which later became the behemoth tree. The fire tree, which was abundant, had been planted in the Shadowlands years ago. From it, the acid tree emerged, belonging to the same tribe that attacked and killed Odimus's mother.

The Felinus Tribe was a mutated Duplication Tree that had the power to duplicate a person's life instead of duplicating the person. The Felinus tribe received their name due to their duplicated lives, with the Duplication Fruit granting them an additional four lives. Each time a member of the Felinus tribe was killed, they became increasingly feral, losing more of themselves each time. In their final life, the person transformed into a wild, feral being, displaying violent behavior more akin to a creature than a human. The Felinus tribe played a crucial role in King Ethydus' capture of Rehnburan, the Void Tribe. These were the only three original mutated trees, but on the battlefield today, three new mutated trees and their serving tribes were discovered. The Kingdom of Light and Energy faced great difficulty as they encountered three unfamiliar tribes. Until this day, King Ethydus had kept the existence of the new tribes of mutated trees on the battlefield hidden, displaying his cunning.

There was a Wind Tree mutation, which was now the vacuum tree. Rather than providing air, it would extract oxygen from the air and your lungs, leading to suffocation and death. Additionally, it cancels any wind ability used against it. The Elastic Tree mutation led to the formation of the Necromancy Tribe, granting them the ability to extend life beyond death and control deceased bodies. The tribe places a slice of the Necromancy Fruit in the mouth of fallen soldiers, turning them into undead bodyguards who fight alongside them. They could only raise a few at a time. The fruit could not affect the living, nor could the undead infect the living. The Plant and Animal tribe mutation becomes the life-drain fruit. Instead of spawning plant life and controlling animals, it drains the life of plants, creatures and human life and then, in turn, increases their strength, speed and health. The fruit's life-draining ability was limited, not infinite. Until the increased power wore off, they could not drain more life to amplify their strength, speed, and health.

Over the next few hours, the battle scene was characterized by terror and intense bloodshed. Odimus and Kyros are swiftly overpowering both men and women in battle, their sole objective being to reach Ethydus without wasting time on unnecessary fights. Odimus and Kyros eventually encounter Ethydus in battle. Without any fear, he approaches them directly after spotting them standing a few yards away. Kyros and Odimus notice that in the middle of the valley meeting before the battle, he was not wearing his helmet, but now his head was adorned with a headpiece embedded with five stones in the Bremium helmet. His Bremium armor was built with the greatest of craftsmanship, more than Odimus had ever seen, yet it looked familiar. He appeared to emit shadowy bursts from all directions, like being engulfed in black flames.

Kyros tells Odimus, "Prevent the guards from attacking while I fight Ethydus. Be cautious, and he will try to attack you with his spear whenever he can. Should I be vanquished, eliminate him so we may emerge victorious."

Odimus confirms the King's command and prepares for Ethydus to arrive and launch an attack. Ethydus, a skilled yet overconfident fighter, refrains from attacking initially and instead stands amidst numerous soldiers engaged in combat. He looks at Odimus and asks, "Do you like the Bremium armor, and what do you think of my spear? Your father made them, so know that as I slay you, it was your father's craft that prevented you from killing me, and it was also his craftmanship that ran you through.

Without hesitation, he aggressively attacks Kyros first. Three of the Shadow King's guardsmen suddenly attack Odimus, and their combined skills rival the First General of Absorption. Kyros initiates his attack by transforming into his Humanoid Manticore form, which he maintains throughout the battle. He effortlessly defends against all of Ethydus' strikes and attempts to hit him. Due to the length of Ethydus' spear, Kyros is unable to make any offensive moves and remains at a distance. Frustrated by Kyros's ability to block him, he transforms into a shadow with glowing orange eyes. He charges towards Kyros, only to be met with a sudden barrier of light from the shield. Kyros surprises Ethydus by leaning over the shield to speak. "Didn't know it did that, did you?" With a roar, the shadowy figure transforms back into a human and starts attacking fiercely. The battle between Kyros, Ethydus, Odimus, and the Guardsman is so intense that soldiers around stop fighting to watch. The violence and intensity of the fighting behind the group of spectators remain unchanged. Odimus strikes down the first guard and then quickly takes care of the second. He engages in a one-on-one fight with a guardsman while occasionally fending off sneak attacks from the crowd. Nevertheless, they are unable to succeed due to the protection of soldiers from the Kingdom of Light and Energy. This skirmish leads to the crowd initiating their own confrontations.

Hearing Kyros make a sound of injury, he turns to see Ethydus landing a strike with his spear on his left arm, leaving it paralyzed. When he tries to rush to his aid, the remaining guardsman steps in his way to prevent him from going to rescue Kyros. Rather than fighting, his main concern seems to be causing obstacles. Odimus fights his way toward Ethydus, witnessing him playfully disabling Kyros' right leg with a gentle poke. Odimus extends his hand and emits an intense burst of light, which sears the soldier's face and appears to have fatal consequences. While running at full speed, Ethydus delivers a devastating deep pierce to Kyros' shoulder with his spear, indicating he is simply toying with him. This causes Kyros to turn back into human form. Ethydus has now ceased playing his games and is now attempting to kill Kyros.

Odimus prevents Ethydus from successfully attacking him by intervening at the last moment. With gravity, he sends Ethydus soaring. However, he flips upside down, drives his spear into the ground, and lands on his feet. Ethydus unveils his bloodline origin, creating rocks to secure his feet and thwart Odimus' gravity manipulation. It appears that he hasn't quite grasped the power of the fruit from the Mother Moon Glodatri. His strategy revolves around using the earth as support and occasionally launching a moderately-sized rock at Odimus, but it doesn't have a significant effect. The last of Kyros's Aura vials have been used, and he is unable to recover fully. There are no Aura medics nearby. Odimus and Ethydus have finally met and are now battling each other. Ethydus, in shadow form, cannot reach Odimus as he lunges at him because Odimus defends himself with a barrier of light using the rune on his forearm. Their battle is not as long and fierce as Kyros and Ethydus'. Ethydus pretends to attack another place on his body with a sizable rock; as Odimus moves to protect himself, his time observance rune activates. However, the Shadow King's move was to draw his guard elsewhere, and his spear is able to tap on Odimus' hand gently. In slow motion, Odimus witnesses Ethydus's deception as he mistakenly blocks the wrong attack, resulting in his hand becoming paralyzed. Ethydus doesn't toy with him; instead, he taps him three more times, leaving him defenseless, and then goes for the kill by aiming for his face with the spear.

Ithilwen in her Cipactli swoops in to his rescue, stopping the attempt to kill Odimus. Holding her sword of power, she positions herself between him and the Shadow King and initiates an attack. Ethydus disarms her within seconds and holds the sword of power to her throat.

Ethydus calls out to Odimus, encouraging him to drop his weapon after witnessing its ability to restore his mobility. From his side armor pocket bag on his belt, Ethydus pulls out something. "Odimus," he says, "I've determined a different fate for you. Based on what I'm seeing, it appears that I'm going to be the loser in this battle." Glancing around, Odimus sees that Ethydus's troops are outnumbered, and there are many casualties on their side. Looking back at Ethydus, he makes a proposition: "Eat the Shadow Fruit, and her life will be spared."

All of Kyros' paralyzed wounds have now healed. He shouts at Odimus, cautioning him against consuming the fruit, "Do not partake, for it will corrupt and destroy you, similar to what has happened to Ethydus."

"The princess seems to be in love with you, as she came to your aid instead of her father's; this fruit isn't worth worrying about over losing her now, is it?"

Next, he cuts her neck, causing it to bleed, and Odimus pleads for him to cease and to give him the fruit. He complies with Odimus's request, and Odimus gazes sadly at the fruit, feeling burdened by his predicament. Upon noticing the fruit in his grasp, his mind wanders to his love for Ithilwen before redirecting his thoughts towards his affection for the *Tree of Light* and the possible consequences. The fear of sacrificing Ithilwen to preserve the *Tree of Light* starts to consume him.

As he begins releasing the fruit, Ithilwen shouts to him, "Good, Odimus! Save the *Tree of Light*! My life is insignificant compared to the lives of billions."

At the moment he starts to release the fruit, he catches sight of multiple potential manifestations of light swirling around the Shadow Fruit. The fact that they are made of light and not shadows is causing him great confusion. Unexpectedly, he notices a small glowing object in the shape of the **Tree of Light's** fruit enveloping the Shadow fruit before vanishing. Instantly, he seizes the fruit and bites into it.

At the same moment, Kyros and Ithilwen let out a cry. A cloud of shadow emanates from Odimus. The cloud rapidly spreads, casting a shadow over millions of soldiers. Millions more soldiers are discovered outside the shadow wall, the overwhelming shadow engulfing most of the military forces causes everyone to cease. Fear and confusion are evident as all look up at the cloud. A tremendous, fearsome whirlwind and roaring storm never before witnessed in the land can be heard by those in the cloud. It felt like the earth could rupture right beneath them. The shadow's power and influence were immense, causing everyone to collapse in fear, some on their knees and others completely lying down. They had a feeling of being immobile. Many people started screaming and wailing because of the terrible sensation they were experiencing. The military forces, without the cloud, began to hear the cries and wails inside, resulting in their terror. The fear causes a mass retreat of Shadowland forces back into the forest, numbering in the millions. People from the Kingdoms of Light and Energy are escaping to the Kingdom of Light to shield their residents.

Inside the cloud, Odimus is devoured by its most violent and destructive part. In an attempt to battle the shadow, he is overcome with excruciating pain and lets out a terrible cry. In all his days, he has never experienced pain, fear, darkness, and misery like this.

Ethydus is also feeling the consequences and effects. However, he starts to stand and smile, convinced of his impending victory. He releases Ithilwen's sword, and now, without it at her throat, she crawls towards Odimus, hoping she can save him but fearing the worst. Overwhelmed by despair and fear, she begins to weep at the thought of Odimus becoming mutated by the shadow fruit. Despite feeling hopeless, she musters the strength to continue crawling towards the man she loves. She is unable to approach him due to a powerful shadow vortex surrounding him. The power of the winds and forces surrounding him is so intense that it feels as if her bones will be crushed.

Kyros has now crawled over to his daughter and grabs hold to keep her safe as she calls out to Odimus. Odimus's fight against the Shadow mutation is weakening, resulting in an increase in the cloud's force. The increased effects all around now have brought Ethydus back down to his knees as he watches in gladness. Within this terrible vortex, Odimus starts to feel as if he's being torn apart at every molecule. He endures excruciating agony as his flesh slowly dissolves into shadow particles, tearing away tiny fragments of his body and transforming into a smoke-like shadow.

In the midst of this terrible horror, he faintly hears Ithilwen calling out to him. He makes a slow attempt to see her but couldn't. Nonetheless, he can make out Ithilwen's voice whispering in the wind.

"Odimus! I love you!"

Ithilwen has finally revealed her love for him, offering him a glimmer of hope. Now, he makes an effort to move his limbs, but only one arm shows any signs of movement. He extends it towards his fallen sword on the ground. With all his being, he commands the sword to come to his hand, granting him the power of Valor. Despite his efforts, he is unable to grasp the hilt of his sword with both hands. He is tired, weak, wishing to be free of this pain and fearing the worst.

With a sudden burst of light, he finds himself kneeling in front of the **Tree of Light**. Behind the **Tree of Light,** is Erayiphim, his Mother Moon, which appears large and radiant consuming everything behind the **Tree of Light**. He no longer feels any pain, and fear has vanished.

Lowering himself to eye level, Mezlikied looks into the eyes of his stagiaire. Mezlikied now kneels down with him and says, "You have fought well, my friend; remember, your name is Odimuvalere."

Standing behind Mezlikied, his mother places one arm on his shoulder and informs him, "Your name translates to Man of Valor." She kneels next to Mezlikied, and his heart longs for her embrace. However, he appears frozen, unable to move, as they speak to him while he kneels.

Another man suddenly appears, standing behind his mother. He places his hand on her shoulder, kneels, and declares, "You can achieve what I could not." The man wore a crown on his head, which matched King Kyron's. Then, he gestures towards Erayiphim, hiding behind the ***Tree of Light***, before turning back and smiling at him.

Then, as they all fade from his sight, he hears Mezlikied's voice, "As I said when I laid down my life for you; Wisdom and light are also charity. I was telling you Odimus, there is no greater charity than laying down your life for another."

The purpose of the vision hits Odimus, bringing him back to the cloud of shadow and his pain returning, yet he regains his strength. He commences pouring his will into the Sword of Valiance, followed by his life force. He lets go of the sword and utilizes the force of gravity around it. Upon summoning the Heart Stone, it immediately begins orbiting around him at a remarkably high velocity. Like the core of the great sun Klibous, the sword begins to spin under the gravitational power.

He understands that when the ancient King glanced at Erayiphim, he signaled him to utilize gravity on the Sword of Valiance and infuse it with his will and life. He also understands that Mezlikied was telling him to sacrifice his life to save all the inhabitants of Luxtenebri and all the tribes of the Mother Moons. Suddenly, a light similar to that of the great sun starts to radiate from the sword while a perfect sphere materializes around it.

Now that the cloud is dispersing, Ithilwen, Kyros, and the King of Shadow nearby can see Odimus.

Ethydus yells, "It's not possible!"

Odimus looks at him and says, "Not for you, but I choose the light."

Returning his focus to the sword, he channels all his energy into activating its power in order to stop and conclude the battle. Reminiscent of the great King of old during the Relic and Rune Wars, though this time it's the Sword of Valiance. Ethydus assumes he is conquering the shadow, unaware of what's happening.

Kyros, however, recognizes his intentions and calls out to him, "Odimus, it will kill you. Don't do this, it could kill us all." He, feeling great fear, knowing first hand the consequences.

Odimus, tears welling up in his eyes, says, "Not this time, my King."

With confusion still lingering, Ithilwen glances at her father and questions, "What is Odimus doing?"

"He is attempting the same thing as the King from our past."

She now comprehends the situation and fights to stand, charging at him. Odimus tells Ithilwen that he loves her, and Kyros stops her from going after him. Kyros instructs her to remove all of her Bremium, but it's s too late.

Odimus commands the release of a blast, resulting in an energy surge that spreads throughout all of Luxtenebri and the Mother Moons. However, this time, only those from the Shadowlands are affected, with everyone from the Shadowlands inside the cloud being killed. The surge of energy hits the military forces that had fled. Nevertheless, they are not killed but transformed back to their natural state before mutation. In shock, they all start examining themselves and each other as they transform back. The wave affects all the moons, including Rehnburan, where Hayleta is hit and starts to transform into a normal woman. Similar to Orthalla, she maintains a large stature, but now she is just ordinary. Slowly, she drops to her knees, buries her face in her hands, and begins weeping. Teleporting to her home to see if she is ok, the Monk elders rejoice at her transformation, kneeling and laughing with joy as they embrace her. They are unaware of what has occurred, only aware of a powerful surge of energy that has affected everything, and she has been discovered transformed. Since they are wise men, they comprehend that this implies a positive event has transpired.

The wave hits the Shadowlands, causing all mutated Trees of Power to wither and die, except for the Tree of Shadow and Absorption Tree, as they originated from those lands and are not mutated. The Tree of Shadow loses support from mutated Trees of Power, causing its roots to release their grip on the **Tree of Light** and wither away to the Shadowlands.

Regarding the Kingdom of Light and Energy forces, the fallen in battle are the only ones who aren't healed; everyone else feels rejuvenated and peaceful. As soon as the energy wave was unleashed, the cloud of shadow vanished.

Now that they're healed, Ithilwen and Kyros rush to Odimus's aid. Unfortunately, when they finally got to him, He is gone. The Heart Stone of Erayiphim is nowhere to be seen, signaling his death and the commencement of the next Guardian's selection. Weeping, she sits on the floor and pulls him into her lap. Kyros grants her the opportunity to mourn by leaving to instruct his forces to gather the dead for burial. Erastus, Adoria, Orthalla, Trenidus, and Fuin have now reached Odimus and Ithilwen from several different locations in the battle. Another member of the team has fallen, and this time, it is Odimus, causing them to sit together and mourn once more.

The following morning, Odimus is dressed in burial attire and placed in a viewing room. Erastus has requested that he be prepared for the Ceremony of Light as his burial, in front of all the people of Luxtenebri. Ithilwen is the only one left in the room after the viewing, and she starts talking while sitting beside him. "When we were at the Kingdom of Light, Kyron pulled me aside after you shared your vision and advised me to reflect on whether I was desiring the right man. I ended up with the man who truly has my heart, and now you are gone." She leans forward and gently kisses his lips for the last time.

Kyros arrives with the Sword of Valiance declaring, "This belongs to him and should be buried alongside him. With everyone having now seen his body, it will remain unknown that they were buried together."

Ithilwen places the hilt of the sword in both of his hands and begins to walk away, but as she does, she notices a scratch on his cheek beginning to heal. She gasps and tells her father to look. Kyros notices his cheek and quickly instructs her to get him up from the viewing table. They raise him and keep him secure in their grasp. Odimus starts to breathe softly through his nose, and his eyes slowly open.

In this sudden turn of events, the Heart Stone of Erayiphim is summoned and starts orbiting around him. Surveying his surroundings, he realizes he is in a viewing room. He gazes at Ithilwen and remarks, "Despite what you thought, It seems you haven't lost me after all." Without uttering a word, Ithilwen bursts into tears and collapses into his arms. Odimus turns his attention to Kyros and admits remorsefully. "It was the only way."

Kyros looks at him like a father to a son and says with a gentle and grateful voice, "I know."

Suddenly, Erastus, his father, appears around the corner. He drops the items in his arms and rushes to embrace his son, wrapping him up like a little boy. Ithilwen is almost knocked over, but then begins laughing and hugs Erastus from behind. In a heartwarming moment, even Kyros leans on his old friend Erastus's back during a group hug.

Upon hearing a loud noise, Adoria sprints to discover its source and encounters Odimus being hugged by the group, leading her to call out to the others. She runs in and becomes part of the groups embrace. Now, the rest join in, laughing and holding their beloved friend Odimus.

Trenidus comments, "It is quite fortunate that you're not from the fire tribe. Otherwise, you would have been turned into ash by now."

Laughing deeply, Orthalla looks at Trenidus and says, "Come here, you." He picks him up and gives a tight squeeze.

The group all let go, and Kyros now asks Erastus. "How is it possible for the Sword of Valiance to have resurrected Odimus?"

"Your majesty, it couldn't have resurrected him, not at all. It appears that the Heart Stone was still with him and was protecting his heart from completely dying until the sword could be rejoined to his hands."

"How are you aware of this?"

With a simple motion, Erastus beckons the Heart Stone to him, and without hesitation, it floats over to his grasp. Everyone is surprised by this. "Mezlikied was my friend all the way back to my childhood. Though he was older, I became dear friends with him through his sister. I was also there on the day he was called, and we were married to best friends. His wife and your mother were childhood friends on the Wind Moon Dalanias before relocating to the Kingdom of Naphdali. We met them there when we wanted to get a couple of Volantuiva to be able to travel to the Academy of Achaicus and back to Erayiphim instead of relying on passenger ships all the time. After purchasing the Volantuiva from them, they both decided to apply to the Academy in search of us. A few months later, we encountered them there - and following; our story began, like a tale as old as time. He became like family to us, helping me raise you both as an uncle after we lost your mother. He was closer to being a brother to me than a friend. Throughout the years I knew him, I studied the Heart Stone and witnessed its attempts to save Mezlikied's life during numerous adventures. I also know that immediately upon the death of a guardian, the moon chooses a new guardian to protect the tribe of the moon to which it belongs. Initially, I didn't pay much attention to the absence of the Heart Stone, assuming the new Guardian just hadn't emerged. But when I saw Odimus in the room and the Heart Stone orbiting him, I knew it had been doing everything it could to keep him alive, desperately hoping for a chance to save him."

Erastus expresses gratitude to the stone and lets it go to Odimus. The stone gives a soft touch to his cheek as it starts orbiting him once more. "The Heart Stone will care for you as long as you live, so remember to care for it in return."

Almost a year has passed since Odimus had saved all of Luxtenebri and the Mother Moons. The guard is rushing around today, more frantic than ever, in preparation for the upcoming challenge.

Adoria reassures Orthalla, who is almost panicking, "You are going to do just fine." She kisses his cheek and warns Trenidus, "Behave, and leave Orthalla alone."

Trenidus laughs and says playfully, "He is worse than I am now, so there's no need to worry about me."

Fuin chuckles, high-fives Trenidus, and agrees "You got that right."

Erastus enters and inquires if Orthalla is prepared, to which Orthalla confirms.

"Then let's go!" Orthalla gets up and walks out the door.

King Kyros politely knocks on Ithilwen's door, and she welcomes him inside. When he opens the door, he finds a woman hurrying around the room, getting her ready in her wedding dress.

"Ithilwen, you look beautiful. Now you and Odimus have decided to embark on the whole Guardian journey together, right?"

Knowing what her father's intentions are, she states, "There has never been an immortal Guardian before, so since we're both immortal, we have unlimited time before we have children. So we have decided to focus on helping the Erayiphim tribe for a while."

"Are you planning to make Erayiphim your home?"

"Father, we will have a home here as we discussed, but together we will venture out often to fulfill his potential manifestations for a while."

"I like the sound of that, although I would like to see some rugrats running around the castle someday."

"Father, someday you'll get grandchildren, but for now, I am currently preoccupied with my wedding."

Erastus walks into Odimus's chambers, "Well, a Prince of the Kingdom of Energy, the great warrior that saved Luxtenebri from destruction and the Guardian of Erayiphim. You've achieved great things, son. I wish your mother could have seen how far you've come."

Odimus, until now, had not remembered to tell his father about the vision he saw on the battlefield, so he proceeded to. Erastus gets teary-eyed and expresses his appreciation, then reminds his son about the wedding.

Odimus and Ithilwen's wedding ceremony has thousands in attendance from all the kingdoms, governments, and Mother Moons. Orthalla is standing next to Odimus, and Adoria is next to Ithilwen, who is asked to give her vows as Odimus stands before her.

"Odimus, I stumbled because of love, and it wasn't easy to recover after losing Othare. Your immortality made me question if I could ever truly be with you, leaving me afraid of falling completely in love again. The **Tree of Light** blessed me with the gift of immortality, giving me the chance to be with you forever. Falling and then being lifted, I finally had the courage to fall in love with you, with all of my being but, it scared me. Seeing the shadow consume you, I knew standing again would be impossible if I lost you, and then you *were* gone. Having you given back to me again has made me again feel scared, weak and afraid. Yet having you by my side every day this past year has made me truly understand that *you* are my source of strength and purpose. I will always be by your side during future battles. I will stand with you against any enemy. And I know that we can overcome any obstacle if we do it together."

Odimus, now teary-eyed, proceeds to say, "Ithilwen, coming from the Moon of Erayiphim, we are able to literally defy gravity. Even if it seems impossible, I'll fight your battles when you're weak. I'll assist you in conquering and overcoming any obstacle in your path. As a Princess of The Kingdom of Energy, you have responsibilities. With the title of Guardian of Erayiphim also comes great responsibilities. You're not meant to support me alone in my responsibilities in this life. I pledge to stand by you, shoulder your responsibilities, and help alleviate the weight you carry. Seeing how we of Erayiphim know a thing or two about weight. Standing together for all Luxtenebri and the Mother Moons is our duty to the Kingdom of Energy and the people of Erayiphim. Together, we can achieve unity and growth for all of Luxtenebri and the Mother Moons by collectively serving the Kingdom of Energy and Erayiphim. Being immortal, I'm literally forever yours."

They exchange a kiss and become husband and wife. Odimus and Ithilwen receive a roaring applause from the crowd as they run down the aisle. Kyros is standing at the end of the line, with Adoria and Orthalla following closely behind. Kyros expresses gratitude to Odimus for confirming their commitment to both the Kingdom of Energy, and Erayiphim. Adoria now proudly shows her hand to indicate her marriage to Orthalla as she and Odimus are now both married. Adoria and Orthalla had tied the knot several months ago. Having learned of Orthalla's royal lineage, they eloped at his coronation. As a result, Orthalla was crowned King, and Adoria was crowned Queen of the Kingdom of Aura.

Odimus hugs her and says, "I love you, sis."

Ithilwen and Adoria scream in an overly dramatic scene, then hug. The couple proceed to climb aboard their Volantuiva, ready for their journey. They ascend straight into the sky and soar toward the atmosphere while the crowd below continues to cheer for them.

Kyron walks towards Kyros and Erastus while bidding Odimus and Ithilwen farewell as they vanish into the sky. He inquires, "Has the wall been completed?"

"The Shadowlands are now sealed off, and no one is allowed to enter, preventing any other Kingdom from serving the Tree of Shadow again."

The wedding of Odimus and Ithilwen happened seventy-five years ago, and peace has reigned since then. Odimus and Ithilwen are now parents of two children. Adoria and Orthalla are the parents of three. Trenidus found a bride but does not have any children. Nevertheless, he acts as an uncle to all the kids. Fuin, who was previously married before his adventure many years ago, has now become a father. All of them are together celebrating the holiday that was established to honor the triumph over The Shadowlands when, suddenly, a man comes soaring over the walls of the *Kingdom of Energy*. Anniphus, who is now very old, gets off his Volantuiva, and everyone comes together to greet him.

He interrupts them to deliver the news, "We have discovered a remarkably large ship found beneath the Ocean of Arthiatus. The ship has markings bearing a resemblance to those found in ancient ruins predating the Harvest Wars, indicating our common heritage. For years, we have been studying it. A fascinating combination of unique designs and machinery we've never encountered before. However, a couple of weeks ago, we started hearing a beeping noise along with a strange map made of light displaying our solar system. Unexpectedly, two dots materialized on the map a few days ago. Our designated spot in the solar system is being approached by the moving dots. We are concerned that it might be a warning of some sort."

www.ingramcontent.com/pod-product-compliance
Lightning Source LLC
Chambersburg PA
CBHW072126300726
48975CB00003B/948